ANNA SPARROWS

His Alpha Unlocked

An Omegaverse Shifter Mpreg Romance

Cover design by Ky at Blue Brolli Graphics

First edition

This book was professionally typeset on Reedsy.
Find out more at reedsy.com

For sixteen-year-old me and anyone else who feels their taste in reading/writing material is weird. Weirdness is where the fun happens. Everyone else is missing out!

Contents

Preface

This book is a part of the *2023 Christmas Omegas* series, and is also Book 1 of the upcoming *Shifters Sanctuary* series, however it can be read as a standalone.

His Alpha Unlocked is a sweet, instant attraction (fated mates vibes) romance. It **IS** an **mpreg** romance, and it does contain **violence, threats, infertility, kidnapping, anxiety, controlling families, a birthing scene,** and some **mild angst**.

This book contains elements suited to readers over the age of 18.

I am still a firm believer in not yucking someone else's yum, so if the above isn't for you, don't force yourself to read it.

Life's too short to read something you don't enjoy.

Acknowledgement

Huge thanks to Kota Quinn for reaching out to my introverted self and inviting me to be a part of the *Christmas Omegas* series, encouraging me to finally write the Omegaverse plot bunny I'd been mulling over. You've helped bring me out of my shell and introduced me to people whose names I would never have thought I'd see mine grouped with. Yours was my first group collaboration, and the best experience I could have asked for. I won't ever be able to thank you enough.

Off the back of that, thank you to Joe Satoria for providing the original cover design as part of the *Christmas Omegas* series. (That cover is no longer available due to the creation of the *Shifters Sanctuary* series, but I will always adore Joe's work.)

I'd also like to thank Ky, my alpha reader, for giving feedback that smoothed out the flow of this novel in its early (super rough) stages, and for talking me through many 'I'm such a fraud, how do I even write a book?' rambles. Ky also designed the new cover for the *Shifters Sanctuary* series and I am beyond excited to unveil it.

Similarly, thank you to Amur and Cindy for being such enthusiastic and helpful beta readers. The tweaks you both suggested really helped make this feel complete and cohesive.

Finally, thank you (yes, *you*) for reading this. I am beyond warmed by the fact that you picked up one of my books when I know just how many other potential reads are out there begging for attention. It means more to me than I can properly express. I genuinely hope that you enjoy the book, but even if you DNF it, thank you for being interested enough to give it a chance.

Chapter One - Oliver

"**D**on't you think it's about time you put the pack first?" My mom's voice came out a little hollow from the speaker of my phone. I rolled my eyes at it as I turned to hang the last of my laundry —a clean dress shirt I planned on wearing out later that night— in my tiny little wardrobe. "You're not *human*, Ollie. You're a shifter. You have obligations."

We seemed to have the same conversation every week. It never went off script.

Ever since I graduated college back in May, the pack expected me to return and 'earn my keep' or some other creative description that basically amounted to wanting their slave back.

As an omega, that's essentially all I was to them, after all. I silently cursed the little crescent moon birthmark that had sealed my fate by declaring my secondary designation to the world before I'd even taken my first breath.

I sighed. "I have obligations to my actual paying job, Mom,"

I reminded her, much as I did every week. "And I've been sending my tithes weekly." I tried not to sound too bitter about that. I wasn't living on pack land and had landed myself a full-ride scholarship through college, so I didn't owe the pack anything as far as I was concerned.

"*Oliver*," my mother's voice was stern, her southern accent twanging as she worked herself up, "it's not just about the money. You're needed here to help with the crops and the manual labor."

At 5'7" and weighing barely a hundred and eighty pounds soaking wet, I didn't think I would be much good for any of that, but the pack didn't care. They never had.

Omegas weren't good for breeding anymore. Not since alphas had faded into little more than mythical creatures. Omegas couldn't impregnate the beta females (not that many even tried, what with generally being gay) and betas couldn't impregnate the omegas, either. The pack literally only saw omegas as bodies to put to work.

Why omegas were still born into a world without alphas made very little evolutionary sense to me, which was why I had chosen to pursue the education that I had.

I had dabbled in various sciences, wanting to try and piece together what, exactly, had gone wrong for shifters in the last hundred years or so. While medical studies had fascinated me, I had eventually majored in zoology and biology. I hadn't even gotten close to scratching the surface on shifter evolution or why shifter society had changed the way it had, but my studies gave me access to resources that helped me on my personal side-quest for answers.

"I'm no good at the farm work, Mom," I reminded my mother, trying to wind up the conversation we were having, knowing we would rehash it all in a week's time anyway. "And I'm happy where I am."

"I bet you've forgotten how to shift," she spat viciously. "Wantin' to live in a dirty city with all those humans. Humans who would just as soon skin you alive and use your pelt for decoration if they knew what you really were."

I didn't bother disputing my mother's assumptions. The less she knew about my routines or where I went to shift, the better.

It's not that shifters were a secret. Not really. But the idea of them being 'other' made humans wary of us and the shifters equally wary of humans. When alphas had still existed, and the packs were more secular, shifters had been even more terrifying to the humans. After all, seeing pregnant men —pregnant omegas— had rocked the status quo just a little too much, and we were hunted and ostracized until we hid away from large cities full of humans, turning our society largely secular and insulated.

But, with betas in male-female pairings gradually becoming the only members of the pack who could reproduce, shifters were able to assimilate among the humans with more ease once more.

By this point, the idea of male pregnancy was relegated to science fiction – a myth, even among shifter kind. Omegas, like myself, were considered cursed sterile at birth.

After I finally managed to get my mother off the phone, I sighed and eyed it warily. A low-grade thrum of trepidation under my skin had me shaking my shoulders and cracking my neck. Maybe it was time to move away? With how badly she was beginning to push me on the issue, I wouldn't have been surprised if the pack came to take me home by force.

I didn't want to go. The pack, while technically my family, was not my home.

* * *

"This is *the best!*" Brandi, a friend I'd made in college, leaned in and yelled into my ear as we danced up a storm in the club. Her long blonde hair, which was brushed to shiny perfection when we had arrived earlier in the evening, was tangled and sweaty, but her smile was wide. "Fuck Zeke. Fuck *men*. Who needs 'em?"

I laughed, shaking my head. Zeke was the latest breakup in a long line of them for my bubbly friend. And, because I was also perpetually single, we were letting loose in celebration of her renewed independence.

"I'm still a man," I told Brandi as the song switched, stepping in closer, winding my arm around her back. She immediately straddled my thigh, grinding against me to the new beat.

"Yeah, but you're gay," the way we were dancing might have suggested otherwise, but it was more about the enjoyment of the movement than anything sexual. However, I was certain that we made a striking pair as we writhed to the rhythm, "so you should be on my side here."

"I'm always on your side, babe," I agreed.

The bass from the music practically vibrated through my bones and I felt alive and invigorated as we continued to laugh and spin and gyrate together. My earlier call with my mother was pushed to the back of my thoughts as I let myself just enjoy the life I was living.

The few friends I had made in college were good people, even if they were all human and oblivious to my secret life. I liked my job and loved the hustle and bustle of city living. It was liberating being anonymous and judged for almost any other reason than having lost the genetic lottery.

I still indulged the urge to shift, traveling out of the city at least once a month. I would visit the nearest forestry to run and hunt and stretch my furred limbs, but it wasn't my sole defining trait.

In my actual life, I was just Oliver Grayson: a nerdy research assistant by day and a flirtatious club rat by night.

"*Oh,* but check out the hottie at three o'clock," Brandi sashayed her hips before she spun around in my hold and plastered her back to my chest, leaning her head back on my shoulder while she continued to give me what amounted to a standing lap dance, "hot *damn.*"

Over the column of her throat, I cast a surreptitious glance to the side, looking for the latest object of my friend's attentions. If there was one thing to be said for Brandi, it was that she bounced back from heartache very quickly.

Despite my lingering amusement, a low whistle traveled up through my belly and out of my mouth before I could even think.

"Right?" Still rolling her hips, Brandi's grin turned knowing, and she wound long arms backwards around my neck, deliberately putting on a sultry show now. "Who let him out unattended?"

The guy in question was sinfully attractive. He was tall and dark haired, with broad shoulders, a slim waist, and thick thighs tightly encased in denim. He had dark, perfectly trimmed stubble across his squared jaw, and he seemed oddly out of place in the middle of the club's dance floor. Far too stoic to be standing among the exuberant and hedonistic displays around me.

"Mmm," I agreed with Brandi, strangely unable to string any words together. Men didn't usually affect me like that. Not instantly, anyway.

Then his eyes met mine, and I forgot how to breathe. The stranger's eyes were as dark as his hair in the dim lighting of the club, but I couldn't tell what color they were. Still, it didn't change how piercing the guy's stare felt.

The other man stayed where he was, awkwardly still in the middle of all the sweaty, writhing bodies.

I could not tear my eyes away. It was magnetism. Brandi continued to grind against me and I moved on instinct to the beat, but my attention was fully focused on the stranger a few paces away.

"Go talk to him," Brandi suggested, cooing the words into my ear once she'd spun back around in a sexy flourish that earned her attention from a number of other men on the dance floor. "It's pretty obvious I'm not his type." Her parting shot was delivered with a slap to my ass, then she sauntered away into the crowd, leaving me alone to do as she had instructed.

She was honestly the best wing woman ever.

I gave myself a little shake before I shimmied through the throng of dancers, my eyes never leaving the burning dark gaze of my prey. As I closed the distance between us, my heart rate increased, but I had no idea why.

Yeah, Mister Tall, Dark, and Devastatingly Handsome only seemed to get taller, darker, and more handsome the closer I got, but looks alone weren't everything to me. There was something *different* about this guy, something I could not put into words, and it sent all of my senses into overdrive. My skin practically tingled as I finally slid in front of the wall of muscle. And, fuck, he smelled divine, too.

"Wanna dance?" I asked the guy from beneath lowered lashes. The coy twink act had never failed me before. Yeah, sure, I had to yell the words to be heard, but looking sweet and demure always hooked them.

Captain Stoicism's lips twitched. He leaned forward, his lips brushing my ear, causing my breathing to hitch as he coolly stated, "I don't dance."

I knew I must look like I'd been slapped stupid. I could feel myself gaping incredulously, even as the attractive man stepped back with the ghost of a smirk on his handsome face.

"You're standing in the middle of a *dance floor*," I argued loudly, thrusting my arms out wide, reiterating my point as people bopped around them, "and you *don't dance*?"

A flicker of something that looked a lot like sheepishness crossed my prey's expression. "Yeah, uh, I..." he stammered, looking around himself as though only just realizing where he was. "I...don't know how that happened, actually."

I could barely make out the words with the noise of the club interfering, even with my enhanced shifter hearing, but I grinned, suddenly feeling like maybe I wasn't the only one having those strange, needy feelings.

Stepping in as closely as possible to the taller man, trying not to breathe in the intoxicating scent the bigger, broader body emitted, I raised up on my tiptoes and loudly asked, "Can I buy you a drink?"

Chapter Two – Beckett

⁓⟋⟍⁓

Holy hell, the thought struck me like lightning, *this guy is stunning.*

I could not take my eyes off the long, lean body of the ballsy younger man who had strutted across the dance floor towards me a few minutes earlier. At that moment, the guy was leaning over the bar, his practically painted-on jeans highlighting the tempting curve of his ass, his light brown hair almost glinting gold from the bar's overhead lighting. He wore eyeliner, making the green of his eyes pop, and there was something about him that had my nerve endings on edge in all the best ways.

That was the only reason I had for being on the dance floor to begin with. One minute, I'd been chatting with my friends, the next, I had caught sight of this insanely pretty young thing practically dry humping an equally pretty woman as they 'danced' and then…*bam!* I was standing in the middle of the God damned dance floor, my feet having followed my dick's interest. I had no idea where my friends had gone, but they would meet me back at the apartment anyway.

I watched as the object of my attentions flirted with the bartender, biting his lip and batting his lashes much like he had done for me back over on the dance floor. It sent a thrill of jealous rage through my body that took me completely off guard.

*Jesus Christ, I don't even know his name. He is not **mine**. He can flirt with whoever he fucking wants.*

And yet the thought was followed by a possessive urge unlike anything I'd ever felt before. It was bizarre. Hell, I almost fucking growled out loud, and that was just plain weird. I mean, what sort of person *growls*?

When Green Eyes turned back to me and winked, though, I gave in and silently acknowledged that, yeah, I wanted the guy. Badly.

After paying the bartender, Green Eyes grabbed the bottles of beer he'd ordered by their necks and sashayed back over to me, a salacious smirk playing on his pretty plump lips. He handed one of the sweating bottles over, then clinked them together, declaring, "To new *friends* and *very* happy endings."

I couldn't help chuckling as I lifted my beer to the toast and took my first drag from the bottle. The cold, crisp liquid was like heaven in the overheated, overpopulated club, quenching a thirst I hadn't realized was there. I hissed in pleasure as I gulped down a good third of the bottle, then pulled it away to offer my new 'friend' a genuine smile. "Thanks."

"My *pleasure*," Green Eyes practically purred back at me, taking a swig of his own drink. My eyes were drawn to the way those beautiful pink lips wrapped around the lip of the bottle, and the way this beautiful stranger's Adam's apple bobbed as he swallowed almost as greedily as I had.

Fuck me, I thought to myself with frustration as my cock strained in the confines of my jeans, *it's been too long since I got laid if this is all it takes to get me so hard.*

"So," Green Eyes eventually spoke, leaning in close so we could hold a conversation without having to yell, "I'm Ollie."

"Beck," I replied, hoping that my voice came out confident and smooth, because one whiff of Green Eyes' —*Ollie's*— cologne had made me lightheaded.

Ollie clinked our beer bottles together again. "It's nice to meet you, Beck. Come here often?"

* * *

Somehow —and I really had no fucking idea how— we ended up on the dance floor together after all. The bass felt like it was thrumming directly through my veins as we ground against each other. I'd never felt like that before. Had never lost my inhibitions and just *moved* with someone to music in public. But Ollie had all but begged me for 'just one dance' until I'd given in. Then it was *me* practically dry humping the beautiful younger man, not some pretty blonde chick in my place.

With his ass against my front, I was sure he could feel just how much I was enjoying this. But then Ollie spun around, pressed his own erection against mine, wrapped his hand around the back of my neck and pulled me down to breathe "You're so fucking hot, it's *killing* me" into my ear. His warm breath sent a shiver of delicious anticipation down my spine.

It was strange that I reacted so intensely to this man. Sure, he was gorgeous, but I had been with beautiful men before. He was a spitfire, though. His personality seemed to brighten his green eyes and made him seem larger than life. Ollie was brazen, funny, and flirtatious – and that all drew me in like a moth to a flame.

Instead of returning the compliment, I fused my mouth to Ollie's in a kiss that started hot and passionate and only became more intense as we made out on the dance floor, still grinding our clothed cocks together to the sultry beat of the music.

Jesus, I thought as tendrils of pleasure licked through my veins, *I'm gonna come in my pants like I'm thirteen again.*

Ollie's tongue tasted sweet against mine, despite the bitter beer we had been drinking earlier. He smelled like clean sweat and the almost floral cologne that had caught my attention earlier. It was soft, slightly musky, and utterly heady. His skin was warm and firm beneath the thin cotton of his shirt, and I couldn't stop my hands from wandering beneath the hem, my fingers teasing at the smooth flesh of Ollie's lower back and sides.

"Bathroom?" Ollie suggested when we separated for air.

I swallowed roughly. That wasn't me. I didn't *do* club fucks. But I couldn't walk away from Ollie.

Almost as if in a trance, I felt myself nodding, and before I knew it, Ollie had taken me by the hand and was leading me through the throngs of writhing, sweaty bodies and towards the bathrooms hidden at the back of the nightclub.

We joined the queue of patrons in the dimly lit hallway, and I idly wondered how many other guys were lined up to fuck, and how many were lining up to actually use the facilities. The encounter was starting to feel cheap now. Rushed and impulsive and...not *wrong*, per se, but not quite what Ollie deserved.

Ollie's the one that suggested it, the voice in the back of my brain said. *Don't look a gift horse in the mouth. Live a little.*

Still, as the hazy, lusty fog from our kissing wore off, and the line trudged slowly forward, I found myself having second thoughts.

My tension must have been obvious, because Ollie ran a soothing hand down my arm from bicep to wrist and then back up again, asking, "Hey, you okay?"

I shook my head on a sigh. "This isn't me. I don't do…" I gestured vaguely towards the bathroom, scrunching my nose, "*this.*"

There was a flash of disappointment in Ollie's eyes, but he nodded in understanding. "Let's take a walk instead? Cool off outside? Get some air?"

Relief washing over me, I nodded.

* * *

The crisp late October night air, even in the city, was instantly refreshing. I closed my eyes, tilted my head towards the starless sky, and breathed in deeply. It was calming. I wasn't quite sure why I'd gotten all twisted up over the idea of a bathroom hookup but, in the open, less inhibiting bustle of the city's streets, it was like I could function properly again.

Maybe *that* had been the problem. I'd never been a fan of confined spaces. The press and cloying heat of the crowd had probably triggered some sort of claustrophobia, and the very idea of fucking in a tiny, filthy toilet stall had tipped me over the edge.

Now, even though New York's streets were rarely void of pedestrians, I didn't feel as closed in.

"You good?" Ollie asked me after the silence between us

stretched on just long enough for it to become awkward.

I startled at his voice. In the noise of the club, we had been yelling at each other. But now, as traffic swooshed past and people around us chatted at normal volumes, I was hearing my new friend's melodic, smooth timbre for the first time. Ollie's voice was deeper than I had thought it might be. Considering the guy's slight build, I'd expected something a bit higher. I supposed it served me right for stereotyping.

"Yeah," I answered, suddenly feeling a bit sheepish. I rubbed the back of my neck. "Sorry about that. I…" Clearing my throat, I forced myself to meet those pretty green eyes. "Crowds sometimes make me anxious. I get claustrophobic with too many bodies around me." I didn't usually tell strangers about my random issues, but I felt I owed this guy *some* explanation as to why I freaked out before we could hook up.

Ollie's expression was warm and sympathetic, but thankfully there was no pity in his gaze. He didn't seem overly frustrated, either, just a little concerned. "Is there anything I can do to help?"

"Nah, coming out here was enough to snap me out of it." I mustered a grateful smile. I could still feel the magnetic pull between us, but the frantic urge I'd felt on the dance floor to fuck and, of all things, claim ownership of Ollie seemed to be fading into a dull desire that niggled at the back of my brain.

I did not love that last instinct at all. I had never been the possessive sort. In fact, to me, possessive tendencies seemed almost abusive. My partners, though few and far between, were grown men with rights to independence. They could go where they wanted, talk to whomever they desired, even dance with other people if they so chose. It wasn't my place

13

to tell them they couldn't or to get all macho and butthurt if they flirted with someone else. I trusted them not to cheat, just as I expected them to trust me. We were equals.

So then why the ever-loving fuck did I want to turn into some sort of cave man with Ollie? Why did I want to growl and bare my teeth (and that wasn't even a metaphor, what the fuck?) at anyone who so much as looked twice at the smaller man? Why did I want to stake my claim and never let Ollie out of my sight?

It had to have been the claustrophobia. Too many people encroaching into my personal bubble, making me feel trapped and irrational. There was no other logical explanation.

Ollie eyed me skeptically and tugged his jacket around his slim shoulders. This was my favorite time of the year, as the seasons turned and headed towards winter, when the air was crisp and cool and not overwhelming. But I was bigger and bulkier than Ollie. I had more layers of natural insulation, and winter was just around the corner.

Feeling guilty at the way Ollie shivered, I scuffed the toe of my shoe along the cement of the sidewalk. "You should head back in," I said. "Get warm again."

"You're not going to?"

I thought about how good it had felt to have Ollie pressed up against me. How badly I wanted to be inside that lithe, inviting body.

How dirty and wrong it had felt to stand in line for the bathrooms with that purpose in mind.

Shaking my head, I sighed and looked down the busy street, where tourists and locals alike still bustled about as they visited restaurants, nightclubs, and shows. Where cars created long lines of lights against the dimmer night air around us and beeped at each other in New York's standard soundtrack of impatience and hurry. I set my gaze on a vague point in the distance and said, "I'm gonna head home."

"Oh," the disappointment in that single syllable was almost palpable. Ollie's hand, warm despite the way he shivered against the crisp night air, landed on my bare forearm. My jacket was draped over my other elbow, and I considered that maybe I should put it on now that I was out of the hot nightclub. Or maybe I should have offered it to him for extra warmth. "I was hoping…" Ollie trailed off as I turned to look back at him. Removing his hand, he shoved it into his jacket pocket and shrugged. "Never mind."

I felt like an ass. But what was I supposed to say? 'Hey, random guy I just spent God knows how long rubbing up against on the dance floor, I think you're worth more than a filthy fuck in a club toilet stall'? Even I could see how weird the sentiment might sound.

"Listen, I—" I started, but Ollie waved me off.

"No, I get it."

I didn't think he did.

He pasted on a smile and then raised onto his toes to kiss my cheek. The site where his lips met my skin tingled long after the kiss ended. "Maybe I'll see you around," Ollie said with a wink as he pulled back.

Already, my entire body was demanding that I reach out and grab Ollie because the withdrawal and goodbye vibes were bringing back all that weird possessiveness. I forced myself to smile back and nod. "Yeah," I agreed, a ball of lead already forming in my gut. I did not want to let Ollie walk away. I did not want to walk away from Ollie. "Maybe."

Chapter Three – Oliver

❧

"What do you mean you didn't bang him?" Brandi demanded, sounding absolutely dumbstruck. "I saw you two fucking, I mean, *dancing*," her correction was teasing, and she laughed from her spot on my bed, sprawled out across the mattress on her belly, her feet kicking in the air behind her, "on the dance floor before you headed towards the bathrooms. And we *all* know what *that* means."

Her long blonde hair was tied back in a braid, and she toyed with the tail end of it while she raised both eyebrows at me. I sighed and flopped onto my back beside her.

"I mean I didn't bang him," I answered patiently, with the tone of someone talking to a particularly dense child. "He had some sort of panic attack while we were waiting for a stall." My eyebrows drew into a frown as I recalled the experience from the previous night. I still couldn't understand the way Beck had made me feel. That magnetic attraction between us had been intense, and I didn't think that I was the only one who had felt it.

Until the bathroom, things had been going well. Conversation had flowed easily, we'd flirted and teased, and our grinding had been electric. Almost literally! I swore that I had felt genuine sparks inside me, an almost magical energy, like the way I felt during a shift.

Then we'd lined up and Beck had gone all stiff (and not in a good way) and weird. Uncomfortable. Anxious. The tension had passed after we grabbed our jackets and made our way onto the street, but so had that delicious, desperate sexual drive…well, at least it seemed to have gone for Beck.

I had still felt it. Had still wanted so badly for Beck to lift me up with those muscular arms of his and brace me against the nearest wall, fucking into me hard and fast, filling me up and…*whoa.*

My thoughts screeched to a halt. I had never —*not ever*— thought the phrase 'breed me' until right at that moment. As an omega, I thought that the latent biological urges were probably to blame, but the concept of being filled with seed for breeding purposes had never felt hot to me before.

Until I imagined riding Beck's undoubtedly large cock (if the previous night's grinding had been any indication) and begging him to breed me.

Jesus Christ, what is wrong with me?

In a way, I was glad that we hadn't managed to seal the deal, so to speak. I could only imagine what kind of reaction *that* might have gotten from Beck if I'd been unable to control my mouth. And I knew that I was vocal in bed. I couldn't help it. Where was the fun if you didn't let your partner know just how good you felt?

"Well, maybe you dodged a bullet with that one," Brandi

said, bringing my thoughts back to the moment. I frowned, bristling on Beck's behalf.

And wasn't that ridiculous?

I couldn't get Beck out of my head. We had spent a couple of hours together at most, hadn't exchanged full names or phone numbers, and yet I was feeling attached in a way that got under my skin.

I didn't *get* attached. Not like that. Not after barely three seconds of knowing a guy.

What the hell is going on with me?

* * *

For me, work was not all drudgery and grind. After college, I managed to find a job as a research assistant for a shifter doctor and scientist. I worked in a small lab with two other shifters, one a beta named Lacey, who had a distinctly vulpine air about her, and another omega named Colt, who scented like a rabbit to me. Our employer, Doctor Weldman, was yet another omega, but I couldn't quite discern his scent. He only appeared to be in his mid to late thirties, but there was something about his eyes and his mannerisms that suggested he was mature beyond his years.

Finding the job was like finding a needle in a haystack, and I loved going to work. Like me, Weldman was fascinated in researching the evolution of shifters over time and, as a fellow omega, seemed determined to discover why we still existed where alphas did not.

"It's been hundreds of years since the last recorded alpha/omega union," he had said to me on the day I'd interviewed. His golden-colored curls bounced around his heart-

18

shaped face with the motion of his enthusiastic head bobbing. "Therefore, I am studying omega evolution over time, as my theory is that we will, with each generation, slowly become more and more like our beta brethren. Or, perhaps, evolve to the point where we can become pregnant by our beta males."

They weren't unrealistic hypotheses, and I was more than happy to sign on for the cause. I also shared reception duties for his little medical practice with the other two lab techs as well. It was a good job, one I was thoroughly engaged and invested in, and I felt I could learn a lot from Doctor Weldman.

Except when I walked in on Monday, I was agitated. After Friday night's failure to hook up with the hottest man I've ever met (an exaggeration fueled by my growing frustration, I'm sure), Brandi dragged me back out on Saturday night where I proceeded to judge and dismiss any potential *paramours* purely based on the fact that they weren't Beck.

Yeah, I was being ridiculous.

I was never going to see Beck again. I assumed he lived in the city, but so did about eight and a half million others. I mean, I had lived there for five years and had yet to casually bump into Neil Patrick Harris, and I had spent a hell of a lot longer keeping my eyes peeled for any sightings of him.

So Saturday night was a bust, too, and I'd returned home even more frustrated than I had the night before.

And the frustration refused to dissolve. Not even jerking myself off in an extra long shower on Monday morning did anything to help.

So, by the time I got to the lab beneath the tiny doctor's office in Manhattan, I was buzzing with the wrong energy.

"Whoa," Lacey said as I dropped angrily into my chair, "what crawled up your ass?"

"Absolutely nothing," I seethed at her, jabbing my finger at the power button on my laptop. Then I lowered my voice and grizzled under my breath, "Which is exactly the problem."

"Preach," Colt murmured from his own computer, pumping a fist into the air lazily while his eyes never moved from watching his screen. "Horny omegas unite."

Lacey snorted and I leveled another glare her way before I tilted my chin up and raised my voice in Colt's direction. "It's nothing to do with being an omega," I groused. "Everyone gets a little frustrated sometimes." I turned back to Lacey. "Come on, back me up here."

She held her hands in surrender. "I'm Switzerland."

"Bullshit," I scoffed. "Are you telling me you never get antsy because you need a good—" Weldman appeared in the doorway behind Lacey, leaning against the frame with an arched eyebrow, and I switched modes immediately, feigning a bright smile and cheery attitude, "—*morning*, Doctor Weldman. How was your weekend?"

A smirk played about the corners of his lips and I felt my face burn. Doctor Weldman, despite being an omega, was just as tall and masculine as any human gym rat I'd seen. Something about him screamed *alpha*, even though his crescent birthmark was right there on the inside of his left wrist. Mine was on the outside of my right thigh, but any shifter looking at my slight frame and almost androgynous features would know I was an omega – I was practically a textbook definition come to life. But Doctor Weldman…well, he bucked those stereotypes. It was intimidating, really.

"I've asked you before to call me Eric, Ollie," he admonished gently, then let the almost predatory grin he'd been suppressing take over his face. "And, for your reference, everyone gets sexually frustrated, yes, but I believe omegas can feel it a bit more intensely at times: a throwback to when meeting a compatible alpha would encourage the onset of a mating heat."

"Told you," Colt muttered, and I threw a baleful scowl in his direction, but he was still staring intently at his computer screen, so I was basically just glaring at his peroxide blonde head. He tended to get tunnel vision when he was in research mode, which was a good ninety percent of the time, as far as I'd seen.

"Anyway," Doctor Weldman continued, shaking his head in what seemed to be fond amusement, "who drew the short straw to cover reception duties today? I'm about to open up the clinic."

Both of my colleagues touched the tips of their noses with their index fingers faster than I could blink, and then everyone's eyes were on me. I fought the urge to growl and throw the temper tantrum I could feel building inside me.

That's just great. Just what I need to really make this day perfect.

I sighed, shut down my laptop, and got out of my chair, forcing a smile at my boss. "I guess that's me."

I didn't hate the receptionist duties, but all I'd wanted was to bury myself in my research —in the passion project I shared with my boss— and to try to forget about my shitty luck with men. Instead, I was going to spend the day dealing with the sick and miserable people of New York.

Lucky me.

I could only hope that these feelings passed and that the day went quickly.

Chapter Four – Beckett

"What crawled up your ass and died?"

I turned to growl at Sandy, one of my roommates. Her teasing words were like rubbing salt into a wound, stinging and gritty, and I was not impressed. But she wasn't at all intimidated by my show of frustration.

Sandy just snorted and reached around me for the pot of coffee I had brewed.

Our apartment was a shoebox, with a tiny ass kitchen and no real living room to speak of, but it had three small bedrooms and a functioning bathroom, and between three of us, we could afford to live in one of the most expensive cities in the world fairly comfortably. Except for at times like these, where my roommates were intruding too far into my personal bubble for my liking.

"Chill, dude," she chuckled. I narrowed my gaze to the back of her bright red pixie cut, startling when she added, "And don't give me that look, you have been in a mood for weeks now."

It was not a lie. My shoulders slumped. I had been wound tight ever since that night at the club across town. Ever since making out with and practically fucking a super hot guy on a dance floor then letting him walk away without exchanging phone numbers or whole names. No amount of jerking off in the shower seemed to help with the ever-present need to find him and fuck him into a mattress, and, if I closed my eyes, I could still smell his cologne, and I could still picture his pretty face clearly.

This was not normal.

Who got fixated so badly that they woke up every morning with a guy's name on their lips and an erection that ached to the point of pain? I had only spent a couple of hours flirting and dancing with Ollie, but the degree of my obsession was disturbing.

So, in addition to feeling like I had a constant case of blue balls, I was irritated with myself for being unable to prevent this random fixation. I was constantly horny and hating myself for it, especially when any attempts to find someone else to help me scratch the itch failed abysmally.

It had been two weeks since that fateful night, and my frustration had yet to fade. Even Halloween had come and gone without my usual enthusiasm for getting into costume and scaring the crap out of the kids who came to the apartment door.

I knew I was being a jerk to my friends, and it was just luck that I worked from home as a freelance graphic artist, so I didn't have to go out and face the public like this. If anything, I had sequestered myself away in my bedroom-slash-home office for as long as I could, only surfacing to use the bathroom or in search of food and caffeine.

I felt a stab of guilt for the way I was behaving. Micah, our other roommate, had made himself scarce. I could hardly blame him.

Grimacing, I leaned back against the kitchen counter and said, "Sorry, Sandy. I suck."

"Love the alliteration," she teased. Having poured herself a coffee, she turned to face me and leaned back against the tiny square of benchtop next to the sink, where the coffee pot lived. There was barely a foot of space between us. After taking a sip of her coffee, which she drank black and sugarless like some sort of weirdo, she eyed me over the top of the cup. "Wanna talk about it?"

For all that she looked like some sort of bad ass punk rock queen, Sandy was the ultimate sweetheart. She was patient and kind, and never failed to stop to help someone in need. She often went without so she could buy extra lunches for the little homeless community who were squatting in an abandoned building near her office. If she thought you were hurting, she would move heaven and hell to try and make things better. We'd met in foster care. She'd aged out of the system first, but had come to get me on my eighteenth birthday, making sure I knew that I had a home with her if I needed one.

Over a decade later, and I was still living with her crazy ass. Sandy was the sister I'd never had, and seeing the concern in her eyes as she cautiously asked me to spill my guts had the guilt roiling all over again.

"I'm…going through something weird," I admitted.

She arched a brown eyebrow. Apparently, it was too much work and effort to dye them to match her hair. I didn't question it. "Something weird?" she echoed.

I nodded. "Yeah. You know that night you and Micah

dragged me out to that random club across the city?"

Sandy's forehead furrowed in confusion. "Like…two weeks ago? For Kate's birthday? And then you ditched us?"

"That's the one," I nodded. "So, I met this guy—"

"Oh no," she groaned, her face scrunching into concern and sympathy, "did you catch an STI? Because doctors are miracle workers these days, and—"

"No, I did not catch an STI." I could feel a smile threatening to tug at my lips. "But mad props for not getting all judgy about the possibility."

"Shit happens," she shrugged my words off, once again reminding me why I love her so damn much. "Catching an STI doesn't make you dirty or a bad person or anything like that. But, still, I'm glad you're not suffering through one." Cocking her head, she prompted, "So, if that's not it…"

"It's stupid," I huffed and crossed my arms, studiously avoiding her gaze. "I met him, and I felt…*ugh*…like, insanely affected by him. Like, it's been two weeks, and I can't get him out of my head. It's fucking with me."

Sandy blinked at me. "So, why not call him?"

This is the point where I could feel my cheeks start to burn. "I didn't get his number. Or his name. He introduced himself as Ollie. That's all I have to go on."

And, at that point, I had started to look for him. I'd started to trawl through Facebook profiles and had considered walking the streets around the club with my Grindr app open, hoping the proximity to where we'd met might equal proximity to his place.

Yeah, I was in a bad way.

"Oh, babe," Sandy pulled me in for a hug, her tiny petite body practically enfolded within mine, her head not even reaching my chin. "I'm sorry. That sucks."

I liked that she didn't try to placate me or tell me that if it was 'meant to be' I would meet Ollie again. She just hugged me and, while it did nothing to make my body crave him any less, some of the frustration did ebb away.

"Just promise me that you've learned your lesson from this and you'll get the next guy's number," she teased as she pulled away from the hug and I nodded emphatically.

"I promise."

* * *

"So, are we doing our usual for Thanksgiving?" Sandy asked me as we sat on a park bench, sharing a pizza from our favorite hole in the wall joint. This was somewhat of a ritual for us, something we'd started as teens in a shitty foster home when we'd needed to escape the house for a little while. Pizzas were cheap and delicious, and eating them in the park was nice. Relaxing.

I stared out over the grass which was beginning to turn that muted color it always did as winter started to set in and considered my reply. Our Thanksgiving 'usual' was to volunteer at a local shelter, dishing out meals to those less fortunate than us, before heading home to eat microwave dinners and catch the highlights from whichever football games had been played during the day while we avidly discussed the hottest players on the teams.

"Sure," I shrugged, still trying to get out of my mood. Thanksgiving was still another couple of weeks away, and after that everything would change to Christmas mania. As it was, festive lights and decorations were already strategically placed over the city.

Christmas was never my favorite holiday. Growing up in the system meant that all the magic of being visited by Santa and showered with gifts...well, to say that didn't happen is an understatement. In my earliest years, I was convinced it meant that I wasn't a good enough kid. I was on the naughty list no matter what I did, and that was heartbreaking when I was five.

When I was older, or at least old enough to understand it had nothing to do with me personally, I was just resentful that my life hadn't been fair. By the time I reached adulthood, I didn't see Christmas as anything special: just a Hallmark holiday where privileged people exerted their privilege, and everyone else pretended to be happy for a day.

Yeah.

So, I was a bit jaded. Add to that my lingering frustration over the whole Ollie situation, and I wasn't feeling particularly thankful or festive.

"Hey," Sandy nudged my knee with hers. "Don't go turning back into Mister Crankypants."

I couldn't help laughing. "Been spending a lot of time with kindergartners, have you?"

"Been watching Yoda, have you?" She shot back mockingly.

"Touché," I inclined my head, then snagged another slice of the delicious, cheesy goodness and bit down on it with relish.

We sat in companionable silence while we ate, and I started to feel like maybe, for the first time in weeks, I was returning to some semblance of normal. Then I saw him.

He was nothing but a sense of movement out of the corner of my eye at first, but I turned my head instinctively, and almost choked on the mouthful of dough and cheese I had just taken.

Spluttering while Sandy gave my back a few solid whumps with her fist, I kept my eyes glued to Ollie the entire time.

He was, of course, oblivious to my presence. Walking along the nearby pathway, chatting animatedly with the blonde he'd been dancing with when I first saw him two weeks earlier, he was just as breathtaking to behold now as he had been then. His slim legs were encased in skinny jeans that I was sure hugged his perfect, perky ass, but the oversized, plush hoodie he was wearing covered him to mid-thigh. His light brown hair was windswept, coiffed back off his forehead and pretty face, and I wanted to kiss those inviting pink lips of his so badly it was almost a physical ache.

"Beck, what…?" Sandy started to ask, but I had stood up and jogged towards Ollie with the same tunneled focus that I had felt in the club.

"Ollie," I said as cheerfully and non-stalkerly as possible as I approached, trying to tame the wide, incredulous grin that threatened to split my face. "Hi!" And then, feeling awkward because he probably wasn't as fixated on me as I was on him, I stuck my hands deep into my jeans pockets and rocked back on my heels. "Sorry. I'm Be—"

"Beck," he said my name on an exhale, and I looked up from my feet to see the surprise and unmistakable wonder on his face. "Wow. Hi."

Then strained silence descended…until we both started to speak at the same time.

"How'd you find—?" he asked, while I went for "What are you—?"

We both stopped and chuckled, and I was becoming more than aware that we had an audience. His blonde friend was staring at me with absolutely no attempt to conceal her interest, and Sandy had followed me over and had her head cocked at Ollie, her eyes slightly narrowed, and her nostrils flared. I didn't know what that was about, but I inched a bit closer to her and kicked out at her shin. She schooled her expression after that.

"I swear I'm not stalking you," I told him once I realized that we were now both waiting for the other to speak. "I saw you and, uh," I rubbed the back of my neck, feeling sheepish – even more so with our peanut gallery watching. Taking a deep breath, I said, "I should have asked for your number the other night. I thought…well, maybe I could take you to dinner sometime?"

"How about tonight?" Ollie's bubbly blonde friend chirped before Ollie could say anything. She beamed at me. "He suddenly has absolutely zero plans."

"*Brandi*," Ollie hissed at her, but she waved him away, still smiling at me. "How does seven sound to you? Give me your phone."

I did as Brandi asked, a little bit dazed by her direct approach. She tapped at the phone, then handed it back to me.

"Great. Now you have Ollie's number, and he has yours 'cause I just texted him from your phone, and he's," she reached into the big, baggy front pocket of his hoodie and her hand emerged victorious with Ollie's phone, "about to save your number and text you his address."

Ollie just closed his eyes, exhaled, then looked up to the sky as if seeking guidance. Or patience. Or both. After a moment, he looked back at me and shrugged. "Seven it is."

Chapter Five – Oliver

C learly, the universe liked the idea of me meeting the man I had been thinking about nonstop for the previous two weeks *way* more than it liked the idea of me fanboying at Neil Patrick Harris.

"So, it looks like Mystery Man missed you about as much as you missed him," Brandi declared once we were back in my studio apartment…if you could call the tiny square of space I lived in an apartment.

Filled with only a bed, a desk, a little freestanding wardrobe, a kitchenette containing the barest of essentials, and finally my 'shoilet' room (which could not be considered a bathroom for how insanely small and poky it was), it was ridiculous how much rent I was paying for the space. But it was mine alone, and it was in New York and away from my pack, and I was happy there.

"Beck has had a name since we met," I reminded her with a roll of my eyes, "which you knew, so I don't know why you insist on that ridiculous nickname for him."

"Uh huh," she pushed off the bed and opened the door to my wardrobe, flicking through the hangers with a little frown on her face. "Except 'Beck,'" I could hear the quotation marks around his name, "isn't a full name, you don't know anything about the guy other than the fact that he has what felt like a big dick, and that he kisses like you're oxygen and he'll die without you."

I hated that she had a point. After I had suffered through yet another one of my mother's calls that morning, Brandi had dragged me out for a walk through Central Park, one of my favorite calming activities at any time of year. The oasis of nature in the middle of such an overpopulated concrete jungle never failed to calm and center me. I had been on edge ever since that night in the club, and it was frustrating that I'd had no way to track down the man who had gotten so thoroughly into my head and under my skin. It was even more frustrating that I was so invested when I knew next to nothing about the guy.

"Not true," I still argued back, because that was just our dynamic. "I know his phone number now. And that he has a friend who looked very unimpressed by me."

A shifter friend. Another wolf, in fact. She hadn't needed to growl or bare her teeth for me to get the message that she was very protective of her human companion. To be fair, though, I would have been the same about Brandi. In fact, I *had* been the same about Brandi in the past, not that any of her human boyfriends had picked up on it.

"Yeah, well, it looked like he was just as excited to bump into you as you were, so maybe she's just worried that he'll get hurt." Brandi looked up from the shirt she had been inspecting and gave me a soft smile. "I can relate to that."

"Don't get sappy on me now, Brooks," I told her, waggling my index finger at her accusingly.

"I wouldn't dream of it." She held out a white shirt with a blue paisley print, tilting her head to the side as she imagined me wearing it. "Yeah," she said, "this is the one. With your skinny jeans and the black jacket."

"I'm nothing but your own personal Ken doll, am I?"

Brandi rolled her eyes again. "Honey, Ken has abs."

I gasped dramatically, pressing my hand to my stomach. It had a softness to it, despite my slim twinky build, and she knew I was sensitive about it. "Fuck you," I complained, but there was no heat to the words.

Still, she had the grace to look apologetic. "You're gorgeous, Ollie. You know it." Then her grin turned positively wolfish. "And if you wear this, you're guaranteed to get laid tonight."

* * *

I met Beck outside my building at seven on the dot. He wore dark jeans, a black dress shirt, and a black leather jacket. His dark hair was cut short, and his beard stubble was practically begging me to nibble along his strong jawline.

I felt my heart rate pick up speed as I took him in, my mouth somehow watering even as my throat went dry.

Holy hell, this man is sexy.

Beck seemed to be taking me in with the same level of appreciation. His eyes swept over me greedily, and I preened under his hungry appraisal.

"Hi," he said when our eyes met, and I loved the husk to his voice. It was a sound that seemed to verify Brandi's earlier words.

As long as nothing I said or did during this date fucked things up, I was guaranteed to get lucky.

My cock stirred at the thought, and I was startled to feel my natural slick building inside me. The latter rarely ever happened with humans unless I was exceedingly horny.

To be fair, it rarely ever happened with shifters, either.

Hell, it had been *weeks* since I'd last gotten laid. Months, if I was being completely honest.

Maybe the unexpected burst of slick came from the fact that I was crazy horny and not from the weird instant connection I felt to this man.

Either way, I tried to calm my raging hormones. I didn't want to sit in a puddle of slick or have to explain the inevitable wet patch later if it got that bad. It never had before, but I had a feeling that if it was going to happen, it would be with Beck.

Clearing my throat, I smiled softly back at him. "Hi," I greeted.

"You look amazing," he complimented, and my smile widened.

"You too." I made a bigger show of eyeing him over, before giving my head a quick shake and clenching my ass. "So, where are we going for dinner?"

He took me to my favorite Thai restaurant, literally two blocks away from my apartment. It was a pretty little space, decorated in fairy lights and shades of purple paint. The accents were all gold, and the plates they served our meals on were white with gold rims. It felt a lot fancier than it ought to, considering how affordable the meals here were.

Beck and I shared our meals, a delicious penang curry and a heaped, steaming serve of chicken pad thai, and drank the imported beers that the server suggested. As we ate, we chatted easily.

I learned that he was a graphic designer, freelancing out of his home, creating anything from website graphics and logos to book covers for his client base. He pulled out his phone when I asked to see some of his work, showing me his website and substantial portfolio.

"Wow," I said, genuinely impressed. "You're talented."

He shrugged, his cheeks turning a little pink with the praise, but he accepted it gracefully, "Thanks. I've been doing it for over ten years. Maybe even closer to fifteen, because I started as a teenager, so…yeah."

I cocked my head at him. "How, um, how old are you?" I was never great at guessing a person's age on sight. "I'm twenty-two, in case you're wondering."

"Shit," he exhaled, sitting back heavily in his timber chair. "I knew you were younger, but…wow. Okay." He cleared his throat. "I'm thirty-one."

Nine years. That wasn't that big an age gap, right? Although, when I was barely of legal drinking age, maybe it seemed a lot to him. I reached out across the small timber table to hold his forearm, which was bare as he'd taken off his jacket before he sat down and had rolled his sleeves up before we started eating. I'd found the whole thing hotter than such a simple action should have been.

Rubbing my thumb over the smooth, exposed skin of his inner forearm, I met his gaze firmly. "Are you okay with that? Or are you freaking out?"

"Over being in my thirties?" he joked. "Yeah, I hit thirty and had a mid-life crisis."

I snorted. "Okay. Firstly, thirty is *not* mid-life. Secondly, you know that's not what I meant."

"Yeah," he moved his arm back, until my palm rested over his. He closed his fingers loosely over mine and squeezed. Thrills of electricity traveled up my arm and directly to my heart, and to my cock and ass.

Jesus. At an innocent touch? Really?

"Nine years feels like a lot," he said while I tried to wrangle my body's reactions back into submission, "but this thing between us feels good, right? Like...important? Different? *Big.*" He swallowed and I watched his Adam's apple bob. "And if it is *something*, like I feel it could be, I don't think nine years will mean much in the long run."

Wow.

Was this the difference between men in their thirties and men my own age? Because nobody I'd ever dated or slept with before had mentioned long-term relationship plans, especially not with me. And certainly not on the first date.

But I was happy to consider this our second date, with the club being our impromptu first.

"Ah, fuck," Beck cursed as I gaped at him. "I'm the creep who's gone too fast. I'm sorry. I didn't mean to freak you out. I—"

"No, no," I rushed to correct him, gripping his hand tightly before he could pull it away. "No, I was just surprised. I mean, yeah, it's unorthodox, but it's not like you were getting down on one knee and proposing. You just said you *can* see us being something serious. You didn't even expect it or anything. Just that it could be. It's," I paused, considering my words, "*refreshing*, you know? To talk to someone who is honest about how they feel. No games. No lies. No guessing." I smiled at him in what I hoped relayed reassurance as well as my genuine curiosity. "So...you're looking for a serious relationship?"

35

Beck snickered lightly, but it sounded kind of self-deprecating. "I wasn't looking for anything until I met you."

From anyone else, that line might have been stupidly cheesy, but I could feel his honesty rolling off him in waves. Similarly, I had to admit that I felt the same way. And that still scared me a little.

I had never considered being in a serious relationship with anyone before, but here I was, getting freaked out over the fact that I *wasn't* freaking out over it.

Yeah, follow that logic, I dare you.

The idea of being with Beck long-term just felt right. But, considering we didn't really know each other, it probably shouldn't have.

Nevertheless, it made it a hell of a lot easier to lower my voice and give him my most sultry, flirtatious look as I asked, "Did you wanna get out of here?"

He paid the check in record time.

* * *

Somehow, we managed to make it back to my apartment before we began mauling each other. As soon as the door was shut behind us, though, all bets were off. I found myself being pushed up against the closed door just as I had fantasized about while we'd waited in line for the bathrooms at the club, Beck's mouth fused to mine, our tongues reconnecting in a frenzied tango while we kicked off our shoes.

Beck kissed like if he didn't, he might die. It was all heat and desire and desperate need. His hands cupped my ass, squeezing and fondling me through my tight denim. Slick threatened to pool in my underwear, but I was not going to stop this. I needed him just as badly as he seemed to need me.

However, it did mean I would need to explain what I was. Not only because him discovering how wet I was might throw him off, but because he deserved to know before we went any further.

Hell, my being a shifter might be enough to throw him off anyway.

That realization cooled my mood almost instantly, and I forced the kiss to slow down, toying with the short strands of hair at the nape of his neck as I urged my racing heart to calm down.

"Hey," with his thumb and index finger curled around my chin, he gently tilted my head back so he could look me in the eye. His dark brown orbs were full of concern. "Everything okay?"

"Yeah," I nodded, then swallowed. "I just…um, before we do this, you should know that I'm, uh, different."

"Different how?"

Not wanting to have this conversation while pressed up against my door, I gestured for him to take a seat on my bed, flushing at not having any other options for him. "Sorry," I muttered, taking off my jacket and slinging it over one of the two bar stools at my tiny kitchen counter, "my apartment is a glorified college dorm." But it had central heating, which was a plus in the chilly winters.

"It's New York," Beck shrugged and removed his own jacket, then leaned forward to toss it over mine. "The fact that you've got a place all to yourself, no matter how small, is impressive." Patting the spot beside him, he smiled patiently. "But I don't think your apartment is what you were talking about."

"No," I agreed. "It's not. I, um…"

"Whatever it is," he reached for my hand, holding it in his,

"I don't think it'll change how into you I am."

Reassured as much as I could be, I took a deep breath, looked down at the worn, scuffed linoleum flooring, and blurted, "I'm a shifter."

"A…shifter?" Beck didn't sound repulsed, just a little confused. "I thought…well, I guess I thought shifters were pretty much a myth. Extinct."

Shaking my head, I sighed. "We don't exactly advertise it anymore. Assimilation and hiding in plain sight is easier than being hunted down for being different. But…well, I don't feel right going into a potential relationship without you knowing. I totally understand if it's a deal-breaker, considering I'm technically a different species, but…"

"Whoa, no. Not a deal-breaker." He released my hand to cup my cheeks with his broad palms and stared at me seriously. "I'm still just as into you as I was before. Maybe even more now because honesty is hot." He waggled his eyebrows which encouraged a small laugh out of me as he pulled his hands away. Then he licked his lips and asked, "What kind of shifter? Or, like, can you just choose at will or something? It's been a long time since I learned about shifters in school. And, back then, it was mostly olden timey history…"

"Olden timey history," I repeated with a snort. But it made sense. Humans had run shifters out of the public eye a long, long time ago. "I'm a wolf shifter, and, no, I'm not affected by the cycles of the moon or anything like that. Not a werewolf. *Those* are myths. But there are other kinds out there. If the animal exists, it's likely there are shifters of the same. We're really good about keeping it hidden. A history of being hunted or experimented on will do that to a species."

I watched his face closely for any sign that he was uncomfortable with the concept, but he only nodded thoughtfully. "Why tell me?" he asked. "Not that I don't appreciate it, but you look perfectly human. You didn't have to say anything."

My cheeks flushed with heat. "That's true, but I'm what's classified as an omega. It's a genetic curse, mostly. Not contagious," I rushed to explain, "but my body is basically built to breed with an alpha. Except alpha shifters went extinct a couple of hundred years ago, so I can't have kids, but my body still thinks it can. It...um...well, hey, you know how women, uh, self-lubricate during sex?" I cringed as the awkward words left my mouth. I was a scientist, damn it, I should find it easy to discuss clinical stuff like that.

Beck's lips twitched with amusement, but he tried to follow my strained ramblings anyway. "Uh...not that I have personal experience with that, but...yeah?"

I could feel my blush getting deeper and hotter. "As an omega, under the right circumstances, my body produces slick. It, uh, usually it happens after lube has already been introduced, but tonight..." I cleared my throat again, shifting my hips against the moisture I could feel threatening to dampen my briefs and jeans.

It took Beck a moment to follow along, and then his cheeks pinked up, too. "Oh. Wow. That's—"

"Weird, I know."

"Hot," he breathed, and I watched as his hand twitched, like it wanted to reach out and explore. "Like...*really* hot, Ollie."

I blinked at him. "Wait...what?"

"Can I..." he licked his lips. "Can we..." Stopping, he gave himself a shake. "Sorry, I just...I'm...I know we're having this serious conversation, but now all I want to do is undress you and discover what it feels like. What *you* feel like."

He brought his gaze back up to meet mine. I could see blatant desire shining in them and, just like that, the smoldering embers of our magnetic connection burst back into the raging inferno of need and desperation that I'd felt for him two weeks ago.

I lunged, tackling him down onto the mattress, my lips moving against his with what felt like practiced movements now. His hands tugged at my shirt, and he growled in frustration when he couldn't just pull it over my head.

"Buttons," I laughed against his mouth, excited by the fact that he was just as worked up as I was, "hang on."

I sat back up and undid the first few down the column of pearly white circles, and then I undid the cuffs as well. That was enough for him to finally pull the whole garment up and over my head, throwing the shirt somewhere near my wardrobe.

Beck's dark brown eyes shone as he looked at me, and I fought the urge to cross my arms over my undefined chest and belly. I could only see pure appreciation on his face, so I didn't think he minded what he saw.

"Beautiful," he breathed, reaching out to smooth his hands up my sides. Then he wrapped them around my back and pulled me in for another hungry kiss. His cotton shirt was smooth against the exposed skin of my chest, and I could feel how warm and firm his body was beneath it.

"Your turn," I demanded, pulling at his shirt now. My whole body felt like it was on fire as desperation to get him naked overtook me.

He groaned as he pulled back to undo his own buttons, big, thick fingers fumbling with the tiny, flat black circles. I brushed his hands away and did it myself, relishing the way popping each button free of its corresponding hole revealed a strip of golden hued skin. Forcing myself to slow down, I took my time unwrapping him, unconcerned that I was leaking slick freely now, far too preoccupied with seeing my mate's perfect body for the first time.

Whoa, whoa, wait.

Mate?

Where the fuck had that come from?

I'd never had that thought before, either. Beck's very presence brought out something primal in me. It felt good and right, and despite the fact that he was a human, I knew I'd be begging for him to breed me before the night was out.

I paused only briefly to consider warning him about my previously undiscovered kink but thought better of it. I might be able to keep the words from spilling over if I bit down on my pillow, right?

By the time I was helping him slip his shirt from his broad shoulders, I felt positively underdeveloped next to him. He was built like a Grecian god, with finely sculpted biceps and pecs hiding beneath lush, dark hair, and a toned abdomen that wasn't exactly a six pack but was certainly all muscle. I was salivating. I was hot all over, as though I was blushing furiously from head to toe. My cock was steadily leaking precum. And my ass? I had never felt so wet with my own slick before.

Just looking at Beck had turned me into a literal puddle of desire and need.

"You like?" he asked me playfully when all I could do was gape at the perfection on display.

"I want to lick every inch of you," I blurted the confession without thought, running my hand through the thick, dark hair of his chest, down the solid plains of his abs and to that enticing V made by his (aptly titled) Adonis belt.

Under the confines of his thick denim jeans, I could see his bulge straining. With my eyes glued to what I was doing, I popped the button above his fly, then lowered the zipper.

His cock, still encased in soft black cotton boxer briefs, pushed outwards as soon as it was given the room to do so, and Beck groaned with muted relief. I gave him no reprieve, tucking my fingers into the combined waistbands of both his jeans and underwear, and carefully tugged them over his hips, then down his thighs. He climbed off the bed to shuck them completely.

I swear to God, my ass clenched around air at the sight of his naked body on display. His cock was, as I'd surmised from our earlier experiences, big and thick. He was uncut, and the skin was flushed dark with his intense arousal, the tip glossy with precum. His cock was so hard that it bobbed in the air in my direction seemingly under its own power, like a divining rod searching for me specifically.

I wanted it in my hand. In my mouth. In my ass.

"Your turn," Beck repeated my words back at me, his tone low and husky with need.

I came back to myself, realizing that my briefs were definitely damp, and I closed my eyes, feeling embarrassed.

"Hey," he all but crooned, "don't do that. Don't hide from me, baby." He pushed me back onto the mattress and crawled over me, peppering my skin with kisses until he reached my lips. His kiss was urgent but closed mouthed. When he raised himself back up, his hands worked at the button of my jeans and then my zipper, hooking inside the waistbands of both as he looked down at me. "Is this okay?"

I reminded myself that I'd told him what I was, what my body was capable of. He'd seemed excited by it, not repulsed.

I nodded.

Unlike the slow reveal of his body which I'd gifted myself, he made short work of getting me naked, tossing my slick-soiled clothes behind him onto the pile with the others. I felt exposed for only a moment as he spread my thighs and then moaned.

"Fuck," he said reverently, "Ollie...Jesus. Look at you. Can I...?"

Splayed out on my bed, I nodded fervently. Still feeling hot all over, I was burning up with the increasing need to have him inside me. "Please," I begged, lifting my hips shamelessly. "Please, Beck..."

He started almost torturously slowly, bringing his fingers up to massage my balls and gently stroke my taint, chuckling as I whined and bucked upwards, even as I felt more slick trickling from me. Then his searching fingers found my hole, and the groan that issued from his throat that time was almost a guttural growl.

He drew out another long, low "Fuck" and slid both his fingers into me with an ease that, if I had been human with zero prep, would likely have caused discomfort and encountered a lot more resistance. "You feel so hot and wet," he proclaimed. "I need you around my cock, baby."

"Yes," I agreed, almost delirious with the raging necessity for him to fuck me already. "Yes, please, yes. N-now," I babbled and spread my legs wider, lifting my ass up from the mattress in not-exactly-silent invitation. "Beck. *Beckett*, please. I can't..." I was on the verge of sobbing. It was like his fingers breaching me had flipped a switch inside me, one I

43

couldn't turn back off.

Using his whole name seemed to force him into action. I'd only learned it over dinner, but it felt right on my tongue. In my soul. Everything about him did.

In a flash, Beck was crawling back over me, and he lined the head of his cock up against my entrance, guiding himself with one hand while bracing his body over mine with the other planted firmly on the mattress. The show of effortless strength had me damn near panting.

"Shit," he froze over me, the burning tip of his cock poised to breach me. His body had gone rigid with tension, and it wasn't the sexy kind.

"What?" I asked, trying to sound patient and not like I was a hair's breadth away from impaling myself on that beautiful, impressive shaft. I was hot all over, and my heart was hammering in my chest, and I *needed*.

Oh, fuck, I needed.

"Condom," Beck grit out. "I'm not…I mean, in my wallet…" He cast a baleful look back over his shoulder, towards the direction of our pile of discarded clothes.

"I'm a shifter," I reminded him, extrapolating, "human STIs don't really affect us. I'm negative, and I can't catch anything if you're positive, even if your viral load is—"

"I'm not," he interrupted, losing some of the rigidity in his shoulders. "I'm negative, too. But you're sure you don't want…?"

In answer, I cut off his question by surging my hips towards his magnificent body, sighing with relief as I felt him slide into me.

"Oh, *fuck*," Beck practically growled the word, his voice deep and beyond husky. It drew into a long groan of a word. He

44

let go of the base of his shaft to brace his body on both hands as his hips propelled him forwards on instinct. "Ollie, baby, you feel...*fuck*."

Yeah, I thought wryly, *that's an apt description.*

Having him inside me was somehow soothing. It was like the building frustration of the two weeks since we'd met was calmed almost instantly. Like my body had very specifically been craving Beck's and now that we were finally united the way it had wanted to be, it could relax.

Except it wasn't relaxing. It felt good. Better than good. Phenomenal. Was there a stronger word than phenomenal? Super-fucking-fuckalistic-expi-fucka-docius? Because it was that.

My entire body seemed to light up as we connected in this most primal of ways. He felt hard and hot and huge inside me, ticking all my sexual boxes and then some. I could feel how flushed my skin was, and I writhed as Beck thrust, whimpering and pleading with him to go harder and faster.

"How...how are you so *tight*?" he asked between his own heavy breaths. "You're so *hot* inside, baby. Hot and tight and wet and...fuck, I'm not gonna last long." He reached between us to grip my cock, stroking it while I continued to beg him for more.

Then he shifted his angle and finally found my prostate.

I saw stars.

Three long, hard thrusts of Beck's hips after that, and I was howling out my release, spurting ropes of cum that splashed his beautiful chest, marking him as mine. That thought was so good, I growled it at him.

Despite the orgasm, I wasn't satiated, which was odd.

Usually, coming hard like that would see me drifting off into a very satisfied sleep. But this time, I still had to have more. I was getting hard again, aching for him again, and he reared back with his eyebrows raised, his hand still wrapped around my dick.

"Is that," he panted, sounding equally desperate to come, "a shifter perk?"

"I don't," I paused to moan as he brushed over my prostate again, "I don't know. It's never...oh, God, *right there!*" I arched my back, encouraging him to go deeper. "Um, it's new."

Nodding, Beck leaned all the way down again, connecting our mouths in a sloppier, messier kiss. Then he slid his arms beneath me, wrapping me up in him, and rolled us over, until he was the one lying back on the bed and I was seated on his cock, somehow taking him even deeper inside me.

His hands went to my hips, guiding me to bounce in place, to ride him and take my pleasure. It wasn't exactly a chore to do, especially not with the view I had.

His chest glistened with sweat, his muscles rippled with exertion, and his face contorted in ecstasy.

"Sit up," I demanded, leaning back, not disconnecting our bodies from where we were connected, but moving with him as he complied without argument. "I want to kiss you. I want to touch all of you. I want...I want..."

It was awkward, but we managed it, shuffling up along the bed until he was sitting up with his back supported by a pile of pillows and the basic timber headboard. I was still in his lap, my legs crossed behind his ass, and our heaving chests were only a few scant inches apart.

Something inside me practically purred at the position and the proximity.

Mate, the instinct said. *Mine*.

46

I curled my arms around his neck, bringing our mouths back together. Another wave of unexpected warmth curled out-wards from my belly, extending to my extremities, demanding that I ride him hard.

So, while kissing him like oxygen was not in fact a necessity, I did.

Beck's hands gripped my hips, his fingers digging into the soft flesh there, likely leaving bruises. He was marking me. I wanted to throw my head back and howl, to let every shifter in the vicinity know that my mate had chosen me.

These feelings should have startled me, but I was lost in the moment. All I knew was that we had a deeper, more primal connection than I'd shared with any previous lovers before. Perhaps it was the two weeks of lead-up making this so much more intense. I wasn't about to complain.

Beck pulled back from the kiss but leaned his forehead against mine. His breath was warm against my face, his lips still tantalizingly close. It was like he also felt the importance to stay as connected as possible.

"Ollie," Beck's voice was gravelly, once again almost a growl, and it spoke to my inner wolf like he truly was my mate calling to me. "Ollie, baby, I'm gonna come. I'm gonna...oh fuck. Fuck, fuck, *fuck.*"

He tensed and released inside me in a hot rush, filling me up the way I'd craved, and I gasped because I swore I could feel it. I could feel his cock when it stiffened and seemed to swell impossibly harder. I could feel it pulse as jet after jet of his orgasm rocketed through him and into me.

Then, inexplicably, he *did* seem to swell more. I felt the pressure and stretch inside me, and I yelped and ground down as the press against my prostate became constant and blindingly blissful.

Beck cried out and, on instinct, I bared my neck to him.

He bit down.

Pleasure unlike anything I had ever experienced exploded from somewhere in my chest. I saw stars and strobing white lights, and I came releasing another burst of cum that coated our stomachs as we moved together. In that moment, I was driven by the same deep-seated urge that had seen me baring my neck. I turned my head and bit him back, right in the smooth, salty juncture where his neck met his shoulder.

He *roared* and I was assaulted by another wave of orgasmic bliss, but it wasn't my own. I don't know how I knew it, but it was an echo of his pleasure.

I didn't have time to marvel over that, though, because he was coming again.

"What…" he breathed, and I could feel his confusion and building panic. "Oliver. What's," he groaned, flooding my insides, *"ungh…*what's happening?"

I'd only ever heard of these sorts of things in stories. They were essentially nothing but legend, historical anecdotes at best.

Alphas did not exist. Alphas were extinct.

I moved experimentally, feeling the way we were locked together, inciting Beck's grip to tighten on my hips again as he cried out another release, the echoes of which I felt in my soul. Even though I had nothing left in me, my cock spurted weakly with the continued pleasure of it all.

"We're *mated,*" I told him with disbelief, wondering if he could feel my emotions like I could his. "You're…you're *knotting* me, Beck." I was careful with the way I leaned back, meeting his gaze with wonder and awe. "You're an alpha."

Instead of a reciprocation of my amazement, I could feel —and see— Beck's panic growing. "I'm *human*, Oliver. What… what did you do to me?"

And, with those words, my heart plummeted to my stomach.

Chapter Six – Beckett

Wｅ were stuck together. Tied. Knotted. However Ollie wanted to describe it, we were stuck. *I* was stuck. Inside him.

How was this my life?

Mated, he'd said. We were mated. I wasn't an idiot, and I could use my context clues, so I gathered that to mate was to do more than just fuck. The feelings resonating out of him, tickling the back of my brain and settling in my chest, made me think that being mated was some link or bond. We had, against all odds, just connected ourselves together magically, for lack of a better term.

The shock of disappointment and hurt that hit me when I asked him what he'd done to me made me feel a stab of guilt, which I was sure bounced back to him. But I was human, damn it. This was the most bizarre experience of my life to date, and I didn't think this mating thing could just be annulled like a quickie Vegas wedding.

Sure, I had told him that I could imagine developing a long-term relationship with him, but I hadn't meant (or expected) it to happen immediately.

I wanted to pull out of him and put a little space between us. I needed to think, to breathe, to try and sort out the jumble of confused, warring feelings inside me, both the ones that were mine and the ones that inexplicably belonged to him.

"How, um, how long does this tying thing last?" I asked into the thick silence that had closed in around us.

He shifted, shrugging despondently, and it gave another tug to the sensitive swell at the base of my cock: flesh that, up until a few minutes ago, had never existed before.

Intense pleasure rocketed through me and I was unable to stop myself from ejaculating yet again.

Ollie shuddered in answer, probably feeling my physical enjoyment like some sort of feedback loop. It was freaky weird and disorienting, and I wondered if there was a way to cut off the feed of my emotions to him. I liked being alone in my own head and I didn't need someone else knowing my thoughts if I wasn't ready to share them.

"Well, this isn't going to be comfortable for either of us for any extended period of time," I decided, trying to be rational. However, I could feel his upset through the bond thing we shared and that made me anxious. I hadn't wanted to hurt his feelings, but surely he could understand how insane this felt to me.

I smoothed my hands down his sides in what I hoped was a comforting gesture. "Come on, baby," I urged him, bracing myself for the discomfort of what I was about to initiate, "let's see if we can turn you around."

Ollie's eyes widened. "But the knot…"

"I know. But if we're stuck for God knows how long, I

wanna get comfy. So, a bit of —ah, fuck— *that*," I cried out sharply as he started to twist around, relaxing himself as much as possible so as to make the movement as easy as he possibly could. Panting through the nearly painful orgasm, I tried again. "A bit of that will be worth being able to…" To what? Cuddle? Did I really want to suggest that when I could still feel how my reaction had affected him?

Thankfully, he saved me from having to finish the thought. "Yeah," he sighed, sounding resigned. "Yeah, okay."

Resolve filtered through to me, steady and strong, if somewhat clinical. Then he exhaled and moved, turning in my lap, the twisting over my knot bordering on torture. It was definitely painful that time, but as he settled with his back flush against my chest, I filled him with more cum as we settled down on the mattress, spooned together on our sides.

The silence that fell once we were more comfortable was anything but the same. Melancholy traveled across our bond and Ollie trembled in my arms, then sniffled.

My heart sank.

He was crying.

"Ollie…" I murmured in abject horror.

He cried harder.

It was certainly the last thing I wanted when I was still inside him, and I tried to squeeze and reassure him in my arms, but he tensed and shook his head.

How had things gone so wrong?

Oh yeah: my body had physically developed a whole new feature and I'd gotten stuck inside him, unable to stop orgasming.

I was still concerned about that, but the panic was starting to recede. In its place, I felt badly for asking Ollie what he had done to me. It was more than obvious that this had taken him just as equally by surprise.

"I'm sorry," I told him softly. "I shouldn't have accused you. I just…I was freaking out. I *am* freaking out. I'm *human*."

He sniffed, then turned his head, trying to level a hard stare at me over his shoulder. "I don't know what to tell you, Beck, but you have a knot. You're *not* human."

"Then how has this never happened before?" It wasn't as though I'd been a virgin.

He shrugged. "Maybe you'd never slept with a shifter before? It's not like you would have known…"

"The slick thing is not a human thing," I interrupted him pointedly. "That's why you told me, isn't it?"

With a heavy sigh, Ollie gave up on trying to maintain eye contact. His head flopped down onto the pillow which was supported by my arm. "Except I've never had that happen with a human before. *Ever*. Sometimes I'd get a little slick during the act, but it wasn't noticeable. Not after lube and condoms." He paused, then said, "I think…I think my body somehow knew that you weren't human. That you—"

"I. Am. Human." I grit out, frustration flaring. "I've never had anything weird like this happen to me before. I've lived a normal life; I don't have super senses or super strength or super *anything*."

Ollie went silent for a little while. "What about now? Do you feel different now?" Then, after a beat, quietly added, "I mean, outside of the bond?"

I considered the question. My heart was no longer racing, and I tried to strain my ears and sniff at the air, as if expecting a sudden change in the depth of either of those senses. Nothing unusual happened. "I don't think so?"

"Hmm."

He was unconvinced. I could feel it as well as hear it. That was still disconcerting, and I wondered again if there was a way to shut the connection down.

"We can't tell anyone about this," he said after more of the mildly tense silence built between us. "Alphas…they're extinct. Hell, all the research I'm currently doing at work is based on that premise. About the evolution of shifter society in a post-alpha world. You…" Ollie stopped and swallowed. "You're an anomaly. Maybe a genetic throwback or something? I don't know. What I do know is, if we tell anyone, we'll have packs and doctors and researchers and God only knows who else up our asses." I could feel the genuine fear building in him as he spoke. "They'd probably want to take you away to experiment, or find a more deserving omega for you to breed with, or—"

"Whoa, whoa," he could probably feel my alarm spiking, answering his own. I pulled him as tightly against my chest as I could, groaning a little as the movement sent a fresh wave of tingles through my knot, down to my balls. How the hell were they not empty yet? "That's not going to happen. For one, I have no intention of telling anyone about my new, uh, accessory."

Ollie snorted.

"And for another," I continued, relaxing as I felt some of his worry recede, "we've got this mate…bond…thing. If science fiction has taught me anything, it's that magical connections like this," I rubbed the center of his chest with my palm, "can't just be ignored or replaced, right?"

"I suppose." He was quiet and contemplative. "I've only ever read about any of this stuff, y'know? It's all word of mouth and recorded experiences from hundreds of years ago. To feel it actually happening to me is, well, it's surreal."

There was a hint of his earlier awe sneaking in alongside his words. It was an echo of the pure joy and amazement he'd felt when I'd bitten him, which had ricocheted into me, lighting me up and extending the bliss of the moment.

"I...I'm *mated*, Beck. As far as I know, I'm the first mated omega in centuries. *Me*. Plain, boring, useless me."

A growl escaped me before I could prevent it. "I won't have you talking about my mate that way," I muttered into his ear, the words also having planted themselves on my tongue. It was instinct. He was my mate, whether I was freaking out about it or not.

A shiver of renewed arousal and joy rocked through him and he threw his head back, exposing his neck and the fresh bite mark there while simultaneously grinding down on my knot which hadn't yet shown any sign of deflating. Seeing the bite mark caused an unexpected surge of possessive pride to lance through me and I dipped my mouth to kiss it tenderly.

Ollie responded with a happy sigh, and I felt his contentment building between us. It was a warm, satisfying feeling. Perhaps not everything about this mating thing was bad after all.

"We're going to have to talk about this properly," he said sleepily. "About," he paused and yawned, stretching his mouth wide. It was adorable, especially when he ended it with a tiny squeak. "About what this means for us."

Us. As in long-term 'us'. As in, not really a hypothetical possible future 'us', but a mystical mating bond is probably going to mean changes to our lives 'us'.

I wanted some time to myself to think about it all, but that wasn't going to happen while I was still locked inside him.

"Yeah," I agreed. "We are." There was no point denying that.

Regardless of my inner turmoil, I was an adult and neither of us was at fault for this having happened to us. If anything, it almost felt like once we had met, we had been compelled to be together…or perhaps that was all the sci-fi and fantasy I enjoyed. Either way, running away to have a freak out on my own wouldn't be fair on him. Especially while he could sense my emotions.

"Mmm," his body was starting to go all loose as sleep took hold of him. "But not now. Later."

I pressed a kiss to his temple. "Sleep, babe. We'll talk tomorrow."

But even as he drifted off, I stayed awake, my thoughts whirring.

Chapter Seven – Oliver

⁂

The first thing I registered upon waking was how I felt empty and bereft of my mate…but also uncomfortably full in another way. I recalled waking during the night, heated and horny once more, grinding down on Beck's knot until we both came again and again, but the memories were hazy, almost as though I had dreamed them. However, the uncomfortable full feeling told me that I had not.

I rolled and scrambled out of bed, for once glad of the postage-stamp size of my apartment because the awkward shuffle towards the toilet felt long enough as it was.

I did my thing, then opted for a quick shower to freshen up, and released a billow of steam into the main space of my apartment when I reopened the door. I had a funny feeling in my chest, like a rubber band pulled tight, and I realized that it was because Beck was gone.

The rubber band seemed to stretch towards the northern end of the city, and I tried not to be upset that he'd left without so much as a goodbye, but it was hard not to be. It wasn't like I hadn't explained why what we'd shared was so special. He could *feel* what it meant to me.

I could equally feel his freak-out, too.

I couldn't blame the guy.

Until last night, he'd thought he was human. If I suddenly grew extra body parts without warning, I'd probably need some time to adjust to the revelation, too.

But to not say anything stung.

It stung a lot.

I distracted myself by getting dressed, and then, when that only took a few minutes, I reached for my phone to call Brandi and maybe bitch at her about how insensitive men could be… until I noticed the text alert on my screen. I snatched the device up and read every single word twice.

'I swear I'm not this guy, but a client messaged me with an urgent update to his website graphics & I can't afford to turn him down. Had to run. But we will talk. Can I see you tonight? Beck.'

It wasn't the affection or reassurance I wanted to hear from my mate, but it was better than being ghosted. I typed my reply back quickly, my thumbs flying over the keys.

'I get it. Plus you probably need the space to freak out in private, right? But talking tonight would be good. I'll be here. XoXo. Ollie.' In addition to the 'X's and 'O's, I also sent a heart emoji.

So much for trying to be cool about it, I berated myself. I couldn't help how deeply I felt the need to shower my mate with affection, though. My inner wolf was practically whining for him. That was also a whole new experience for me. My lupine side wasn't usually so close to the surface, not even when I hadn't shifted in weeks at a stretch. But now it seemed to have a whole new dimension, like being mated and claimed had awoken some new part of it.

Hell, maybe it had.

There was so very little actual documentation about the mating and claiming process between an alpha and an omega. The knowledge had died out with the alphas, and so much of what was left had to be taken with a grain of salt, written as it was through the eyes of generations far removed from the last known mated pairs.

Except now *I* was part of a mated pair. I'd been knotted. I had a claim mark (now covered with a strategically chosen scarf) and could feel the connection to my mate in the back of my mind and in my heart. While I could honestly say that I didn't know Beck well enough to love him, the mating bond seemed to make the previous stirrings of emotions and attraction more intense.

The analytic part of my mind said that I should probably start documenting the entire experience, noting everything I could from our first meeting onward. It would be invaluable anecdotal information. Except I had no plans to share it with anyone. My fears from the previous night still stood. I could just imagine the attention that Beck and I would get if anyone found out what had happened.

An alpha.

Beckett was still denying it, but that's what he was. I could feel it in my bones. My wolf could feel it. Now that I knew it, it made sense that I had been so unsettled since we'd met. My omega had recognized him for what he was and wouldn't have been satisfied with anyone else. Maybe over time it might have forgotten, but meeting him the second time had cemented that all-consuming need to connect with him.

And boy had we connected! He'd knotted me!

Never in a million years could I have imagined how good that would feel. On paper it sounded strange and even a little scary. After all, the idea of being locked together means being vulnerable and trapped. But I didn't feel either of those things. Yes, the prostate stimulation was amazing, but the intimacy of the experience once the shock had passed and Beck's panic had receded was on a whole other level to any of my previous sexual encounters.

Then there was the bond itself. The give and take between our souls, sharing emotions and, judging by the rubber band compass inside my chest, proximity added a whole extra level of comfort and intimacy.

All combined, I felt sorry that shifters couldn't experience this anymore.

Did betas experience this sort of thing when they mated? Or were these sensations unique to alphas and omegas? I made a mental note to try and research these questions on the side.

I'd kept an eye on my phone but there was still no response from Beck. I couldn't feel his emotions as clearly as I could the previous night, and I wondered whether the proximity affected that part of the fledgling mating bond, or whether it had been stronger because he'd been knotting me at the time, or...God, there were so many possibilities.

I was ecstatic to be able to research this firsthand, but I was also overwhelmed. I had no idea where to start, what to focus on. On top of that, I had all these urges inside me, demanding that I find my mate and spend more time getting to know him. How many of those were being driven by the bond and how many were my usual 'new relationship' instincts, I couldn't actually say.

When my phone rang, I answered it happily, not even

bothering to check the screen.

"Hey," I said a little breathily, preparing for Beck's deep voice to soothe some of my wolf's whining.

It was not Beck.

"Oliver," Mom sounded confused to have been greeted so flirtatiously and I cringed.

Shit.

"Uh, sorry, hi, Mom," I sat down heavily on my mattress, then scrunched my nose as I registered the state of the sheets. They'd need a wash. "Is everything okay?" We'd already had our weekly call the day before.

In the background of the call, I could hear the sounds of her TV. She liked to tune in on the cheesy, evangelical Sunday sermons presented by a shifter preacher in a cult-like church that went by the ridiculous name of *Moonmusic.* The whole thing gave me the creeps, but she loved it.

"Your father and I are going to come and visit you," she said, and my heart rate picked up speed.

No.

No, no, no, no, no.

"Mom," I tried not to let her hear my panic, "I live in a shoebox. There's no room here for you guys."

"We'll get a hotel room, Oliver. Surely you've heard of those?" From anyone else the words might have been playful and teasing, but from her they were a reprimand. She sniffed down the line. "Besides, we'll only stay the one night. Long enough to help you pack your things and—"

"Wait, *what?*" The panic was building to a real fear now. "I'm not moving back to the pack, Mom. I told you."

"And I told you that you have responsibilities here." Her tone was final.

Oh God. Oh God, oh God, oh God.

I couldn't tell her that I had a mate. I couldn't tell her that my mate was an alpha. I couldn't tell her anything. I needed to buy myself some time. Time to talk to Beck. Time to plan a way out of whatever it was the pack wanted from me.

In the background of her side of the line, I could still hear preacher Joe Morstein sermonizing about something that was likely only going to line his pockets somehow. Irrationally, I blamed him for my mother's sudden decision to come for me. Freaking shifter cult mentalities.

"Wait until after Christmas," I blurted. "Please, Mom? Give me one last Christmas in the city."

I did love Christmas in New York. Even though the movies had given me a bum steer and it didn't normally snow until January, there was still something magical about the way New York dressed up for the holidays. All the lights, the decorations, the trees. Santas on street corners and carolers and window dressings and parades! I loved it all.

"Ollie…" Mom sounded frustrated, but I could hear the barest hint of fondness breaking through. We hadn't always been at loggerheads, Mom and me. When I was little, we were close. She was the reason I loved Christmas so much. We would bake cookies together, dress the tree, write letters to Santa… it had been a magic all of its own, really.

"Mom, please," I begged again, my voice wobbling. "One last Christmas in New York."

She sighed. I heaved in a deep breath. "Then you'll come back to the pack?"

I had no intention of following through, but I dejectedly agreed. "Yeah, Mom. I'll come back."

Christmas was less than six weeks away. At best, I had maybe seven weeks to have a plan in place.

No matter what, I was not going back to the pack.

Chapter Eight - Beckett

I hadn't lied to Ollie. I really had woken up to a barrage of texts from an anxious client begging me to do some quick work for him. He'd agreed to pay me extra for the inconvenience and for putting a rush on it and, as a freelancer, I was in no position to turn down the work. Still, leaving Ollie's apartment while he was in the shower was a dick move, I could admit it. But he was right: I did need a little space to think about everything that happened the night before.

The strangest feeling developed in my chest the further away from Ollie's place I got. As I rode the subway uptown towards my apartment, it was like a cord being strung tight, directing me back towards him. I couldn't feel his emotions anymore, but there was still a vague hint of his general well-being in the base of my consciousness. If I'd thought that the previous night was a fever dream, or a hallucination or something similar, this was enough to convince me otherwise.

I had a mate.

I...wasn't human.

Having grown up in the foster system, I didn't have parents to demand answers from. Not for the first time, I wanted to track them down somehow, but now it was because I needed to know what I was. What they were. How could I have been left to think I was a regular human being when that was obviously not the case? Surely, if I came from a family of shifters, I should have been raised among my own kind.

Or maybe they hadn't known.

I'd often speculated that my mother was a scared teenager when she'd had me and abandoned me in one of those baby boxes they have at some churches, hospitals, and police stations. What if my father had been a shifter and she hadn't known?

It was as much a possibility as any other.

I continued to think it over as I trudged up the street from my subway stop, around the corner and then up the front steps to our apartment block. Just as I was fishing my keys from my pocket to open my apartment door, it swung open.

Sandy's arm shot out and she grabbed the lapel of my jacket, yanking me inside as she let the door slam shut behind me. Her eyes were wide and she got up on her toes, pulling me further down to her level as she plunged her nose into my neck and inhaled deeply.

I pushed her away, bewildered. "What the fuck?"

"You...you smell like..."

I scrunched up my nose. "Sex. Yeah, I know. I didn't realize it was that bad, or I would have showered before I left Ollie's. I—"

"No," she stepped back into my personal bubble and sniffed again. "Beck, you smell like shifter. Like a wolf. And not just because he's all over you. *You* smell like a shifter." She frowned.

"But you smelled human yesterday."

"Wait," I inched backwards, shaking my head, unable to compute what she was saying or, worse, *why*. "How…? What…? *Sandy?*" I swallowed roughly, understanding hitting me.

I'd known Sandy since I was a kid. She was my big sister in all the ways that counted. The only family I had, even if we weren't biologically related. And this was something huge that she hadn't trusted me with. It hurt.

"Beckett," she reached for me and I took another step away. Her face fell, and she let her hand drop to her side. "It's not safe to just tell humans what we are," she justified, and I understood. I did.

And yet…

"You're my sister," I bit out, unable to keep the hurt from my voice. "Did you honestly not trust me enough, not know me well enough to tell me? What, did you think I would come at you with a pitchfork or something? Run screaming out onto the streets?"

"Beckett…"

"Stop that. Stop trying to *Beckett* me." I jabbed myself in the chest with my index finger, punctuating each word in my next sentence. "I am your brother, Sandy. And I would have supported you even if you'd said you were secretly a mime."

I had a thing about mimes. It was a long story.

Sandy, at least, had the grace to be apologetic. "I'm sorry," she said softly. "It's just…I never thought it would have a reason to come up. We're an insular secret society, and we don't advertise our existence because that hasn't ended well for us, historically speaking."

"Yeah, I know," I thought back to Ollie telling me the same thing. "But I wasn't just some random, Sandy. I was —I *am*—

66

your brother. We tell each other everything. At least, I thought we did."

She had been the first person I had come out to when I was seventeen. The only person whose opinion had mattered to me at the time. And she had given me all the unwavering support and acceptance I'd needed. I couldn't believe that she hadn't trusted me to do the same for her.

"Beck," I could see her fingers twitching. Her desperation to close the space I was putting between us and hug me was almost palpable. "We did. We *do*. It's not as easy as..." She sighed and her shoulders slumped. "I'm sorry. I should have told you. You can hold it against me for as long as you need to, but, Beckett, you don't smell human anymore. But you don't smell beta or omega..." Her eyes went back to being wide and imploring. "What happened?"

As much as I wanted to stay mad at her, I couldn't. In fact, I was relieved that I had someone to talk to about all this new craziness in my life, and I was even more grateful for it being Sandy. Even if I was hurt that she'd kept her true nature a secret from me, there was nobody else in this world I would trust to help me through whatever these changes meant for me.

I led Sandy to the couch in our tiny living room, and we sat side by side, turning in to face each other as I gave her a summary of everything that had happened since I had first laid eyes on Ollie in that club. To her credit, she listened patiently through the whole story, not interrupting or asking questions the way I'm sure she wanted to do.

When I was done, having blushed through the description of our mating and the unexpected evolution of my cock, her eyes were huge and practically bulging from her head.

"Holy shit," she breathed, and she scanned my face for any sign of deception. "Your new boy toy didn't put you up to this, did he? This isn't some elaborate prank?"

"Why would he…" I started, then understood that Ollie would have recognized Sandy as a fellow shifter and vice versa. "Oh." Trying not to frown, I shook my head. "No. No, he wouldn't do that. He's a sweet guy. You'll like him. Uh…" I narrowed my eyes at her. "Unless all you shifter types are territorial and stay out of each other's ways?"

"We have packs, dude," she rolled her eyes. Then they got wider again. "Holy shit, you're an *alpha*. No pack has seen an alpha in hundreds of years. You could wander in," she made a show of walking her fingers through the air, "and demand control of any pack of your choosing. Well," she sniffed the air again, "any wolf pack."

"That's archaic," I told her, feeling a little lightheaded. Ollie's concerns from the previous night made more sense all of a sudden. Being an alpha, the only known alpha at that, sounded as though it would give me a lot of power *and* put a huge ass target on my back. Then I cocked my head. "Why wolves?"

"Because that's what you are. Or, at least, that's how you scent."

"Right. You said that before." Running a hand through my hair, I hung my head. "This is all so weird."

Sandy didn't disagree with me. But she did reach for my knee to squeeze it. "You should try shifting," she suggested, like it was the simplest thing in the world to do.

"Oh, sure," I sassed back, "what do I do? Just close my eyes and think wolfy thoughts?"

"Well, it's not too far off that, really. Just, um, more like meditating and reaching inward for your wolf and…I don't know, I just *do* it. I never think about it."

"Uh huh," I wasn't convinced. "That sounds kind of airy-fairy. And what happens if I manage to do it? How do I change back?" I could just see myself getting trapped as a wolf for the rest of my life. No thanks, hard pass on that. And that was assuming I was actually a shifter and not just a human with a bizarre medical condition based solely in my cock. (I had no intention on seeking medical advice in either instance.)

Sandy rolled her eyes. "You just follow the same feelings in reverse. I don't know how to explain it to you. It's instinct, Beck. The same kind of thing that led you to mating, knotting, and bonding with someone you only met once. It'll just happen." She looked around our tiny living room and sighed. "But here's probably not the place to try."

"I wasn't planning on it," my response was dry. She curled her hand into a fist and punched my thigh. "Ow," I complained, even though it hadn't hurt. "That's abuse."

"Poor baby," she cooed without a lick of sympathy. "You seriously have no interest in seeing if you can shift?"

I huffed. "I didn't say that. But with everything being so raw, and I still haven't even showered, I'm not exactly ready to just embrace all of this, you know?"

I was still reeling. I was still panicked and uncertain about what this all meant for me and Ollie, both in the short and long term. The sensation in my chest tying me to him was uncomfortable and alien. Being aware of his state of well-being at all times was disorienting, especially when a spike of anxiety that wasn't my own hit me out of nowhere.

I clutched at my chest, though the feeling seemed to radiate through my whole being. It was only fleeting, sharp and fast, but my echoing anxiety echoed long after it passed.

"What's wrong?" Sandy demanded, all sense of playfulness gone.

I couldn't answer her. Instead, I pulled my phone from my hip pocket, leaning to the side to access it, found Ollie's number and pressed the button, bringing it to my ear. The call went to voicemail.

I shot him a text checking in and then glared at my phone, waiting for his answer.

"Beckett, seriously," Sandy pushed while I continued to stare at my phone screen with my leg bouncing with nervous energy. "What's going on?"

"I felt…" I rubbed at my chest again. "He was panicked. I can't feel all of his emotions from this far away. Not like last night. But I felt that." I was rambling. "So…it must have been something big, right?" I glowered back down at my phone screen, demanding, "Answer me, Ollie."

"I'm sure he's fine," my best friend reassured me. She rubbed my knee. "Can you still feel him?"

I closed my eyes and breathed deeply, actively searching my consciousness and the strange new connection in the recesses of my mind. My own concern had overridden my ability to feel him, but he was still there. Still connected. He felt okay, but I was still uneasy. For the first time since this started, I wished it was more like it had been the night before. Being able to read his emotions clearly was better than this state of not knowing what was going on.

"He's fine, isn't he?" Sandy prompted.

I nodded. "I don't think there's anything immediately wrong, no…"

But that huge spike of fear niggled at me. I wouldn't be okay until I knew that he was. Was that part of being his mate? Or was it the way I would have felt if none of the weird shit had happened?

I liked to think that I would have been just as invested if I'd remained a normal human…but I wouldn't have known that something had scared him, either.

God, this whole situation was messed up and confusing.

When my phone screen lit up with a text a few minutes later, I was relieved to see it was from Ollie.

'I'm fine,' it read, *'my Mom just spooked me. We'll talk about it tonight.'*

The fact that he thought it was something we needed to talk about didn't fill me with confidence. But he'd said he was okay and, with no reason to believe otherwise, it settled me.

* * *

I worked my ass off for the rest of the day, getting the new files to my client by his deadline. Working helped to clear my thoughts and forget the twist my life had taken overnight, if only for a few hours. But once it was done, I found myself heading back downtown towards Ollie's apartment.

Sandy had offered to come with me, but I was an adult. Whether I was human or shifter, I had made my own decisions to that point. I could only blame biological imperative so far: at no point during my time with Ollie had I felt as though I couldn't stop and walk away. It had been my choice to pursue him, both in the club and after I saw him again in the park. It had been my choice to go back to his place. It had been my choice to sleep with him and follow my instincts beyond that.

While I had managed to forget the alien feeling in my chest and gut pulling tight towards Ollie all day, it was hard not to acknowledge the way the sensation loosened the closer I got to his apartment. Tension I hadn't realized I was carrying melted from my shoulders. Under normal circumstances, I wouldn't feel like that over a guy I had only just met, but I was coming to accept that circumstances weren't normal.

Ollie was my mate. It made sense that I should want to be near him. Especially when we had only bonded less than twenty-four hours earlier. Some inner part of me wanted to whine and curl up with him again, spooned together, sharing emotions and affection the way we had while we were tied together. His petite frame fit so well with mine, and if I closed my eyes, I could remember his scent and the warmth of his skin against me.

We needed to talk, but by the time he was opening his front door, those instincts had taken over. Thankfully, Ollie was just as anxious to reconnect as I was. He flew into my arms, wrapping his around my back, and tucked his head under my chin with his ear pressed to my chest.

"Mmm," I murmured, almost certain that I would have purred if I was the right species, "hey."

"Hey," he echoed, nuzzling against me.

We stood like that in his open doorway for longer than could be considered normal or appropriate, but eventually the urge to be pressed up against each other dissipated enough that we could pull apart and close the door behind me.

"Sorry," Ollie said. His cheeks were flushed adorably pink, and his green eyes seemed somehow brighter against the color. "I just…"

"Needed that," I finished for him with a nod, then rubbed the back of my neck. "Me too."

His kissable lips turned upwards into a sweet, understanding

72

smile. "This is going to take some getting used to. But…" the blush on his cheeks darkened, "I'm glad my mate is a good guy."

Guilt settled in my gut. I hadn't felt like a good guy when I made him cry while I was lodged inside him. Nor did I feel like a good guy when I left his apartment without so much as a goodbye that morning.

He didn't react to the feeling, though, and I probed inside myself, searching for that connection we shared. It hadn't changed again, even though I was within touching distance of my new mate.

Interesting.

"I can't feel your emotions," I blurted. "But last night I could. Oh, and when you got super scared earlier today." Cocking my head, I asked, "What was that about?" I looked him over, only barely refraining from patting him down. "Are you really okay?"

Biting his lip, Ollie shrugged. "Last night we were freshly mated and you were still tied to me. There's not a lot written about these bonds, but I guess it was more intense because of that." Then he sighed and gestured for me to take a seat on his bed. "As for the other stuff…we should talk."

"Three words no man ever wants to hear," I joked anxiously, but sat down on the edge of his mattress all the same. It felt so much like the previous night that I got a wicked sense of déjà vu. It almost made me smile.

Ollie did smile, but it didn't reach those expressive green eyes of his. "My pack is demanding I go back and 'fulfill my duties' to them. They've been at it for a while. Ever since I graduated college, actually." He paced the small stretch of linoleum between the tiny kitchenette and the bed, rubbing his left hand up and down his right arm. "Then, this morning, Mom said they were going to come and get me. Just pack up my stuff and force me to come home."

"You're a grown man," I argued, bristling for him. "They can't force you to go anywhere."

He shrugged and I didn't need to feel his emotions to read the dejection on his face. "In their eyes, I owe them. I'm just an omega. I don't provide value. I can't extend the pack, and my chosen degree and profession don't help with the farming or running the town."

If that was true of most of shifter society, I was glad to have been raised human. "I'm not letting them take you anywhere." The possessive sentiment was out of my mouth before I could edit it. I cringed because I didn't have any more right to control him than his pack did. "I mean, you don't have to do anything you don't want to do, Ollie. I'm not going to let anyone force you to do anything. I'm not going to force you, either, but..."

His chuckle interrupted my rant and he sat beside me and took my hand, squeezing it. "Thank you. I appreciate that."

"When are they coming here?" I asked, already looking around his room, wondering if we could pack the essentials and hide him out at my place. Sandy would understand, and Micah was barely ever home anyway.

"After Christmas. I managed to buy myself that much time, but it won't hold them off forever."

I did the mental math. "So...six weeks. Okay." I unwound a little. "That's enough time to plan a way to get you out of it."

I wasn't expecting Ollie to sob and throw his arms around me, but he did. He buried his face in my neck and trembled in my arms. "Thank you," he murmured. "I'd hoped..."

Ah.

I understood, and I couldn't blame him for being unsure of where I would stand with all of his personal drama.

Smoothing my hands down his back, I kissed his temple. "We're mated, Oliver. We need to talk about what that means, and about all the changes that have happened and what might still happen, but Sandy seems to think this will be permanent and that it's a big thing. So, you're stuck with me, and I've got your back."

Chapter Nine – Oliver

aving Beckett's support was bracing. We spent the rest of Sunday night just cuddling, reassuring the bond —and ourselves— that we were together in all of this mess. We talked late into the night about our feelings surrounding everything that had happened, and had sex again when our bodies could no longer resist the urge to reconnect in the most primal way possible. I still marveled over that desperate need to be filled by my mate, the way my flesh seemed to burn until he sated my need and locked himself inside me.

I was relieved to discover that, while he still wasn't sure about what it all meant, Beck was beginning to accept the fact that he wasn't human. He'd spoken at length with his best friend, the wolf shifter I'd met in the park, and that seemed to have helped him feel more at ease with the concept of being one of us.

And he *was* one of us.

I could scent it on him. He was a shifter, a wolf like me,

and his scent was warm, comforting, and strong. Something about our mating must have brought it out of him, but I was at a loss to know what or how it had happened. The scientist in me demanded answers.

Beck, however, didn't seem too bothered about knowing the whys of it all. He was more concerned about how it would affect life going forward. Being separated for the day had put a strain on both of us, but neither one of us thought moving in together immediately was a good idea.

We resolved to continue dating like any normal couple but agreed that if the need for physical contact became too strong for either one of us, we would reach out to the other and sate the bond's demands. It wasn't exactly a hardship to have to cuddle up in his big arms, after all. Or against his solid chest. Or to have him spooned up against me in bed, one of his thick thighs thrown over mine, pinning me down in the most delicious way...

Yeah. Nothing hard about any of that.

Well, except for my dick.

I woke up in the early hours of Monday morning feeling almost as desperately horny as I had on Saturday night. My hole was slick, my cock hard and leaking, almost as though I hadn't had sex in months rather than in a handful of hours. It was still dark outside, and the alarm I had set on my phone had not yet gone off.

Behind me, I could feel Beck's answering erection at my back. He was down to wearing only his boxer briefs because he hadn't packed an overnight bag, but I had turned the thermostat up so my apartment was warm despite the onset of winter outside. I was only wearing my pajama pants and briefs, but the few layers of thin cotton between my ass and his cock felt like insurmountable obstacles.

A whine tore through my throat and I couldn't help grinding back against the bulge at my back.

"Mmm," Beck stirred, "mornin' baby." He pressed a kiss to my throat, right over my exposed mating bite, and I felt the precum dribbling down my cock.

"Beck," I whined again, pushing back against him, "please…"

He chuckled. "You have to work today," he reminded me gently, and he soothed the annoying words by nipping at the bite mark with blunt teeth, "so we don't have time to get knotted together again, do we, hmm?"

I hated that he was right. I was so horny for him, so desperate to have the bond between us renewed once more. To feel satisfied.

"But," he continued, sounding amused and kind of smug, "we can take care of this," his hand slipped into the front of my pants and I cried out as it wrapped around my shaft, "in other ways, can't we?"

"Anything," I babbled, thrusting into the loose fist he made. "Anything. Please, Beck. Please. I need you."

I whimpered when the warmth of his chest disappeared from my back, but he shushed me and guided me to lie back. "I've got you, baby," he said, winking. Then he started to kiss a trail down my body, over the softness of my abdomen and down to the waistband of my pajamas. I raised my hips to help him pull them off, and I gasped as he continued to pepper me with kisses over my needy cock then down over my balls and lower still.

"*Beckett*," I breathed, half incredulous and half in anticipation. He spread my thighs wider, then slid his big palms beneath my ass and lifted me up so his mouth had access to my slippery hole.

At first, he just kissed at my ass cheeks, but I was strung tight, waiting for the main event.

My mate did not disappoint. He started slowly, licking the puckered entrance first with the searching tip of his tongue, then with the flat of it. He moaned, then dove in with a gusto, twirling his tongue around my hole until I relaxed enough to let the searching muscle inside.

Fuck, but Beck knew what he was doing. He teased and speared me with his tongue, alternating between deep dives and kitten licks. Then he pulled back, muttering, "You taste phenomenal, baby," before rolling me onto my front and getting me to position myself on my knees, with my head down and my ass up.

'Downward dog' was a beautiful, beautiful yoga position, I decided, not even tempted to make a wolf joke. No, that was a lie. I was going to rename it 'downward wolf' by the time this was over. And, okay, I knew that the pose I was in wasn't quite right for the joke I'd made inside my own head, but who else was there to correct me?

I cried out again when Beck spread my cheeks and dove back in, the new position helping that magic tongue of his to work in deeper. It felt like he was trying to lap up all of my slick, his tongue working in proxy of his cock.

Speaking of cocks, when his hand traveled under me and grasped mine, it was a sensory overload. I wasn't sure whether to fuck into his fist or rock back onto his tongue. Both experiences were blissful and overwhelming.

"Fuck, Beck, I'm gonna come," I warned him mere seconds before I shot my load over his fist and onto the rumpled sheets beneath me. My hole clenched as my cock pulsed and spasmed, and his moans of enjoyment only prolonged my orgasm.

He pulled away and I flopped and rolled onto my back, making sure to stay out of the wet patch. Beck stretched out at my side and I pulled him in for a sloppy kiss, tasting my slick on his tongue, slightly sweet but otherwise not all dissimilar to precum.

He was still hard against my thigh, and I could not let that stand for long.

So, having caught my breath, I pushed him onto his back and shimmied down the mattress, worshiping his body the same way he had done mine.

His cock, just as large as I'd remembered, sprang free from his boxer briefs as soon as I peeled the waistband down. It was purpled at the head, glistening with the evidence of how much he'd enjoyed eating me out, and I couldn't wait to return the favor.

His taste exploded on my tongue as soon as I suckled at the head, salty and a little sweet, his warm musky scent calling to my inner wolf like nothing else could. I wrapped my hand around the base of his shaft and pumped slowly as I tried to work as much of him into my mouth as I could reach. I was never going to fit him all down, but I'd have fun practicing.

His hands threaded through my hair, but he didn't push my head or slam his hips upwards. He had epic control, letting me treat him however I so chose, and I sucked and licked and pumped that gorgeous, delicious cock of his until he was shaking with the need to empty down my throat. The entire time, he was murmuring praises about the feel of my mouth, the heat of it, how good I was at sucking him like that, and it all served to egg me on.

I allowed my other hand to wander. I fondled his balls,

tickled the skin behind them with my fingertips, and then traced back over them and upwards to the base of his shaft where I found the beginnings of his knot swelling up.

He groaned loudly when my fingers tickled the swell and I grinned around the organ in my mouth.

Bingo.

Within moments, Beck was a babbling, pleading mess. His knot was sensitive, and with every squeeze of it while I sucked him, he'd unravel just a little bit more.

"Ollie," he breathed, "Ollie, baby, that…oh *fuck* that feels so good…don't stop, don't…*ungh!*"

I had no intention of stopping. Not until he came, anyway.

His fingers tightening in my hair and the minor thrusts of his hips were his tells. I squeezed his knot again, tightening my fist on my next upstrokes, and I hollowed my cheeks.

Beck howled his release, repeating his praises among a litany of curses, and I swallowed as much of his cum down as I could. There was a lot of it, more than I had ever taken from previous lovers. But then, this man was an alpha and I'd just been toying with his knot. What else had I expected?

Beck slumped back when it was all over, flinching away from my hands and mouth as I wrung out as much pleasure from him as I could, his cock spurting weakly when I gave his knot one last squeeze.

"Come here," he demanded, pulling my back up to his side. I went willingly.

We kissed again, and he didn't seem bothered by the taste of his release on my tongue. We rested in silence, content to snuggle and relish in our mutual afterglows before my alarm finally sounded and I groaned.

"Come on, babe," Beck gave me a little shake, "gotta get up

and face the real world at some point."

I tried not to think about it. After the craziness of the weekend, returning to the daily grind was off-putting, no matter how much I usually enjoyed my job.

I tried a different diversionary tactic.

"I like that you call me that," I confessed. "Babe. Or baby. It's…nice."

Beck's lips found the top of my head. "I'm glad. I didn't really think about it. It just felt right."

"Story of the whole weekend," I snorted and then squealed as he attempted to tickle me.

"Get up," he instructed. "Work calls, remember?"

I sighed. "Yeah." The plus side was that I could use Doctor Weldman's resources to research our bond without raising too much suspicion.

My mate laughed and moved to get out of bed himself. "Come on," he repeated. "I'll join you in the shower. That's good for the environment, right?" He waggled his eyebrows.

And, even though I knew showering with him would probably make me late for work and would not, in fact, save even a drop of water, I agreed and followed him into my tiny cramped bathroom.

This felt like the start of something good.

Chapter Ten – Beckett

Over the course of the next few weeks, Ollie and I worked out a schedule that seemed to suit our lives and satisfy the bond. We went on dates like any regular couple getting to know each other would —bowling, playing pool, ice skating at Rockefeller center, basically a romcom montage of fun little interludes— and I would go back to his place on those nights and make love to him, locking us together before we drifted off to sleep.

We remained separate for Thanksgiving, even though Sandy insisted that Ollie was welcome to join us, and tried to have a plan of attack (or, in our case, defense) for when his pack would inevitably insist he go home with them. The best we'd come up with so far was for him to move in with me and hide from them, but we didn't actually believe that would do much more than buy an extra few days. Faking his death had been vetoed for the same reason.

"We could tell them you're mated now," I suggested as we snuggled in his bed a month after we got together.

Ollie was exhausted, run ragged from the stress of his pack's threat looming over his head and the extra hours of research he had been putting in, trying to find more information about our situation. He yawned widely and shook his head, closing his eyes as I toyed with the ends of his hair.

"That'd just put a target on your back," he said, repeating the same argument he'd raised since this all started. "You're the only alpha alive on the planet, as far as I can tell. They'll either - oh, sorry." He stopped again to let loose another yawn. "They'll either try to use you to control all the packs around them, or they'll think you're too much of a threat and will…" he trailed off, unable to say the words. A tear trickled down his cheek and he brushed it away angrily.

"Okay, babe," I soothed, not wanting to further upset him. "It's okay. We won't tell them, then. We'll work something else out."

He didn't say anything more, just snuggled in closer and fell asleep with his head pillowed on my chest.

Like that first night a month previous, I stayed awake for hours longer, my brain trying to come up with a solution to our problem.

I couldn't come up with one.

* * *

"Are you ready to do this?" Sandy asked me, bouncing on the soles of her feet. On her other side, rugged up in thermals and a big, puffy jacket, Ollie looked just as excited, even with the dark circles under his eyes.

We'd traveled together to Catskill Park, which was a couple of hours drive from the city. It was a popular hiking destination, considering its location in the Catskill Mountains, and in the snowier months it was also home to ski retreats. But, more importantly, it was apparently a favorite destination for shifters living in the city to travel out to and shift whenever the need took them.

Over the past month, both Sandy and Ollie had discussed their individual needs to do so, so there we were. I had been convinced to join them because I still hadn't attempted to shift myself. I hadn't felt the urge, too driven to just be with my mate whenever possible.

I shrugged at them both. "What if I can't do it? What if I'm not a real shifter? Just some weird half breed?"

They scoffed in unison.

"You're an alpha," Ollie said, as if that explained everything.

Sandy nodded her agreement. "There's no way you could be an alpha and be unable to shift. How would you deal with predators or challengers to your status?"

"Uh, I don't have a status," I told her, speaking down to her like she was a particularly dense five-year-old. "And I don't have to deal with predators because I live among humans and, until a month ago, I thought I was one."

Sandy and Ollie exchanged a look that spoke volumes about how stupid they thought I was being, and then started to strip. My eyes went wide, and I instinctively moved to shield Ollie from Sandy's eyes.

She rolled hers. "You're still thinking like a human, Beck. We need to get naked to shift, or we'll destroy our clothes and that's just a waste. I'm not eyeing your mate and he's not looking at me. It's a shifting thing."

None of that meant I had to like it.

Sandy sighed. "Anyway, I'm freezing. I'll see you on the

other side. Remember," she pinned me with a pointed stare. "Don't overthink it. Reach for your wolf and follow your instincts. It'll happen."

Then she closed her eyes, exhaled, and started to shift. It looked painful, her body contorting and sprouting fur, limbs shifting and shortening right in front of me. She grew a tail and dropped to four legs and then, within moments, Sandy was gone, and a brown colored wolf was standing in her place.

"You've got this, babe," Ollie said from behind me. I turned to face him.

"What if—"

"It'll be just like the mating," he told me, repeating sentiments that had been discussed over and over again during the course of the month we'd been dating. "Your body will know what to do."

Then I watched him go through the same process as Sandy. It seemed slower for Ollie, or maybe that had something to do with the fact that I could feel him changing through our bond. It wasn't painful, as far as I could feel, but I definitely felt something different about him once he was in wolf form. It was like another part of me suddenly woke up.

Ollie's wolf was of a small build, like Sandy's, only his fur was sleek tones of silver and gray with a white chest. His eyes were as green in wolf form as they'd been in his human form, sharp and intelligent. I knew it was him behind them, even though I was looking at an animal instead of my boyfriend.

Mate, a voice in the back of my head corrected. It was growly and impatient. I was beginning to realize that it was my inner wolf. It had always been there and, now that Ollie had shifted, it was demanding to be let out.

Before I tried to shift, though, I took the neatly folded piles of clothes that my companions had shed and I put them aside, under a nearby bush. Then I removed my own clothes, my teeth chattering in the cold of winter. I felt like an idiot, standing naked in the middle of a freezing forest, but the whine of the gray wolf at my side steeled my resolve to do this thing.

I closed my eyes as both Sandy and Ollie had done, and I took deep, meditative breaths like I had been told to do. Drawing on how Ollie's transition had felt through the bond, I reached inwards, not quite sure what I was looking for, until a spark of something in my consciousness took hold. It felt like Ollie, sweet and grounding, but with an edge of sensation not unlike the spark I'd felt when I'd bitten down on his neck as we'd mated. It was, as best as I could describe, *magic*.

I let the sensation pervade my thoughts and my senses and then I was twisting inside. It felt wrong and disorienting, a push and pull of my limbs and organs, like being on one of those carnival rides that spins so fast you defy gravity. But it also felt *right*. My whole being lit up with lightness and joy, like I was finally coming home. As the first feeling faded and the second one settled over me, I opened my eyes. Excited yipping greeted me, and Ollie and Sandy pranced around on the frosty ground, the claws at the end of their paws clacking against stones and hard packed dirt.

I opened my jaw to tell them how amazed I was, but all that came out was a series of excited barks. Right. I was a wolf.

I could somehow sense their joint amusement, though, as they moved forward, sniffing the air and then my neck and snout. Ollie nuzzled his comparatively much smaller head beneath mine, and I took the chance to sniff him in return.

Mate, my instincts cheered.

He pulled back and licked my nose, then we rubbed our cheeks together and I felt completely whole.

Sandy broke the moment with a whine of her own, demanding that I greet her, too. Even though she was my older sister and she was more experienced at this shifting thing, I got the submissive wolf vibes from her lowered posture. She approached me with a sense of strange reverence, keeping her head lowered until I scented her. Then she raised her snout and licked my cheek before rubbing hers against the same spot. Though I wasn't mated to her, I could feel how moved she was by this whole experience.

It felt like they were more than family, and suddenly I understood what it was to be an alpha. Though unconventional, this was my pack, and I would do anything to keep them safe.

I tried to radiate these vibes at them, making wolfy sounds that likely made absolutely no sense, and then the three of us were off, bounding through the frosty forestry, chasing each other and yipping like excited pups.

It was the most liberating feeling in the world. All my senses were heightened, and all of my human troubles melted away to the back of my consciousness. It was just me and my pack, roaming the woods and bonding the way nature intended. I loved every second of it.

As we tired and the day drew to an end, I paused in a clearing, tilted my head to the sky and howled my delight. It was a wild cry, a joyous sound as much as it was a declaration of my intent to protect what was mine. Ollie and Sandy howled, too, and a flock of birds batted wings in a flurry as they fled from a nearby tree.

Even though we'd stopped to drink from a gently trickling stream on its way to icing over, by the time we returned back to our clothes, I was starving and thirsty. The feeling manifested tenfold when I managed to reverse engineer the shift, following Sandy and Ollie back into human form.

We dressed hastily against the freezing cold air, and Sandy rummaged through the backpack she had also stashed away, pulling out three thermoses full of steaming hot chicken and vegetable soup. I could have kissed her.

"So," she asked after I'd swallowed down half of my thermos's contents in three large gulps, "how was shifting for the first time?"

I grinned back at her. "That was…wow."

Ollie leaned against me, sipping at his thermos cautiously. I looked down at him, concerned. "Is it too hot?"

He scrunched up his nose. "No. It's just…not appealing right now." He shot Sandy an apologetic look. "Sorry."

She waved him off. "I went through a phase where I couldn't stomach anything other than pumpkin pie after a shift. I have no idea what that was about. Bodies are weird. Just make sure you're hydrating at least." She reached back into the backpack and pulled out a bottle of water and tossed it to him.

He caught it deftly with his free hand. "Thanks."

I took his thermos from him so he could drink from the water and watched, satisfied, as he guzzled down half the contents.

"Good boy," I murmured, taking it back from him to drink a few mouthfuls myself before passing it back to Sandy.

He rolled his eyes, but I could tell he was preening under the praise. I suspected he had a bit of an under-explored praise kink. It wouldn't be under-explored for too long if I had my way (and I would.)

We trekked back to the area where we had parked the rental

car and by the time we got there, Ollie looked about ready to drop. He was yawning widely and dragging his feet.

"Maybe shifting when you're already run ragged was a bad idea," I said, frowning as he slumped into the passenger seat with a deep sigh. He closed his eyes and rested his head on the headrest.

"No, I needed that," he insisted, yawning again. "I'm feeling more settled. I'm just exhausted."

"Not eating probably didn't help, either," I continued from my spot in the driver's seat.

He snorted. "You're such a mother hen."

"Alpha wolf," I sassed him back, smirking as he cracked an eye open to glare half-heartedly at me. Sandy had slipped into the backseat and leaned over the center console between us.

"Maybe you're fighting off a flu?" she suggested.

I frowned as I turned the key in the ignition. "I thought shifters were immune to stuff."

"Human STIs, yeah," she shrugged. "But not stuff like influenza or stomach bugs. If an animal can catch it, chances are a shifter can, too."

I didn't follow the logic, but I believed her. "Right. Good to know." Then I looked over her head to Ollie. "We can stop and get you something lighter? Like stuff to make a clear broth or something? Freshly squeezed OJ?"

He shook his head and then went back to his pre-nap position. "Nah, a nap will help. I'll be right as rain when we get back home, I promise."

"Okay," I acknowledged, still concerned. "But if you change your mind, just tell me, okay? I need my mate in fighting shape."

Ollie snorted again. "*Fighting*, huh? Is that what we're calling it?"

My cheeks burned. "Around my sister it is."

She cackled as she settled herself back in the backseat and that feeling of rightness —of *pack*— settled over me again.

Even though we had less than two weeks to sort out a plan to deal with Ollie's family, I was riding on a high, feeling good about life in general.

I was even starting to look forward to Christmas!

With the way Ollie was nuts about it, it was difficult not to find myself swept up in his enthusiasm. These days, his tiny little studio apartment looked like the North Pole had exploded inside it. He'd strung tinsel and fairy lights around the small space. He'd hung a giant felt cut out of a Christmas tree on the door that led to his 'shoilet' (his word for the tiny bathroom, not mine). He played carols on repeat and his bedding was now all Christmas themed. And our date nights had begun to revolve around visiting various Christmas displays in the city. The previous week, we'd even gone to the annual Tree Lighting Ceremony at Rockefeller Center. If my mate loved Christmas, I was not going to be the one to ruin it for him.

We hadn't spent Thanksgiving together, so I hadn't been able to take him to the Thanksgiving Day Parade, which was also New York's unofficial Christmas Parade. I felt guilty about that, having been so certain that a city like New York would have something else in place specifically for Christmas. Because I'd spent my life not paying enough attention, I hadn't realized that was not the case.

But Google had informed me that some of the small towns upstate had their own Christmas festivals in December. Rhinebeck, for example, was lauded as being one of the best. It had an entire day of festivities set up, culminating in a Christmas parade and pageant. The *Sinterklaas Festival Day* sounded absolutely magical, even to a slowly reforming Grinch like myself, and I'd been excited to discover that we hadn't missed it. While most years it seemed to be scheduled for early December, this particular year had seen it scheduled for the weekend before Christmas and I had plans to take my mate there for a romantic getaway. It was only a couple of hours away from the city, after all, and we could get ourselves a cute Airbnb for the night and celebrate an early Christmas together.

I couldn't spend a lot of money on gifts, but this was something special I could give to my mate: the man I was certain I was falling in love with.

Chapter Eleven — Oliver

"**W**hoa," Brandi said as she met me at the nearby Donut King where we bought our coffees on our daily shared commute to the subway station, "you look like crap."

"Gee, thanks," I muttered, stepping in line ahead of her, "that's what every guy needs to hear."

She flicked my shoulder, but the jacket I wore was thick and puffy, so it only registered as a dull 'pfft' sound against the material. "Seriously, does that boy toy of yours let you sleep?"

"Let's get one thing straight," I told her haughtily over my shoulder, "*I* am the boy toy in our relationship, being the youngest and prettiest and all."

My BFF laughed and shook her head, then held her hands up in surrender. "Forgive me for not stereotyping," she sassed. But then she eyed me with genuine concern as we shuffled forward with the queue. "Seriously, though, you look wrecked."

I felt wrecked. For weeks I had been constantly exhausted,

my shifter senses on overdrive. I'd thought that I had just been overdue for a shift, but that had barely revitalized me over the weekend just gone. My reflection in the mirror that morning had been ghastly. I'd looked wan, my skin sallow and eyes lifeless, dark circles beneath them like I had been on a three-week bender. But I was sleeping more than could be considered normal or healthy, so I didn't understand what was wrong with me.

It didn't help that I wasn't eating right. I couldn't stomach most foods and those that I did manage to get down would inevitably make their reappearance an hour or so later – not that I had told Beck that. If he knew I was throwing up, he would have forced me to visit a doctor, and I did not have the funds for that kind of expense. However, I knew that wasn't much of an excuse. I did work for a doctor, after all. If things got bad enough, I'd ask Doctor Weldman for a consult. That wouldn't cost me anything: a perk of my current job. I just didn't want to face more bad news when I was still stressing over what to do about my pack and their plans for me.

"I think I might be coming down with something," I admitted.

Instead of giving me a wide berth, my best friend flicked her long blonde braid over her shoulder and stepped in closer, bringing the back of her hand to my forehead. "You don't feel warm," she observed.

I shrugged. "Maybe I'm fighting off a stomach bug or something."

She frowned. "Or maybe you're anemic? You should get your boss to run some tests."

"True," I acknowledged as the line shuffled forward again. It wasn't as though shifters were immune to those issues, either.

Not that Brandi knew what I was. Still, her idea had merit. "I'll cave and talk to Doctor Weldman today."

We were only a few spaces away from the counter at that point. I was desperate for my caffeine hit. It wasn't great coffee (some might argue that it wasn't even good coffee) but it was cheap, accessible from my apartment, and it did the job. I sighed as I waited impatiently, then turned back to Brandi with a soft smile.

"What about you?" I asked her. "Did you end up going out with that guy you met last week? I wanna say...Jim?"

"John," she nodded, and her own smile went a little secretive. "And I did. He's...different. A little old fashioned. Actually wants to take me out on dates."

I thought about Beck, and I chuckled. "Is he older than us? Because Beck is totally the same. He's taking me away this weekend for a whole romantic Christmas thing. It's sweet."

Brandi grinned. "To Rhinebeck, right?"

"Uh, yeah, how'd you—"

"You did say he was looking into it. I mentioned it to John and now he wants to take me this weekend, too." She was bouncing on her toes, encased as they were in stylish heeled boots. "Oh, oh! We could meet up! Double date!"

I thought about how excited Beck was at the prospect of a romantic getaway for just the two of us and felt torn by indecision. Brandi looked so excited and hopeful and, to be truthful, I'd never been on a double date before. And never with my best friend.

"I'll talk to Beck," I told her. "I'm sure we can maybe meet up and do dinner or something."

She squealed, uncaring of the looks we were getting, and then pushed me forward towards the now open cashier.

We paid for our drinks, accepted them a few moments later, and then headed out onto the bustling sidewalk, chatting about the festival we were both apparently going to attend. It was a little annoying that Brandi was crashing my romantic weekend with her own, but it wasn't as though thousands of people didn't flock to the festival each year. We wouldn't have to spend any time together, and Beck and I could still enjoy our getaway.

By the time I got off the subway at my stop and trudged into the little Manhattan clinic, I was back to being exhausted. The caffeine hit hadn't lasted long, and I was contemplating drinking the crappy coffee we brewed in the lab when a wave of dizziness hit me.

"Hey, whoa, you okay?" Doctor Weldman caught me as I grabbed blindly for a surface to steady myself on.

"Just dizzy," I told him, closing my eyes and trying to control my breathing. The last thing I needed was to get all worked up to the point where Beck could feel the fluctuation in the bond. His mother henning was a little absurd. "I'm okay, Doctor Weldman. Thanks. I'm sorry, I—"

"It's Eric," he reminded me gently. "And I'm the doctor here, so let's sit down for a second, okay?"

My cheeks burned and I allowed him to lead me into his tiny little consulting room. Sure, I had planned on talking to him at some point, but I hadn't needed him to see me almost pass out.

I sat in the comfortable chair beside his desk and he sat in his bigger, high-backed rolling desk chair, swiveling to face me. "Don't take this the wrong way, Ollie, but you're not looking so great today. In fact," he softened his voice, "you've been looking a bit wrung out for a while now. What's going on?"

I didn't know if he was asking as my boss or in the capacity of a medical professional, but it all came pouring out anyway. How exhausted I was all the time. The new food aversions. The random vomiting. The inability to keep my eyes open by the end of the day. The sudden dizzy spells. How shifting hadn't helped.

"Am I, like, anemic or something?" I asked him. "Or fighting off a weird bug?"

"It could be either of those things," he agreed, frowning. "Or something more insidious."

My eyes widened and my hands shook. A lump formed in my throat. "Like…cancer?"

"Obviously, that's a worst-case scenario and unlikely," he assured me. Then he smirked. "If you were a woman, I'd say the symptoms were all indicative of pregnancy, but that's not possible, obviously. Not unless you've been hiding an alpha away!" He laughed a little at his own joke.

I felt all the color drain from my face. I was a terrible poker player.

Doctor Weldman —*Eric*— looked immediately concerned, all levity gone. "Ollie?"

Pregnancy, my mind repeated.

I was an omega. I had been mated by an alpha. Knotted and filled with his seed over and over again. Hell, for that first weekend, I'd been practically insatiable, constantly slicked up and practically burning with desperation. It was almost like I'd been in heat.

Holy fuck.

It wasn't 'almost' anything! I *had* been in heat.

I'd never once stopped to consider that Beck being an alpha might mean I wasn't completely unable to have kids after all.

Not once. I'd even fucking thought about begging him to breed me, but I'd never imagined that he *could*.

"Oh fuck," I breathed, trying not to hyperventilate. I expected that the overwhelming sense of intense panic I was feeling would definitely translate through the bond, and I didn't know how to prevent that.

"Ollie," my boss rolled his chair across so he could place his hands over my trembling pair. "Deep breaths. In…" he mimicked the action for me, and I tried to follow his lead, "that's it. Good. And out." I exhaled shakily. "Good. Again. In…and out."

We went through it a few more times, but my hands continued to shake and the panic refused to recede. I felt like I was going to be sick.

'Morning sickness,' chimed a snide little voice in my head.

Swallowing back the bile, I willed that voice to shut the fuck up.

"Oliver, you're worrying me." Doctor Weldman said, frowning deeply.

"I…I…I…" The words wouldn't come. Couldn't come. If I admitted what I was all of a sudden certain about, I'd be outing what Beckett was. What we were to each other. Even though I trusted my boss, I knew that telling anyone would be a risk. Not that I'd be able to hide something like this from a doctor.

Hell, my belly would be hard to hide in a handful of months and that would give us away. Not just to Eric, but to the whole world.

I was so fucked.

Not to mention how Beck would react. He was only just starting to accept the fact that he was a shifter. We were still taking the dating thing slowly, even if we were bonded together forever. We were trying to treat everything as naturally and normally as possible.

Pregnancy under other circumstances might be natural and normal, but it certainly wasn't the usual for two cis-gendered men. Though, with my designation as an omega, could I *really* claim that this wasn't normal for me? Ultimately, I'd known what my body was capable of.

"Doctor Weldman," I started, still shaky.

"Eric, Ollie. I've asked you—"

"Eric. Right. Sorry." I bit my lip. "Eric, I…" Was I honestly about to tell him? Was that wise? But he was a doctor, he was a shifter, and he had very similar goals to his research as I did. He was the most trustworthy person I could think of going to about this, even if the thought terrified me.

"You…?" he prompted gently.

I took another deep breath. "I'm pretty sure I'm pregnant."

Eric arched an eyebrow, got up, walked over to his office door and shut it. He crossed his impressive arms across his chest and stared down at me.

"Oliver," he began patiently, "I know that as an omega—"

"I'm not crazy," I cut him off. "I…I'm mated. To an alpha. He, um, he knotted me. I didn't know he was an alpha, and he thought he was human, and we were just drawn to each other, y'know? And then I'm pretty sure meeting him put me into some sort of mating heat and…"

"Whoa," Eric held up his hands in surrender against the rambled onslaught of information. His eyes were wide, and I could see the gleam of excitement in them. Then his rational side kicked in. "Ollie, what you're saying sounds…" he paused, reaching for the right euphemism to imply that I was losing my mind, I just knew it, "far-fetched."

"Do you have an ultrasound machine?" I asked him.

He frowned but humored me. "How many weeks along do you think you are?"

I shrugged. "No more than four or five." My cheeks burned. "That was when we first mated." I started unraveling my scarf to show him my faded bite mark.

"Even if we were to presume and count the initial two weeks for ovulation that we consider in a female pregnancy," he mused aloud, coming back over to his chair, sitting down and leaning in to inspect my mark, "that would still only place you at six to seven weeks gestation. That's assuming the offspring of an alpha-omega shifter couple gestates at the same rate as the offspring of two betas or two humans. As such, it might be too early to pick up a heartbeat on an ultrasound machine. You know they're not generally used until after nine weeks at least. And finding hCG in your blood or urine could indicate cancer rather than a pregnancy, especially as you're a shifter and not technically human."

I appreciated that he was trying to take me seriously, even though his doubt was obvious. "Please try the portable unit," I begged him. "And if nothing comes up, we can try a full ultrasound." We didn't have the equipment on hand for that, or I would have demanded it to start with.

My heart was still hammering in my chest. From the moment Eric had jokingly mentioned the possibility, I didn't need any further confirmation. I just needed help that Beck and Sandy wouldn't be able to provide, which meant convincing my boss and mentor that I wasn't crazy.

He ducked out of the consulting room to the storage room next door and was only gone for a few moments before he returned and locked his office door.

"Climb up on the table," he gestured towards the exam table, "lie back, shirt up, unbutton your pants and slip the waist down a bit."

I did everything he told me to do, glad for the warmth of his rooms. He squirted some of the lubricant onto my belly, apologizing for not having prewarmed it, and then brought the wand of the portable ultrasound to the same spot. It was low down on my belly, right above my pubic bone, and he pressed firmly with the wand.

It was attached to a small speaker unit, and he turned the volume up so we could listen while he searched my lower abdomen.

Moving the wand slowly, all we heard at first were normal bodily swooshing sounds, staticky through the little speaker. But then, after traveling slightly left of center, it came through loud and clear: a rapid *whoosh-whoosh-whoosh*ing sound that couldn't be anything other than a fetal heartbeat.

"Holy shit," Eric inhaled, pressing in harder with the wand, chasing the sound. He listened in awe for a moment before looking up at me with wonder. "Oliver..." He trailed off and licked his lips anxiously. "Ollie, you really are pregnant."

I'd known it. I had. But it was something else to hear the heartbeat and to have the trained medical professional confirm it.

I opened my mouth to speak, but I was back to being dizzy, my own heart feeling like it was beating just as quickly as the one on the speaker.

"Ollie?" Eric was back to being concerned.

He had a right to be, I supposed. Because as I lifted my head to reassure him that I was fine, my eyes rolled backwards and the world around me went black.

Chapter Twelve – Beckett

The panic hit me as I was adjusting the text placement on an ebook cover commission. I moved my mouse too suddenly, misplacing the word, but I didn't care. It was an easy fix, whereas the feeling in my gut was not.

I scrambled for my phone, hidden under a pile of notes on my desk. With a few swipes, I had Ollie's contact up on the screen and I brought the phone to my ear. I was disappointed but not surprised when the call rang through to his voicemail.

His panic wasn't receding.

For him to feel so strongly, and for so long, something had to be wrong.

The only thing I could imagine was that his pack had come for him early. After everything he had told me about them, it wouldn't have surprised me if they had. I got up and paced the length of my bedroom, wondering on the action I should take. If it was indeed his pack, revealing who and what I was might make things worse. But I couldn't just let them take my mate.

I concentrated on the physical pull towards him. It felt like he was still in the direction of the lab where he worked. He'd walked me past it a couple of weeks ago, telling me about his job with a passion and enthusiasm that had made me so happy for him. It wasn't often that people found jobs that they truly loved, but Ollie was invested in his.

He wasn't moving away, either. The bond wasn't tugging or straining in a different direction. He was panicked, but he was staying still, most likely at work.

That made me pause.

What if the spike of anxiety was work related? What if I was being hypersensitive and overreacting? I'd noticed myself becoming increasingly protective of Ollie and I had put that down as a consequence of the mating bond. What if my response now was just an extension of that?

I redialed his number and listened to the call ring through to voicemail again, frowning.

If it was indeed a work-related issue, Oliver would know that I could feel his worry and he would try to reassure me. I resolved to give him a few minutes to sort whatever the problem was out, and if he hadn't tried to call me back or text me after that, then I would find him and reassure myself that he wasn't in any trouble.

So I continued to pace, my own work forgotten.

After five more agonizingly slow minutes with radio silence from Ollie, I gave up and grabbed my jacket from the back of my chair, sliding it on over my arms and back before I hastily wrapped my scarf around my neck and grabbed for my wallet and keys on my desk.

I was just stepping out through the apartment door when another small spike of Ollie's anxiety hit me, followed by the strangest sensation of his consciousness dimming, the panic vanishing completely. It was kind of like the way he felt when he was asleep, but abrupt and harsh, like he was suddenly gone.

He'd passed out.

With that realization, I raced down the hallway and bypassed the rickety old elevator, taking the stairs that led to the ground floor two at a time. I burst out of the building and onto the sidewalk. I hailed a cab, thankful that the early morning rush was over and unwilling to waste time on waiting for the subway. I barked out the address for Ollie's lab and bounced my leg in agitation as the cabbie weaved through New York's constantly unwieldy traffic. I remained laser focused on Ollie's status through the bond, exhaling in relief when that strange dimmed feeling changed back to his normal state.

When his fear flared again, I knew something was definitely wrong. It was unusual for me to feel his emotions at all anymore, unless we were knotted together. For them to be coming through so clearly meant that he was feeling them deeply.

A block away from the lab, the cab hit heavy traffic.

"I'm getting out here," I told the cabbie, who grumbled about the inconvenience of being stuck where he was. I thrust a handful of bills at him. "Keep the change," I said, then pushed open my door, climbing out of the yellow sedan as quickly as I could manage.

I followed the loosening imaginary band inside me, letting it guide me to my mate. I tried to push feelings of reassurance and calm towards him as I neared, knowing that he would be able to feel my approach. Whether it worked or not, I couldn't say.

Only a few minutes after leaving the cab, I burst into the little reception room for the doctor's office above the lab, housed in a pretty brownstone. There were a few people seated on the faded floral armchairs that lined the perimeter of the room. There was also a tiny plastic table with proportionately tiny plastic chairs, a plastic cup full of broken crayons and a stack of coloring pages set out for children to entertain themselves. I paid none of that much mind as I moved to storm past the reception desk, following the pull of my mate.

"Sir," the guy at the desk called after me, his tone increasing in insistence. "Sir! You can't go back there!"

I ignored him, hearing him push his chair back to follow me, but I didn't care. I had tunnel vision and stopped at the door that led to Ollie. I tried the handle, but it was locked.

"Sir," the guy from reception said forcefully, and I turned to growl at him.

His brown eyes widened and he took a step back. He was petite like Ollie but looked closer to my age. He had hair so blonde it looked almost white, but his eyebrows were dark brown. I knew he was a shifter, because Ollie said everyone on staff was, but I couldn't recall his name or the kind of shifter Ollie had said he was, and I wasn't in the mood to try and sniff him out. I was still learning that skill and it was hit and miss. The way he reacted to me, though, I could only assume it was not an apex predator like myself.

"S-sir," he stammered. "I need you to—"

"Ollie's in there," I snapped. I didn't have the patience to play games. "Ollie's in there, and he needs me."

The receptionist guy frowned and folded his arms. "One, how do you know Ollie? Two, how do you know he needs you? Did he call you? Because neither he nor Doc said a thing about anyone coming." Having regained his confidence, he looked me up and down. "They said they weren't to be disturbed and that appointments would all have to be pushed back this morning."

I fought the urge that told me to get in this guy's face and turn into a raging, aggressive asshole. I might have been an alpha, but I was not that guy. Even with my concern for Ollie warring away inside me, I forced myself to breathe deeply and speak calmly. "I'm Ollie's…partner. And he's unwell. So, if you don't mind," I turned back to the door to knock on it, but it swung open.

I blinked at the tall, muscular man who opened the door. He was decidedly not what I had expected when Ollie had told me his boss was a doctor and medical researcher, and an omega like him. This guy was big, buff, and handsome. He was clean shaven, with a heart-shaped face and a mop of hair composed of messy, golden curls. He had big, blue eyes that stared intently back at me, and he was dressed in khaki business pants and a crisp, white business shirt. He couldn't have been older than forty.

Behind him, Ollie was sitting up on the exam table, wringing his hands in his lap. He wouldn't look at me.

"Thanks, Colt," the doctor said in a smooth, authoritative voice. "I've got this. Can you apologize to everyone waiting?"

The receptionist guy —Colt, I corrected myself— gave me one last wary glance before he headed back down the hall.

The doctor silently ushered me into the room and then shut the door behind me. Then he looked me over with curiosity. "So you're the alpha," he said, and I frowned. He offered me a tight smile. "Don't worry, the room is soundproofed. Shifter ears and medical confidentiality, you know the drill." He rolled his wrist as he spoke.

"Right." I said, then leaned around him to gaze at my mate. "Ollie? Babe, what's going on?"

He'd told his employer that I was an alpha, that much was obvious. But *why*?

Watching Ollie shrink in on himself made my inner wolf whine. I wanted to go to him, to nuzzle him and hold him and fix whatever the hell had gone wrong.

"I think you should sit," the doctor said when it became apparent Ollie was not in a talkative mood. I fought the urge to growl at this guy who stood between me and my mate. "Beck, was it?" He stuck out his hand and smiled pleasantly. The guy had dimples, too. If I'd been a lesser man, I might have been intimidated by how attractive he was. "Eric Weldman."

I shook the proffered hand. "Beckett Smith," I responded as politely as I could. Then I inched around him and headed over to the exam table, hopping up next to Ollie and wrapping an arm around him. His breathing hitched and he stiffened for a moment, before turning into my embrace and burying his face in the crook of my neck.

My hackles rose and I looked at this Eric guy in askance. "You knew I was an alpha," I said, even though I wanted to demand answers about why my mate was so upset.

"To be fair," Weldman responded calmly, sitting in his high-backed rolling chair and scooting it forward towards the table. He sat forward, clasping his hands between spread legs, the picture of casual professionalism, "I can scent it on you. You've got a subtle power about you that betas and omegas don't." He cocked his head. "Do you have a birthmark?"

"Not that I'm aware of."

Ollie mumbled something incoherent into my neck.

"What was that?" I asked him.

He pulled back and flushed pink. "You, um, you have one on your butt."

"I do not. I've seen my butt in the mirror every day my whole life. I don't have a birthmark."

He shook his head. "It's, um, just under the curve of your left cheek."

I didn't want to accuse him of lying, but I had never noticed such a thing before and I told him so.

"What sort of shape is it?" Weldman asked, and I tried not to be weirded-out by the question. He held up his hand. On the inside of his wrist, a port wine birthmark in the shape of a crescent moon took up barely an inch of skin. But I blinked because Ollie had the same mark on his thigh.

"We're marked as omegas," he explained gently. "All omegas bear this mark somewhere on their body. It serves to reason that alphas would have a mark as well."

I sighed. "Well, that makes sense. But I never had a mark on my ass before."

"What if it appeared at the same time as everything else?" Ollie asked, and I was relieved that he was starting to sound himself again. I could still feel a low thrum of anxiety resonating from him, though, which meant that he was more shaken than he looked or sounded.

Weldman nodded. "You said the knotting and claiming seemed to bring out Beckett's previously hidden shifter scent and abilities."

I knew my eyes had blown wide. "You told him about…" I made a vague gesture over my crotch.

Ollie paled and looked away. "I…I had to."

"Babe, help me understand," I pleaded softly. "The last time we talked about it, we agreed that other shifters knowing would be a bad thing."

I watched him bite his lip and noticed the tremble in his body. I cuddled him closer, wanting to comfort him. "I'm not mad. I'm confused. I'm new to this shifter thing and I trust your judgment, but—"

"I'm pregnant."

His words stopped me short. I blinked. Once. Twice. Three times.

"Honey," I started carefully, "you're a man."

"He's an omega," Weldman corrected me. "And you are an alpha." There was a hint of awe in the way he said it. Given all that Ollie had told me over the past month, I thought I could understand why. Especially when the guy's research was all about shifter evolution and why omegas still existed if they couldn't bear…oh.

Oh!

I felt Oliver tense up at the same moment the pieces fell together for me. That first night together, he had said that he produced slick to make the whole mating thing easier. That it was a throwback to being able to get pregnant by an alpha.

I was an alpha.

He was an omega and I was an alpha.

I was an alpha who had knotted him. Who had claimed and bonded with him. Who had filled him with cum and stayed locked inside him on more than one occasion.

It only takes one time, my high school sex ed lessons echoed in my brain unhelpfully. At the time, I hadn't really cared too much because I'd known I was gay and I was probably never going to have to worry about accidentally knocking someone up.

"Oh my God," I suddenly understood Ollie's panic with clarity. I swallowed hard. "Babe..."

"I didn't think," he murmured, looking down at his hands. He was still wringing them together. "I didn't...not even after you knotted me. I never thought about why alphas existed. It's even the basis of my freaking research and I just...didn't think."

"You've spent your entire life believing yourself infertile," Weldman interrupted in a warm, calming tone. "Oliver, it's understandable that your brain wouldn't immediately make the connection that the sudden discovery of an alpha might lead to-"

"It should have!" Ollie argued, then immediately looked shamefaced. "Sorry. I don't mean to snap. I...I just...this has come out of nowhere and I'm only twenty-two and, oh yeah, how will we keep the whole alpha thing a secret if I'm waddling around with a baby bump?!"

These were all valid concerns, but I was leaning more towards what would happen *after*. It wasn't him being pregnant that scared me, it was the product thereof.

A baby.

I was *not* ready for a baby. I'd never even wanted kids.

I was gay. Surprise babies weren't supposed to be a thing for me. I wasn't supposed to be able to accidentally get people pregnant. That was one of the many benefits of sleeping with other cis-gendered men. Or, at least, it had been until I magically changed species mid-coitus and quite obviously knocked another man up.

Great job, Beckett.

I knew I was going to cowboy up and be a proper parent. Having grown up in the system, I was *not* going to risk my own kid ending up with the same shitty fate. No matter how this had happened, it had happened, and I couldn't change that now.

But Christ on a cracker, a baby?!

Ollie and I hadn't even been dating for more than a month or so. I was barely getting comfortable with the idea of being forever bonded to him, a veritable stranger, and now we were going to be parents together?

"We're going to do this all off the books," Weldman told Ollie. "You can trust that I won't tell a soul, Ollie. I'm..." he hesitated. "I have resources. Connections. Access to information and history that most don't. It's going to be all right."

Ollie shook his head. "And Lacey and Colt?" he asked pointedly. "Are we going to force them to keep their mouths shut somehow? What about your shifter patients? At some point, someone is going to notice, and the news will get out, and the humans will hunt us, and the shifters will want Beck for themselves..."

"I'm not going anywhere," I assured him, regardless of my desire to run from my new responsibilities and not look back. I couldn't do that to Ollie. I cared about him, and not just because of the bond we shared. "But this does mean we really do need a plan to evade your pack after Christmas."

I'd witnessed a few calls between Ollie and his mother over the past few weeks. The more I heard her spouting off about the 'good of the pack', the more I couldn't help but feel like their pack was actually a cult. It made the hairs on my neck stand on end and my protective side bristle. I could only imagine what they might do if they were to realize that Ollie was pregnant. It would rock their status quo, and history had proven that never ended well for cults.

"Lacey and Colt are just as passionate about our research as you and I are," Weldman insisted, speaking as though I hadn't cut in. "And having first-hand experience with a bonded alpha and omega pair, especially through a pregnancy…"

"We're not your lab rats," I hissed at him.

Ollie put his hand on my chest. "Beck, stop. He doesn't mean it like that."

My wolf really didn't like hearing my pregnant mate defending another man, but I stomped down on the possessive jealousy. That shit was getting old fast. "Then how did he mean it?"

The doctor held his hands up in surrender. "I would love to ask you questions, to study your bond and try and work out whether your existence as an alpha is a fluke or whether there might be more of you out there. But Ollie is also a friend, and I would never harm or betray a friend." The corners of his lips lifted. "And, within nine months, he will be glad to have had a friend with medical training."

Beside me, Ollie blanched. "I hadn't thought about giving birth."

Well, neither had I until he said the words. I squeezed my hand around his bicep and wondered how much of my mounting terror he could feel.

"We'll work it out, Ollie," Weldman assured him. "Like I said, I have resources. I—"

"What kind of shifter are you anyway?" I blurted and sniffed the air. "Because the receptionist dude…Colt? He was something like a rodent, right?"

"A rabbit," Ollie interjected offhandedly. Then he smiled at me with pride. "Hey, you're getting better with your scenting."

I grinned. "Thanks. Sandy's been making me practice."

Then I gave myself a shake and narrowed my gaze back at Weldman. "But you…you smell…" I inhaled deeply, and my inner wolf told me to back away and get my mate to safety. "Like an apex predator of some kind…but nothing like the bears or lions or others that Sandy's been trying to train me with." Her training had involved a lot of trips into Times Square, where the heavy population of tourists guaranteed a mixture of scents to explore.

Weldman's smile turned toothy. "I'm not any of those things, no."

Also, he was cagey. That did not bode well.

"Listen, bud, if this was a cheesy fantasy novel, you would be coming off as the potential villain right about now," I told him.

He rolled his eyes and crossed his arms. "You're not going to believe me if I do tell you."

"Try me."

We locked gazes and I tried to channel all of my alpha posturing. Ollie and Sandy had both said that, as an alpha, I inherently outranked any other shifters.

Eventually, it seemed to work. Weldman threw his hands in the air and declared, "Fine. I'm a dragon. Are you happy now?"

Ollie inhaled sharply but Weldman had been right: I didn't believe him.

"Dragons aren't real," I argued. "All the other animals? Totally legit creatures that exist. You couldn't have gone with hippo or something?"

The doctor snorted. "Hippo?"

"Those things are killing machines," I insisted. "I'd rather take my chances with a bear than a hippo."

113

"Right," he drew the word out like I had lost my mind. I was starting to feel like maybe I had. Then he sighed and shrugged. "Dragon shifters exist. We're close to extinction, given that we are a male only race and the last of our alphas died hundreds of years ago, but…"

"If your alphas died, how is it you exist? Are you a half-dragon?" I was curious.

He rolled his eyes. "The last known dragon alpha was my father."

"But…"

Holding up a hand, Weldman sighed again. "I'm a *little* older than I look."

I wasn't going to ask. "Okay," I acceded, deciding that there was no way to prove or disprove his claims at that point, "so, you've got even more reason to want to lock me in a cage and force me to make little dragon babies."

"You're a wolf," he spoke as if I was an idiot, "for obvious reasons, you couldn't breed with a dragon."

"Well, unless…" Ollie said, frowning, "unless he only became a wolf shifter once we were bonded. Like…what if being an alpha is kind of like having an O negative blood type? Like, he could, uh, donate blood to all other blood types? Because he was definitely human before we mated."

I frowned trying to follow the logic.

Weldman pursed his pouty bow lips in thought. "Was he able to knot you before he claimed you?"

I recalled all too clearly the way the base of my cock had swelled that first time. I'd felt harder than I had ever felt in my life, like I had a never-ending supply of cum and like I had needed to push everything I could into Ollie's wet, tight heat. I remembered the way he had cried out and writhed in my lap, the way he had bared his neck and I had taken advantage and bitten down.

My cheeks heated with the memory.

"Yeah," I answered before Ollie could. "Yeah, I…" I paused and cleared my throat. "I was, yes."

"Hmm," Weldman rolled his chair to his desk and started tapping away at his computer. "So, assuming you didn't scent like shifter yet, it's possible that Ollie's onto something. Perhaps alphas are universal? Perhaps the claiming is what sets things in place and awakens your latent shifting ability, linking you with whatever breed of shifter you've bonded with?"

I sat up straighter. "So, you're saying that if I hadn't initiated the bond, I would have stayed human?" I paused and thought of the knot. "Mostly human?"

Weldman nodded, and he had a look on his face that I recognized. It was just like Ollie's 'itching to research' face. It softened him. "And I wonder…" He skimmed through some articles, but then abandoned the pursuit to turn back to me. "Would an unbonded potential alpha be able to donate sperm to omegas of all breeds, or does a claim need to be initiated for the seed to take?"

My eyes bulged for what felt like the ten thousandth time during the short conversation. I bit back the urge to cover my junk and sent a thank you to the universe that I had actually claimed my mate and locked in my breed, as it were. One unplanned pregnancy was more than enough for my lifetime, and there was no chance in hell I would have signed up to donate my genetic material, sub-species on the edge of extinction or no.

"Or, now that you've settled into a specific breed," Weldman continued in thought, oblivious to my musings, "whether your sperm is still viable with other wolven omegas, despite your mating bond." He turned back to his screen as Ollie bristled beside me. "There is some anecdotal data which suggests some alphas took more than one omega mate during the dwindling of their numbers."

"Absolutely not," Ollie growled out with a possessive edge I hadn't heard from him before.

It was fucking hot.

"Sorry, Eric," he didn't sound at all apologetic this time, "but I'm not sharing my mate." He sidled in closer to me, physically staking his claim. It was adorable. "Not any part of him, sperm included. Not even for science."

I kissed the top of his head, thrilled by his declaration. "Good boy," I murmured, and he blushed prettily.

Weldman's face fell, but he nodded. "I understand. From all accounts, especially in the early days of your bond, any threats to it aren't likely to be well received. But," he looked at me imploringly, "I would like to take some samples purely for research purposes. I promise not to impregnate any omegas without your knowledge or consent."

That didn't fill me with much hope. Still, he was probably the only even remotely trustworthy person who could help Ollie through his pregnancy.

Oh, God. That word set off a series of palpitations again.

"I agree to those terms," I started, and he lit up like the Christmas tree in Rockefeller Center, "as long as you promise to help Ollie through…" I couldn't say it out loud. Instead, I placed my hand over my mate's belly and finished lamely, "everything."

Weldman nodded eagerly, extending his hand to shake on

our deal. "I wouldn't dream of suggesting anyone else look after Ollie and your child, Alpha."

Well, I thought bemusedly as we all seemed to straighten with surprise and a tingle of what I could only call magic as he addressed me so formally, *this is new*.

Chapter Thirteen – Oliver

When Eric suggested the ultrasound so that Beck could hear the baby's heartbeat for the first time, I was almost certain that my mate would run through the office door Wile E Coyote style. Beck paled and tried to assure the doctor that it wasn't necessary, but Eric insisted.

There was a strange dynamic between them now. Eric, as a dragon (and wasn't that a surprise?) and also the oldest of the three of us, was usually a commanding presence, but he had formally ceded rank to Beck and that seemed to settle over them with a wave of magic similar to the one I had felt when Beck had bitten me. It wasn't as strong, but it felt right. Like an invocation of the way things should be.

"Your other appointments…" I started, knowing that we had pushed his day's schedule out by at least an hour at that point.

Eric waved me off. "I've already had Colt cancel my mid-morning appointments. This is far more important. You, Ollie, are far more important."

That felt strange to hear. I knew he cared about me as a good boss should care about their employees, and even as a friend should care about their friends, but the gravitas he spoke with implied something deeper than that. Reverence, maybe?

I supposed I was the first omega to turn up pregnant in a couple of hundred years. Well, the first we knew of, at any rate. If others had existed, they'd kept very well hidden. From a scientific perspective, I could understand Eric's awe. I just wished I wasn't the living, breathing test subject.

Still, I was familiar with that set of his jaw and the stubborn glint in his eye, so I gently pushed Beck off the table and lay back down, assuming the same position as earlier.

Eric was much more excited to get the ultrasound running this time around. I kept my eyes on Beck the entire time. He was freaking out. I didn't need the bond to tell me that. I couldn't blame him: this was huge, and I was freaking out, too. It didn't escape my notice that he couldn't say the word 'pregnant', but it had surprised me that he had put his big, warm palm over my abdomen earlier, non-verbally protecting his unborn child.

Jesus Christ, a child.

I hadn't given much thought to anything beyond being pregnant, but pregnancy meant a baby – a little person we had to be responsible for and raise to adulthood. It was literally a lifetime commitment. Yes, our accidental bond was also a forever thing, but we probably could have lived separate lives if we'd really wanted to. But a baby? A child? That wasn't something we could pretend didn't exist.

Eric squirted some more of the cold lube on my belly and applied the ultrasound wand, fiddling with the dials on the staticky speaker again. He went straight for the spot we'd heard the heartbeat earlier and, after a few moments of pressing down uncomfortably hard on my lower belly, the *whoosh-whoosh-whoosh* sound, just as fast as before, came through the speaker.

"Is that...?" Beck asked, narrowing his gaze at the transducer wand in Eric's grasp. Then he looked at Eric's face with the same unconvinced expression.

"Baby's heartbeat," Eric said cheerily, in the kind of tone I expect he used on all the expectant parents he performed prenatal checkups for. "It's supposed to be fast," he added.

Beck swallowed roughly. "Wow." He looked back at the wand and my belly and swallowed again, then finally at me. "This is..." He trailed off.

"Huge?" I suggested. "Scary? Un-fucking-believable?"

"All of that," he agreed. "Ollie, I..."

"*Oh*," Eric's surprise tore both of our attentions towards him. He was moving the wand and the speedy whooshing sound was warping in on itself, seemingly doubling. My face fell as I understood what I was hearing, but my brain refused to compute. Eric looked up at us, genuine excitement brightening his face. "Hear that?" He asked us.

"Please don't say—" I began, begging with him not to confirm yet another horrifying revelation.

"Twin heartbeats," he ignored me.

Beck sucked in a sharp breath. "Tw—" he started, then cut himself off, shaking his head in emphatic denial. "*No.* Really?"

"That's definitely two heartbeats," Eric replied. "You're wolves, so perhaps litters are—"

"*Litters?*" Beck's voice went high and thin. His eyes were wide, and his skin was pale. "Please tell me there aren't more hiding in there."

120

A burst of hysterical laughter erupted from the back of my throat. I had to wave off the incredulous look Beck shot me.

"Sorry," I bit back another laugh. "I think I've finally cracked."

It was all too much. Being mated, being an omega with an alpha and keeping the secret, going from strangers to bonded for life, then, ultimately, learning that we're going to have not one but *two* kids made me feel like my entire world was unraveling. Not to mention the impending pressure of my pack coming to steal me away. I was laughing because it felt surreal. Like I was suddenly part of a far-fetched soap opera rather than living my real life. And, if I didn't laugh, I would cry.

Beck's gaze softened into understanding.

We had so much to talk about now. So much more than we had even a few hours ago, and I had to admit that I was a little scared that this might be the thing that pushed him over the edge, too. The thing that sent him running for real. After all, he wasn't the pregnant one. He could walk away, ignore the call of the bond, and live life like any other shifter.

I was the one who couldn't run away. I considered asking Eric about omega terminations, but my stomach roiled at just the idea. I didn't want to do that. I would never judge another person for choosing to do so, but even if the option was there, it wasn't for me.

No, from the second I'd realized that I was pregnant, I'd known I would have my baby. That didn't change because there were two babies to consider, though it would make things more complicated.

"Go home, Ollie," Eric instructed, wiping off my belly with a wet wipe he had warmed between his large palms. "I'll still pay you for today, and I'll start doing deeper dives into omega pregnancies and births, but you've had a shock, and you were lightheaded enough when you got in."

I opened my mouth to argue with him, but he shook his head.

"I'm going to suggest you take some iron supplements, as well as some folic acid. Eat small meals regularly to try and combat the nausea and stave off the dizzy spells. Take a day or two to come to terms with what's going on, then come back to work."

I nodded mutely. I couldn't exactly argue with my boss when he was also my self-appointed doctor in all of this mess, could I?

* * *

Beck kept his hand on the base of my spine for the entire trip back to my apartment, but he didn't say a word. Not even when we stopped at a bodega for a little bottle of orange juice to fight off another wave of dizziness. I attempted to probe the bond, searching for a hint of his feelings, but there was nothing there. It was almost like he'd found a switch to sever the transmission, because there was no way he wasn't freaking out the same way I had earlier. The same way I still was.

I had made my peace with being essentially infertile. I'd always thought that if I ever had kids, it would be through adoption (especially if I fell in love with another omega), or a surrogate using my human —or beta— partner's sperm. Never in my wildest dreams had I ever imagined that I would get pregnant. That I would be the first omega in a couple of centuries to do so. Well, not unless there had been other alphas out there in the world, living in successful secrecy.

Surely Beck wasn't the only one. Maybe there were more overseas, or even hiding in other parts of America. I could definitely understand why they would want to keep it a secret.

Eric and I would have to put feelers out into the shifter community. As a dragon, he probably had contacts with deeper pockets and more prominent social positions, likely all over the world.

To think I'd been working for a dragon all this time! I had so many questions I wanted to ask him about the history he had witnessed firsthand, and about the staggering amount of knowledge he must have amassed in his extended lifetime.

When I let us in to my poky little apartment and shut the door behind us, Beck's hand left my back. I immediately missed its presence.

"You should probably eat something," he said, but he didn't meet my gaze.

Yeah, he was definitely freaking out. I couldn't blame him.

I pulled a box of crackers out from the cupboard beside the fridge and nibbled on one to appease him, acknowledging that the snack did seem to settle my remaining nausea. I didn't know if it was the slight hit of salt or the dryness of the cracker, but it helped.

"Beck…" I started, not quite sure what I wanted to say. I wanted to apologize for not making the biological connection in my head. For not thinking about the potential consequences of him knotting me.

His face was pale as he looked up at me from the edge of my mattress, his feet planted firmly on the scraggly, worn carpet. His elbows rested on his knees, and he held his clasped hands in front of his mouth. He was the picture of stressed out.

Guilt ate away at my insides.

Hot tears threatened behind my eyelids. "I'm sorry," I said with a wobble in my voice. My throat was tight. "I didn't think. I didn't—"

"Babe," he sighed and reached for me. Placing my hand in his, I allowed him to tug me down to sit beside him. He wrapped his big, strong arm around me and cuddled me to his side. "This isn't your fault."

I scoffed. "No?" I asked him, the first of the tears finally spilling over. "Because *I'm* the omega. I'm the one who grew up knowing about shifter biology. I fucking research it, for fuck's sake."

"And like your ridiculously hot boss you've never warned me about said," Beck calmly argued back, making me snort with amusement, "you've spent your life convinced that you're sterile because you're an omega. What happened between us was unexpected. We got so wrapped up in the fact that I wasn't human anymore, neither one of us thought of the implications of actually being a mated pair. You explained what you were and what it meant before we even had sex. After I knotted you…after we worked out I was an alpha…well, I could have made the same connection, too. But I didn't."

"I feel like freaking out over changing species lets you off the hook for that."

"Okay, but then you're also off the hook because you were freaking out about me being something that shouldn't exist, too."

Sniffling, I couldn't do much more than nod. "It's not like we can change it now," I managed to get out after an awkward silence. My voice was still thick with emotions, but I felt drained and hopeless. "But you don't have to stick around," I continued, the words making my heart ache. "You didn't ask for any of this."

Beck's lips brushed the top of my head before he rested his cheek over the same spot. "Neither did you, babe. I'm not going anywhere."

"But you can't tell me you want this."

I didn't really want it. Not then. Not so early into our relationship.

I could feel him tense up, but he still held me close. "We can't undo it," he murmured, neither confirming or denying my statement, "and I won't let my kids grow up like I did."

I was struck silent by the jumbled feelings his admission provoked. I wanted to tell him that a sense of obligation was not a good enough motivator to commit to being a parent, but at the same time, I was warmed by the fact that he obviously cared enough about our children to want a better life for them. I felt guilty all over again, but also strangely hopeful that we might actually be able to make a future work.

"I don't want them to grow up like I did, either," I confessed quietly. "The pack hierarchy is…well, let's just say it's archaic. It has all the hallmarks of a cult, and I don't want that for my kids."

Kids *plural*.

Of which there would be two.

I was definitely struggling to wrap my head around that.

"You're not going back to your pack," Beck insisted, squeezing me tighter against him. "We've already decided that."

"They're going to go *insane* when they discover this," I went on, placing my hand over my abdomen. "I kept an alpha all to myself *and* I let him breed me?" I shook my head. "I'm in deep shit."

If nothing else, I imagined they would have wanted the first successful mating between an alpha and omega to exist within the confines of the pack structure, with an omega more pliant and willing to let them meddle. God only knew what my pack would do once they discovered that an alpha existed. *My* alpha.

A low, possessive growl echoed in the room and for a moment I thought I had let my thoughts get the better of me. But the sound hadn't come from my throat. It had come from Beck's.

"I'm going to protect you," he said, his voice deep and gravelly. It sent shivers up my spine and sparked a curl of arousal in my belly. My need for him only grew as he placed his hand on top of mine, over the soft tissue of my stomach, "all three of you."

Well, damn.

* * *

The next few days were strained between us. I was still exhausted to my marrow, feeling nauseated more than I felt 'normal', and Beck was physically present but quite obviously lost in his thoughts. Not that I blamed him: I had grown up knowing what my body was physically capable of, but working out that I was actually pregnant had thrown me for a loop.

Nevertheless, Beck stuck by my side, feeding me dry, salty crackers and Gatorade as he brooded and silently fretted. I didn't push him to talk. I was still beyond relieved that he'd chosen to stick around at all. I didn't think I'd manage on my own, even though I'd told him that I could.

I missed the camaraderie we had been building between

us, though. It almost felt like we were back at square one: awkward strangers who hadn't already been on multiple dates and mapped out each others' bodies with hands and tongues. It sucked, but I was determined to wait until Beck had sorted through his thoughts before I started pushing the issue.

But the breaking point came when Beck cautiously suggested that going away for our planned romantic getaway to Rhinebeck mightn't be the best idea for my safety now that I was expecting.

In our many conversations with Eric, who was thoroughly invested in learning everything he could about our bond, Beck had confessed that he was starting to feel more possessive and protective and that it felt more like ingrained instinct than emotion. Eric had hypothesized his reasons, citing the bond and Beck's inner alpha, but none of that made me feel any happier to hear that those new instincts had my mate wanting to cancel our pre-Christmas plans.

"No," I whined, horrified to feel tears prickling in my eyes. A lump that for once wasn't bile, but was still completely unwelcome, lodged in my throat. Grief and disappointment threatened to drown me from the inside and the way my mate's eyes widened told me that he'd felt the intense feelings through the bond. I didn't want him to feel manipulated, but I couldn't contain the emotion either. "Beck, please? I've been so excited to go."

Even though we had been on dates like any other couple, the thought of having my own Christmas-themed romantic weekend away with the man of my dreams —with my mate!— had made me giddy when he had first asked me to join him. It had been so sweet that he had researched towns with parades, knowing how much I wanted to see one. And the cozy cabin he'd chosen for us, all timber with fireplaces and miles of privacy, had cinched the deal. It was going to be just us, our first little holiday as a couple, our first Christmas celebration together. I didn't want to lose that. Especially not because of whatever knee-jerk reaction he was having over the news of my pregnancy.

If nothing else, a romantic getaway should help us reconnect. We could hide out and talk in a neutral setting. Hell, we could even shift in the woods and let our wolves sort things out their way.

All of those thoughts came tumbling out of me in a rush. "I'm barely even pregnant," I argued with a sniffle, cursing myself for not being able to control my tears as I pleaded for him to change his mind. "Nobody can tell by looking at me. There's no reason we can't continue on like a normal couple in public for a while. Not until I'm showing. And it's not like my pack will come looking for me there, right? I just...I just want us to be *us* again, you know? Like, I know things are gonna change fast, but can't we just have this one thing? Can't we just forget that this week happened and have a romantic weekend together?" Tears were coursing down my cheeks as I worked myself up. "I know that's selfish, but..."

"Hey, shh." Big arms enveloped me and tugged me in for a hug. I breathed in his scent and allowed it to settle me as his voice rumbled through his chest. "I'm sorry. I'm just being a paranoid jerk. Of course we can go." Beck sounded amused as he huffed, "But we're not just going to forget what's going on, babe. It doesn't work that way."

"You know what I meant," I grumbled. "Things have been weird since we found out."

"It's a lot to process," he responded softly. "But I'm getting there, Ollie. And I meant what I said: I'm not leaving. We're going to make it work. It's just going to take time."

I wished we were more established in our relationship. That we had a more stable foundation underneath us. I wanted to hear him tell me that he loved me, and I wanted to be able to return the sentiment. Not that those three words would fix everything, but they helped to soothe the uncertainty, didn't they? I'd never actually exchanged them with anyone before. But I did know that right then would have been too soon to do so. All I could do was trust that what we had was enough, and that Beck really was going to be okay with the changes coming our way.

* * *

"Thank you for doing this," I repeated for what felt like the thousandth time as we pulled our little red rental car into a park on a side street a short walk away from Rhinebeck's bustling thoroughfare. I'd been thanking Beck since he had picked me up outside my apartment, after he'd lectured me for carrying my own damn suitcase down the few flights of stairs so I could meet him by the curb.

The drive upstate had been idyllic and we were finally starting to talk to each other without any lingering tension or awkwardness. Well, there would have been less awkwardness if I hadn't spent the ride thanking my mate every ten minutes, but I couldn't help it.

I was grateful to him for so many things and I needed him to know it. Even if he was still processing the baby bombshell, I was grateful that he hadn't left me to cope on my own, and that he was making an effort to talk it through with me. I was grateful that he was going to keep me safe from my pack, too. But mostly, I was grateful that he had given in to my pleas and was still taking me away for a romantic weekend: something no man had ever done for me before. Especially not for Christmas.

It was special. Beck made me feel special. Even while he was still freaking out, I didn't doubt that he cared about me or wanted to be with me. I'd been right all those weeks earlier: most men my own age didn't have the maturity of a man Beck's age. I'd spent too long barking up the wrong trees, but I was thankful to have finally found the right one in the end.

We'd made it to our cabin where we had dumped our bags and taken turns in the en suite bathroom, freshening up before we headed back out to the town. Brandi and I had arranged to meet up in a little café before the parade. She was excited to introduce me to the guy she'd started dating, and even though I was still a little annoyed that she had essentially copied my romantic weekend plans, it was sweet to see her so buoyed over this new guy after the last few asshats she'd dated. I'd never met anyone quite as unlucky in love as my best friend.

Beck reached over the center console and squeezed my thigh. "You need to stop thanking me, baby. I wanted to do this for you. For us."

My heart squeezed and I swallowed roughly. "I know. But I meant giving up some alone time to come meet Brandi and John."

"She's important to you," he said with a nonchalant shrug, "so that makes her important to me, too."

It meant the world to me to hear him say that. Brandi was pretty much all I had in the world now that my pack had made their intentions crystal clear. Plus, the sweetness and reassurance in Beck's tone went a long way to easing whatever residual fears I had about us as a couple. We hadn't had sex since we'd learned about the babies, but as long as we were still sharing intimate moments like this one, I knew we were on track again.

Unbuckling my seat belt, I leaned across the console and sighed happily when our lips connected in a sweet, chaste kiss. My heart fluttered and I fought back the urge to say words I didn't think he was ready to hear. I wasn't exactly ready to say them, either, but I was starting to feel them. How could I not, when he was working so hard to make sure I was happy? Nobody else had ever done anything like that for me before. I pulled back slightly, barely leaving any space between our mouths.

"Th—"

"If you say 'thank you' one more time," he chuckled against my lips, leaving the idle threat hanging.

"Mmm, are you going to punish me, Alpha?"

He groaned and shifted in his seat, visibly adjusting himself in his pants. "Keep that kind of talk up and I'll drive us back to the cabin right now, Brandi and parades be damned."

I gasped. "You wouldn't!"

With a dramatic sigh and a roll of his eyes, he said, "Get out of the car, babe. Otherwise I'll make good on that threat."

I laughed, pecked him on the lips once more, then climbed out of the passenger seat. Beck came around the car and we linked our gloved hands together. I practically rode on a cloud the entire walk to the café, genuinely feeling like everything between us was going to be okay.

So, when we walked into the brightly colored café, the bell

above the door jingling merrily over our heads, I knew I looked like a besotted teenager. Brandi called out to us and waved, gesturing for us to take the two free seats at the table she had somehow managed to snag, and I went happily.

It wasn't until Beck tensed at my side that I realized we might have an issue after all.

Chapter Fourteen – Beckett

John was a shifter. I hadn't needed Ollie to tell me that when Brandi introduced us. I'd scented it on him. *Wolf*, my instincts said. *Threat*.

There was something about the guy that rubbed me the wrong way. But then, over the past few days, a lot of things had. Weldman said it was likely my alpha wolf becoming extra protective of its mate and unborn pups (not a word I was comfortable with), and Ollie agreed with the doctor's hypothesis. But this gut feeling wasn't the same as the irrational urge to wrap Ollie in bubble wrap, or to growl at anyone who looked at him with appraising eyes.

No, this was a deep-seated sensation that John couldn't be trusted. It was like the time in my Junior year of school, when Billy Robards asked me to keep his backpack in my locker. I'd known there was something off about the request and, sure enough, when they did a 'random' locker search that same day and found a bunch of stuff he'd stolen from a little old lady whose house backed onto the school grounds, I was glad that

I'd said no. My gut was revolting now, just as it had back then.

Ollie and I had offered to meet up with Brandi and John in a quaint little café just off the main thoroughfare in Rhinebeck late Saturday afternoon. When, reeling from the news that Ollie was pregnant, I had suggested we cancel our trip, Ollie had not been able to contain the wave of disappointment and grief which filtered through the bond. He'd been looking forward to our romantic weekend away and, to be honest, so had I. So, I'd quickly rescinded my attempt to cancel.

Besides, as Ollie rightly pointed out, it was still early days. His pregnancy was nowhere near obvious to others. As long as he followed Weldman's advice to control the morning sickness (Jesus, how was this my life?), there was no reason he couldn't continue on living as normal. And he really, really wanted to see the parade and experience the festival.

Looking into his pretty green eyes, I couldn't turn him down. Not even when he said that Brandi was also going to be there with the man she had started dating and that they wanted to meet up.

"Just for a double coffee date," Ollie had assured me. "Then we'll go our separate ways again, enjoy the parade and the other cool Christmas stuff some more, and then head back to our cute little cabin for some *other* festivities." He'd sealed the deal with a cute, if somewhat hilarious, suggestive waggle of his eyebrows.

But, sitting across from the big, hulking man Brandi had cheerfully introduced to us, festivities were the last thing on my mind. He looked ridiculously oversized for the tiny, overheated space we were seated in. He was dressed all in black while the rest of us wore knitted Christmas sweaters and matching brightly colored scarves. He was taller and broader than me, and I could swear his knuckles had fading bruises on them, though he had muttered something about the cold and slipped black gloves on when he'd seen my glance fixate on them.

He practically radiated 'bad news' and 'red flag' vibes. I wanted nothing more than to throw Ollie over my shoulder and hightail it out of that café, alpha or not.

Brandi and Ollie sipped at mugs of hot cocoa, heavily decorated with cream and sprinkles, chatting happily. Ollie's hand squeezing my thigh tightly under the table was the only sign I had that he was aware of the tension between me and John, or that he was at all concerned about the guy being a shifter. I didn't like the looks John kept casting between Ollie and me, his big caveman brow furrowed over bushy dark eyebrows.

"...a coincidence that John wanted to bring me here, too, right?" Brandi was saying, and my internal alarms blared.

"Yes," I responded dryly, meeting John's eyes, "a big coincidence."

My sarcasm went over Brandi's head, but Ollie just squeezed my thigh tighter in warning. Whether it was to say 'behave' or 'don't antagonize the WWE wrestler dude', I had no idea. Still, I heeded my mate's warning and backed off.

Smiling a bit more genuinely, I asked where they were staying. Thankfully, the motel he had managed to snag a room in was just outside of the town proper and in the opposite direction to our cute cabin. Distance from this guy seemed paramount.

Our coffee date seemed to drag on forever. I was not unaware of the subtle flaring of John's nostrils, or the way he was clearly trying to scent me and figure out why I didn't scent like a beta or omega. I couldn't explain how my scent was different, only that it was. Ollie said that it was almost like an electric scent – buzzing with power. I couldn't scent it on myself, but once the other shifters knew I was an alpha, it seemed to click for them mentally.

The last thing I needed was this John guy working out what I was. Somehow, I didn't think he'd keep our secret like Eric and Sandy were.

"You're from out of town, aren't ya?" he asked Ollie directly, interrupting the conversation about the candy store Ollie wanted to visit.

Ollie squinted with suspicion and nodded. "Yeah," he said, but he didn't offer any further information.

"Don'tcha miss your family?" John pressed.

My hackles raised.

So did Ollie's. He shook his head and pasted on a mildly condescending smile. My mate was feisty when he wanted to be. "My family and I don't really see eye to eye," he explained vaguely, in a tone of voice that anyone should be able to read as a request to drop the conversation.

John did not.

Leaning forward over the tiny café table, the other man said, "But I imagine you've got family obligations."

Brandi bristled on Ollie's behalf before either of us could even blink. Scowling at her date, she shook her head. "His family are some sort of weird hick cult," she tried to explain, oblivious to the fact that everyone else at the table knew exactly why the pack gave off that vibe. "New York's a much better fit for Ollie. They want him to...to...be a farmer or some shit out in Bumfuck Nowhere, Virginia. But, and no offense, honey," she added as an aside to Ollie, patting his hand before turning back to John, "look at him. He's *not* built for hard labor. He's a science nerd doing a science nerd job."

Ollie snorted, despite the tension building over the conversation. "Thanks, babe."

Brandi blew him a kiss before turning narrowed eyes back to her date. "Why are you so interested in this stuff, anyway?"

John shrugged. He'd pulled his phone from his pocket and typed away at the screen before calmly putting the device away again. "I've seen his type before, is all."

"His *type?*" Brandi seethed, clearly affronted. She folded her arms across her chest and glared. "The fuck is that supposed to mean? Also, you *just* met him. You don't get to be a dick to my best friend like this. It's not okay."

The pit in my gut only grew as John didn't seem at all bothered by how badly he had upset his date. He just rolled his eyes and made no attempt to apologize or calm the situation.

Eyes widening, Brandi sat back in her chair. "Wow," she said, shaking her head before tilting it back to ask the ceiling. "Why do I keep picking up assholes?"

Ollie patted her shoulder and looked beseechingly in my direction. My heart sank as I understood.

So much for a romantic getaway for just the two of us.

I sighed, folded up my napkin and tossed it onto the table, next to my barely touched coffee. "You can stay with us," I told her, pushing my chair back. "We'll go get your stuff from the motel and—"

"Oliver, you can't avoid your pack forever," John cut me off angrily, pushing out of his own seat and looming over the table. "You do have obligations and I'm not leaving this stupid ass town without you."

Brandi gaped at him as we all scrambled to our feet. She

stood protectively in front of her best friend, pint-sized and fiery. She pointed her index finger at John's chest. "You…you *used* me! You're part of that cult?" She grabbed for Ollie's wrist and inched them both backwards until I could stand in front of the two of them. "What kind of stalker freak does something like this? Jesus, I should have known you were too good to be true."

The jig being up, John huffed and ignored her, glaring at me. "I don't know who the fuck you think you are, but his pack has a former claim on him. Step aside."

We were starting to draw attention in the packed little café, but I didn't care. My inner wolf was growling and snarling at this threat to my mate and pups. I curled my lip and held my ground. Yes, this guy was bigger than me, but I was the alpha. It was time to wield that to my advantage.

Outside the large bay window, the crowd was growing thicker in preparation for the parade, herds of people heading towards the main thoroughfare in groups. I hated the idea of losing my mate in the throng of people, but our bond would allow me to find him anywhere.

"Ollie," I directed over my shoulder, eyes not leaving the man in front of me, "get to the car. Drive to where we're staying. I'll find you both there." I would have told him to shift and run, but that wouldn't help Brandi, and it would likely leave a scent trail anyway.

John smirked as the bell over the door tinkled. With the rush of cold air that swept into the warm café interior, I scented the presence of more shifters. *Fuck.*

A look over my shoulder confirmed my fear. Two more men, as big and burly as John, had entered and were making their way towards us.

Even as my brain panicked, my instinct took over. I pulled at my shifter senses in the same way I would when I shifted, but instead of shifting, I growled deep in my throat and felt myself almost radiating power. "*Stop,*" I commanded the men and, bizarrely, they did. At least for a moment, anyway.

Their eyes went wide as they looked between themselves before they shook off the effect of my gravelly instruction. Their attention was on me, though, and not on Ollie.

"The fuck was that?" John demanded. "What the hell are you?"

"Run, Ollie," I insisted, ignoring the question. "Go out the back. I'll find you."

I don't know if he was compelled by the weird power I'd tapped into, or whether he was just doing it because it was the smarter option, but he grabbed Brandi's hand and took off, weaving his way through the other tables and chairs towards the kitchen. John and the brutes moved to go after him, but I growled out another command that they stay put and it made them stumble.

"Seriously, what the fuck is this shit?" John whirled on me, though he waved the other two on to continue their pursuit of my mate. I hoped I'd bought Ollie enough time to get out and lose them. I focused on our bond, trying to deliberately sense him through it.

He wasn't panicked enough for me to feel him, though I could sense that he was still on the move. The rubber band feeling inside my chest pointed me in the vague direction of our rental car. That was a relief.

John took a menacing step closer. "What are you?" He sniffed at the air, frowning. "Sorcerer? But you're a wolf." He was trying to puzzle me out. As an alpha, I was not going to run. I was higher on the food chain, even if he didn't realize it. "Not beta. Not omega. But…" he trailed off, his eyes suddenly as wide as saucers. *"Impossible."*

"Kneel for your Alpha," I growled out.

His jaw dropped and I watched him fight the compulsion to obey.

"Impossible," he repeated.

And, despite my concern for my mate, my lips pulled into a smug smirk. I held my arms out wide. "And yet, here I am."

Chapter Fifteen — Oliver

"What the hell is going on, Oliver I-Can't-Remember-Your-Middle-Name Grayson?" Brandi demanded between puffs of breath as we raced around the back of the buildings and towards the crowds making their way to Montgomery Street.

I cringed. "Just *run*," I answered, swallowing back bile. I didn't know if it was morning sickness or panic making me feel like I was going to throw up, and I didn't particularly care either way.

John was from my pack. He and his goons had been sent to stalk me and take me home by force. I should have known better than to trust that my mother would stick to her end of the deal. Not that I had been planning to uphold mine, either, but that was beside the point.

I could hardly believe that they'd dragged my best friend into their machinations, though. She was human! They had no right to use her as a pawn to get to me!

"Ollie!" Brandi hissed. She had every right to sound

frustrated and hurt.

"I'll explain," I panted, willing the urge to vomit away by sheer will, "I promise. But once we're safe."

We wound our way through groups of people, hopefully camouflaging ourselves among the thousands of bright Christmas sweaters and beanies. I pulled my green knit beanie out of my pocket and tugged it over my head for additional anonymity, and Brandi did the same with the red one she had been wearing when she had met us at the café.

We slowed to a walk, essentially adding ourselves to a group of twenty-somethings huddled together on the sidewalk, waiting for the parade. Hiding in plain sight felt like a better option than heading to the car like Beck had told us to. After all, we'd be sitting ducks in the car or at the cabin by ourselves. Here we could blend in, and there were too many sounds and smells for the shifters to track us.

"Didn't Beck say to go to the car?" Brandi asked while I did my best to stay alert, keeping my senses peeled for sight, sound, or scent of John or the other brutish looking betas from the café.

"We're safer trying to blend in here," I told her. My stomach roiled again, and I did everything in my power to keep my lunch down. "Trust me."

"Trust you?" She sounded a little hysterical. She even laughed kind of manically. "Why should I when you haven't told me what the hell is even going on? How did John know your family? How did he even know I knew you? And what's so special about you that you're worth pulling a stunt like this? Not that I don't think you're special," she hastened to add, a little of her ire deflating. "But I only think you're special because of our friendship. No, wait, that came out wrong, too."

Despite the anxiety still zinging through my veins, I chuckled. "Relax, my skin's thick enough that I can handle your weak ass insults."

"Ollie," she all but whined. "What is going on?"

Nobody else in the still-growing crowd was paying us even the slightest attention. There were too many ambient sounds and smells for our pursuers to be able to find us easily. So I sighed and steeled myself. "I'm a shifter, Bee. And John is, too. He's either a member of my family's pack, or he's been hired by them to take me home by force. But I'm not going. I can't go back."

Brandi's blue eyes went wide with shock. "A shifter? Really?" She sounded awed rather than disgusted or betrayed, so I took that as a win.

Nodding, I gave her the breakdown of my situation as an omega and my pack's demands that I return to them. I explained the deal I'd made with my mother, bitterly complaining that she had broken her end of that deal by sending John and his goons after me.

Brandi snorted, "No offense, babe, but you were also planning on reneging."

"Yeah, well…" I waved her argument off. "They broke the agreement first."

She nibbled her bottom lip, suddenly thoughtful. "Beck's a shifter, too, isn't he?"

There was no point denying it, so I nodded.

"Beta?" she guessed after few beats of silence spent with her face scrunched in thought. I remembered Beck telling me that he had learned about shifters in school, and I supposed Brandi was drawing on similar memories.

143

I swallowed, but I was saved from answering as the tightness in my chest loosened noticeably. Concentrating, I realized Beck was close by. Knowing that he'd be able to find me if we ever got separated was a relief, but I wasn't willing to test the geographical limits of the bond too far if I could help it. Simultaneously, I cursed myself for not paying closer attention during my time spent explaining things to Brandi. I wasn't worried about Beck finding us, obviously, but I should have been keeping alert for our pursuers.

"Ollie?" Brandi prompted.

I opened my mouth, but Beck's growled words beat me to replying as he came up behind us.

"I told you to go to the car and drive."

"I know," I turned around, trying to placate him, "but what if they had others waiting at the cabin? It's easier to lose shifters in a crowd like this than in the wilderness."

Beck's eyes widened and then flickered over to Brandi.

I rolled mine. "I told her. She's cool."

"You told her?" he repeated in disbelief, even as he stepped in behind me protectively, his large palm splaying over my belly. A shiver went up my spine as he brought his lips to my ear and whispered, "Everything?"

Swallowing against the unexpected jolt of arousal from his touch and his breath coasting over my skin, I shook my head. I wasn't stupid enough to go blurting out phrases like 'I'm pregnant' in such a public setting. I felt him sag a little in relief.

I wanted to ask him about what happened after we ran, but I knew that conversation would have to wait.

Cheers started going up in the distance; a sign the parade was approaching. Despite everything that had happened, I still wanted to see the parade.

"Can we stay and watch?" I pleaded. "We're just as safe here as anywhere right now."

It took a moment of contemplation before he sighed and nodded, pulling me just a bit tighter against him. "Only because I'd hate it if those assholes took this from you. I know how much you've been looking forward to it."

It was so sweet to hear. I knew that things were a bit weird for us right then. We were, for all intents and purposes, only just starting to really get to know each other. But we were also mated and bonded with kids on the way. It was a strange sort of limbo between newly dating and comprehending what it meant to be committed to each other for the rest of our lives.

I was still struggling to wrap my head around it, and I knew Beck was as well. We hadn't had sex since discovering I was pregnant, either, which I thought might be adding tension. It certainly was for me.

My mate smelled divine. Ever since I'd gotten pregnant, he only smelled more enticing. When I wasn't battling morning sickness, I was fighting back the desire to jump my mate and insist that he knot me. I didn't quite understand why. I mean, I was already knocked up. What was the additional mating going to do?

As more cheering erupted down the street, I craned my head to catch the beginnings of the parade. Even with my sharper eyesight, I couldn't see much. Flashes of color, streamers, and tinsel glinted in the sunlight. But the atmosphere was electric. There was excitement and anticipation in the air. Everyone was joyful.

It was enough to let me forget that somewhere out there, a bunch of hired muscle was lurking and looking for me. For the moment, I felt safe where I was. Beck's strong arms around me and his scent were reassuring, and the happiness of the crowd surrounding us was infectious.

The music of a marching band filtered towards us on the crisp winter breeze. Trumpets, a drum, flutes…they all came together to create a familiar tune. *Santa Clause Is Coming To Town*. I bounced on my heels and Beck chuckled.

"You really are into this, aren't you?" His lips were pressed to the shell of my ear and his voice was a delicious rumble at my back.

I felt my cheeks flush. I'd warned him that I was one of those people who went nuts over Christmas. I loved everything about the festive season, basically channeling my inner five-year-old as soon as Halloween decorations made way for Christmas trees and fairy lights. I'd play carols on repeat, decorate my shitty little apartment, watch the parades on TV and check out every single window display in the city. There was something magical about the whole season.

"It's cute," Beck added, his tone affectionate. His palm moved to cover my belly again. "It'll be good for them, too."

A lump lodged in my throat, and all I could do was nod.

Beck hadn't really spoken about our soon-to-be children like that before. We'd briefly discussed the practical aspects of what my being pregnant meant for us and for our future, but I had been giving him time to process. After all, he'd never imagined that he would get another man pregnant and he had never wanted children. The fact that we were having two at once was a scary enough concept without adding the complicated feelings of never wanting any to begin with.

"I never had experiences like this growing up," Beck kept on talking, and the arousal I had felt at the press of his mouth to

146

my ear and the tickling warmth of his breath faded the more I focused on his low confession. "Being a foster kid, I was lucky if I even got Christmas presents, you know?"

The lump in my throat refused to budge, but the emotion welling up in me was equal parts empathy for the little boy he once was, and rage at a system which had failed him. Even in my pack, my childhood hadn't been terrible. I loved the holidays for a reason, after all.

"But our kids?" Beck mused, seemingly not at all perturbed by my ongoing silence, "They're going to have all of this. Even if I'm a grumpy ass, you're going to decorate our home and make sure there's enough enthusiasm for the both of us. And maybe...maybe it won't be so hard for me to learn to get into this kind of stuff. I mean, despite the guys trying to drag you back to your pack, this is actually kinda fun."

I let out a strangled, wet chuckle, unable to prevent my tears from spilling over. The future he was painting for us sounded idyllic. If I closed my eyes, I could imagine it vividly. Two little boys who looked like him, with thick dark hair and olive skin, bouncing around a cozy suburban home decked out in tinsel and fairy lights and popcorn strings. Putting decorations on a tree, uncaring if it looked unhinged and nothing like a professional set up. Singing Christmas carols together at the top of our lungs until Beck himself joined in, laughing. Bundling the boys up in brightly colored winter jackets and watching the joy on their faces as they took in a parade much like the one we were about to see...

"Hey," concern filled his voice and he shifted, moving around from my back so he could tilt my face up to look at him. "I didn't mean to upset you."

I shook my head, still choked up. "Blaming hormones," I

decided quietly, forcing a watery smile. I grabbed for his gloved hand with mine, squeezing it as tightly as I could. "I want that future with you."

Beck's frown lines smoothed out and he bent to kiss my lips softly. "We'll have it," he promised, and I wanted nothing more than to believe him.

"Hey, love birds," Brandi interrupted our moment, and Beck huffed an incredulous laugh, using his glove-covered thumbs to wipe away the remnants of my tears while she said, "the parade's coming."

I pushed up on my toes to see over the crowd, unable to prevent a wide smile from taking over my face as the marching band finally came into view. They were dressed as Santa's elves, wearing a mix of green and red tunics and curly-toed shoes. They wore matching hats, and every outfit had gold embellishments.

There were dancers, too, I realized. People carrying long ribbons in silver and gold, catching the late afternoon sun as they twirled in the air. They wove through the band, some doing cartwheels and flips with effortless grace. In the distance behind the long stretch of band, I caught glimpses of what looked like kids in snowmen costumes.

The crowd of people cheered, clapped, and a lot even sang as the band marched ever closer. It was hard not to feel joyous in that moment.

I snuggled in against Beck's side, relishing in the warmth of his body pressed to mine and the comforting weight of his arm across my shoulders.

"Aww," Brandi said as the kids in costumes appeared, tossing individually wrapped candy canes into the crowds from the little buckets they carried, "look at the reindeer!"

I poked my head through a gap in the crowd, wondering whether she meant actual reindeer, or more kids in costume. It turned out to be a mixture of both, with more dancing elves helping to keep the procession flowing. And then, behind all of that, was a large, heavily decorated float carrying Santa himself in a sleigh.

As soon as the kids in the crowd saw him, they started calling out to him. I had to fight the urge to do the same. There was just something magical about Santa. From his pillow-stuffed red velvet costume, to his bushy white beard and rosy pink cheeks, to his twinkling eyes and friendly smile, everything about him made me feel five years old again. His booming "Ho ho ho, Merry Christmas!" as he passed was a soothing balm to whatever remained of my rattled nerves.

I waved and cheered just as loudly as the kids around us as he got closer, much to Beck's continued amusement.

"Do you have a Santa fetish?" he teased as the float containing the jolly man in red slowly passed us by, once again asking the question as a seductive murmur in my ear.

I couldn't help but close my eyes, the tremors of arousal from earlier returning. I wanted to commit every part of this parade to memory, especially these unfiltered moments with my mate.

Beck's grin was clear in his voice as he added, "Because I could find a costume…"

Bursting into laughter, I spun in his arms and hit at his solid chest with open palms. "Ew, gross."

"What?" he chuckled. "You might have some sort of Santa Silver Fox attraction thing going on…*ouch!*" I smacked him even harder, but his complaint was drowned out by his laughter. "Okay, okay, no sexy Santa for you. Got it."

"Ugh," Brandi huffed at my side. "It's not that I'm not happy for you, Ollie, but the PDA is killing me right now. I just got dumped remember?" I turned back around to catch her screwing up her face and cocking her head to the side. "Or did I do the dumping?"

"You dumped him, babe," I assured her while Beck snorted into my ear, his arms wrapped around me from behind again. I pinched his arm. "Be nice," I warned.

"I didn't say anything," he argued back, but I could hear the smirk in his voice.

"Ugh," Brandi repeated, unable to contain her own smile, "stop already." She gestured over us with her pink glove. "You're even worse together than I imagined."

My clever retort died on my lips as her face drained of color, her eyes fixing on something behind us. Immediately, Beck and I straightened, all sense of playfulness gone.

He tossed the car keys to Brandi before I could blink. "We're parked a few blocks down behind the café. Little red Nissan." He looked over his shoulder, just as I turned to see John and his goons pushing into the gathered crowd, noses up, scenting the air. After rattling the address of our cabin off, Beck urged Brandi to run. "We'll shift," he told her. "We'll catch you up. Take our phones and wallets. Quickly."

In a blur of motion, we gave her our valuables and watched her run off, weaving through groups of people still watching the tail end of the parade. "Duck," he instructed, "move."

My heart was back to hammering in my chest and I hated that my pack had still managed to ruin our romantic weekend after all. I'd gotten to see the parade in the end, but at what cost? What if they managed to grab me? I couldn't afford for them to do that. I couldn't afford for them to learn about my condition.

Straining my ears, I tried to blend in among the groups of people, but the crowd was starting to thin out now that the tail end of the parade had passed.

"There!" I heard John yell, and I didn't turn around to confirm that we'd been spotted.

"Shift!" Beck cried from directly behind me. "Shift and *run*, Ollie!"

I didn't stop to think. Didn't bother taking off my clothes beyond my gloves, scarf, and beanie. I started to run, forcing my body through the change while I was in motion. It wasn't ideal. I got caught up in my clothes and tore my way out frantically with my teeth. My muscles protested the rapid change, and I hoped that the general hubbub of the festival would distract most of the humans from the shifters morphing directly in their midst.

The second I was free of my clothes, I dropped my head and ran full pelt through the crowds, darting through and around groups, circling back, generally trying to make my scent trail as confusing as possible in my wake. I hoped Beckett was smart enough to do the same. I could feel my mate's proximity through the bond, but I couldn't allow myself to focus on it. We had to lose these guys.

It struck me that John had no idea where we were staying and if we could get into the car with Brandi, the other shifters couldn't track our scents. It would be smarter to attempt to flee that way than to lead John and his thugs through the woods and directly to us.

Changing course, I forced myself to race away from the concealing crowds, heading down side streets in the direction of our parked car, hoping that I wasn't too late. I also hoped that Beck would have the sense to follow me, but even if he didn't, I could always track him through the bond.

My heart thudded painfully in my chest as I rounded the corner to see our rental car pulling away from the curb. Adrenaline sent me bursting forward, yipping and whining, begging Brandi to stop the damn car, even though she couldn't hear me.

I chased the little red vehicle down the length of the street, my mind racing, trying to come up with a backup plan if I couldn't catch up. Obviously, I could race through the woods and double back on my tracks as I went, doing my best to muddle my scent for my trackers. Or I could change back to my human form, then try and find some clothes and a way to pay for a ride to the cabin, assuming the group following me didn't catch up in time.

Thankfully, though, brake lights came on and our car slowed to a stop at a red light. With my adrenaline waning, I gave one last sprint and forced my body to change as I came up to the car, willing the light to stay red.

It did.

My hand closed around the passenger side door handle and I wrenched the door open, throwing myself bodily into the passenger seat, my chest heaving as I tried to catch my breath. I closed my eyes and leaned back against the headrest, ignoring Brandi's squeal of surprise. I could feel Beck closing in on the car quickly.

"Don't drive yet," I demanded. "Beck's right behind me."

"Jesus, Ollie," Brandi admonished, and I turned my head, cracking an eye open in question. She was staring firmly ahead at the road, her hands gripping the wheel tightly. "You scared the crap out of me. And, also? Put some damn pants on."

I rolled my eyes but covered my junk with my hands anyway. "You've seen this all before."

Having crashed in each other's dorm rooms and apartments over the years, we'd gotten changed in front of one another more times than I could even recall.

"Still, I'm driving. I don't need—" Whatever she was going to say was cut off as she squealed again when the rear passenger door was yanked open. Beck's big, broad body slid into the back seat and he perched himself in the middle, slamming the door shut on his way in.

"Light's green," he panted with urgency, looking through the rear window over his shoulder, "*drive.*"

Brandi floored it, making the tires skid on the potentially frosty road, but she was quick to get the car back under control. I watched in the rear-view mirror as three wolves came into view just before Brandi turned the corner.

"That was too fucking close," Beck growled.

Bile rose in the back of my throat while tears of guilt pricked the backs of my eyes. "I'm sorry," I muttered, looking down at my hands clasped over my dick. "I shouldn't have begged you to stay."

Beck sighed and found the little pile of our belongings on the seat beside him. He passed me Brandi's beanie and I lay the material over my lap. It was a testament to how serious the mood was that I couldn't even find amusement in the way Brandi's nose scrunched in distaste over my chosen loincloth, or the way she murmured, "You are so washing that for me."

"No, baby," Beck eventually said in response to my earlier words, "I didn't want to let those fuckers ruin our plans either."

I just shrugged, feeling despondent.

In the silence, Beck began directing Brandi through the suburban streets, using the maps app on his phone to plot the most complicated way just in case our pursuers could trace the car's path after all.

I stayed quiet, not even responding to the obvious furtive glances Brandi kept shooting me, having 'accidentally' glanced down at my naked mate's body. Guilt continued to roil my gut. I still felt like everything was my fault. Our mating. Being pregnant. My pack. Beck had been living a perfectly normal life until I came along.

Beck pulled me aside when we got to the cabin. I half expected him to demand to know what was wrong, but all he did was pull me against him in the cold early evening air, warming my front with his. He pressed his nose to the top of my head and breathed in deeply. "I almost lost you," he said quietly. "I'm not going through that again."

Even though I felt awful for turning his life upside down in only a matter of weeks, my traitorous heart sang at his declaration anyway.

"Come on," he pushed me towards the open doorway. "Let's get you inside. Freezing to death after all of that would be counterproductive."

Chapter Sixteen – Beckett

W e had pizza delivered for dinner and I was glad that, by the time we got ready for bed, Ollie was back to being upbeat, if a little distracted. I couldn't hold that against him. His pack —his family— had tried to have him kidnapped and dragged back to them kicking and screaming.

For the first time in my life, I was glad that my parents had done me the kindness of abandoning me at a hospital as a baby. I couldn't imagine growing up with a family who treated me like Ollie's did him. At least I had known that my foster families were never really mine. I knew they didn't care because they didn't have to care. But Ollie's family? They didn't value him because of a gift of genetics, something nobody could control.

My inner wolf growled indignantly.

My pups (a word which came far too easily to mind) wouldn't be treated that way. It didn't matter if they were born omegas, betas, alphas or completely human: they would know we loved them for who they were.

And I *would* love my children. I cared too much about their well-being, even while they were nothing more than a pile of cells each, to think otherwise.

Yeah, it was going to take a while to completely get over the shock of getting my boyfriend pregnant, but my wolf was already fully invested. That went a long way towards settling my own nerves somehow. Maybe because my wolf *was* me and vice versa. I was still getting used to being a shifter, too.

We left Brandi asleep on the futon in the little living room of the cabin where she was quite content to curl up in front of the fireplace, though she had loudly lamented the loss of her clothes and toiletries. Thankfully, she understood there was no way in hell we were going back for her things. At least, not that night. We could reassess in the morning, because I also understood how costly replacing a chunk of one's wardrobe could be.

As it was, Ollie and I needed to buy new winter coats, as we had abandoned ours when we shifted and ran. With babies on the way, and the likelihood that we would need to leave New York for a while, that kind of cost was not something we could afford to repeat.

In the tiny little bedroom, with its own fireplace crackling away, Ollie curled into me on the Queen bed, nuzzling his head beneath my chin. The light from the flames bounced off his pale skin, making him flicker shades of orange. The timber walls around us were rustic and soothing to my wolf, but it was Ollie's body pressed tightly against mine which made my anxiety settle.

He smelled so good. Sweet, with a hint of musk. As he shifted, the restless, anxious energy beneath my skin morphed into something else. Something carnal.

We hadn't had sex since finding out about the babies. That was partially because Ollie seemed constantly exhausted or nauseated, and partially because I had been freaking the fuck out. But now, after almost having my mate snatched out from under my nose, I was overwhelmed with the desperate need to claim him all over again. To fill him with my seed and mark him as mine from the inside out. Every shifter he came across in the next few days needed to scent me all over him, to know that he was my omega.

My human side knew these instincts were animalistic, but I still felt unsettled by how possessive and chauvinistic they were. Ollie was his own person. I didn't own him. He had an identity outside of being my mate, or the maternal father of my pups. He was more than a breeding tool. More than an incubator.

But my wolf wouldn't be swayed. He wouldn't be content until he was buried deep in our mate's slick, waiting hole, knotting him and filling him up with cum.

"Uh…" Ollie brought me out of my thoughts with a curious smile in his voice. "Are you thinking happy thoughts, Beck?" He rubbed his abdomen against me. Specifically, he rubbed his abdomen against my aching cock.

I dipped my head to capture his lips in a kiss. "Very happy thoughts now," I agreed as we parted again, leaving only a sliver of space between our mouths.

"Mmm," he moaned quietly, writhing his body as he sought out more contact. "And would you look at that – so am I."

With my right hand trapped beneath him as we lay on our sides, I let my left hand sweep down his back, sneaking under the elastic waistband of his pajama pants. I couldn't help cupping the perfect curve of his ass cheek, squeezing the smooth, lightly furred flesh with intent. Ollie arched his back, tilting his head back with the movement, exposing the long, pale column of his throat, marred only by my claiming mark. It shone silvery on his skin, scarred perfection. It made the beast inside me practically purr with satisfaction and pride, which was odd given that our species was lupine and not feline.

"Beck," he whimpered, squirming under my touch, "please. I need you."

Giving his cheek another squeeze, I shifted my hand to tease at his crack. The tips of my fingers met with moisture and my lips curled upwards. "Already wet for me, baby?"

In a far cry from his embarrassment on our first night together, Ollie nodded vigorously. His breath was hot as he practically panted out his reply. "All for you. There's so much slick. I'm leaking for you, Beck. *Alpha*. Only for you."

Swallowing roughly, I explored the seam of his ass, my searching index and middle fingers finding his hole dripping as promised. "Fuck, babe, you weren't kidding."

He whined as I pressed against his rim, his body sucking my digits in with ease. At times like these, I was reminded of the physiological differences between him and other men I'd been with. His body was made to take my cock, opening up for me with very minimal work on my part. And his slick…God, I couldn't put into words how much I loved it. It was like the most high-end lube I'd ever come across. It felt heavenly on my fingers, and when I pulled my fingers from him and sucked the honey from them, the flavor was heady. Sweet in a way I'd not anticipated the first time I had tasted him, but with a hint of salt and something just *Ollie*. Kind of like precum but thicker. Richer. My cock dribbled as soon as the taste hit my tongue.

"Inside me," Ollie babbled, his eyes shut and head thrown back, "I want you inside me. I *need* you inside me." His hands tugged fruitlessly at the waistband of my pajama pants. He was uncoordinated in his desperation, and fuck if it wasn't the hottest thing to witness.

With my dick aching at his words, I made short work of pulling his pants down over his hips and long legs, tossing them over the side of the bed before wriggling out of my own and sending them in the same direction. We'd gone to bed shirtless, warmed by the fire burning just a few feet away from the bed, and I was glad that getting us both naked had barely taken thirty seconds.

I took Ollie's cock in my hand, spreading his precum over his shaft as I stroked him languidly. My own dick was demanding that I give him what we both wanted, but I didn't want to rush it.

I wanted to reconnect with my lover properly. My instincts might have been urging me to smother my mate in my scent, painting his insides with my seed, but my head and my heart wanted to draw this out. I wanted to savor the feeling of Ollie's lithe body against me. I wanted to relish in the scent of his arousal and in the sweet sounds he was making.

I wanted him to know that I cared about him as more than just my mate or the man I had accidentally bonded with. He was also the cute guy I met at a nightclub. The guy I danced and flirted with and could not get off my mind. The man whose company lit me up from the inside, regardless of the mystical connection between us.

We had gone on fun dates together. We had shared our pasts

with each other. We had talked about the things we wanted to achieve in the future.

I loved his sense of humor. I loved his ridiculous attachment to Christmas and the holiday season. I loved the way he geeked out over science journals, and his secret obsession with reality TV.

Before we found out about the pregnancy, I could admit to myself that I had been on my way to falling for my boyfriend. For my accidental mate. I'd been getting used to the idea of making our unexpected bond work for us in the long run. After all, dating him was fun. And just because we were a mated pair didn't mean we had to rush our relationship. We could still behave like any other new couple: going out, getting to know each other, getting comfortable with one another's quirks…it was all going to be fine.

But then the baby thing happened, and I felt like I'd gone reeling all the way back to square one. Not only was I magically connected to this perfect stranger, but we had also brought children into the equation. The stress of impending fatherhood (not something I had thought would ever apply to me) on top of everything else had made me pull back. Sure, I stuck around to support him, but the intimacy between us had all but vanished.

That had been wrong of me, and I was planning on making up for it as best I could.

"B-Beck," he stammered, thrusting forward into my hand, "oh *God*…"

"That's it, baby," I urged him, "fuck my hand. Take your pleasure from me. I've got you."

Babbling and whining, Ollie did just that. I watched the rapture on his face and reveled in the precum leaking from his cockhead in a steady stream. He didn't come, though. Instead, he rocked his hips, his cheeks flushing an alluring shade of pink, his voice thin and desperate as he started to beg again.

"Please, Beck. *Alpha*. Please. Knot me. I need it. I need your knot. I need...I need..."

He sounded on the verge of tears, but I wasn't trying to torture him. I was trying to focus on his pleasure above my own.

"Shh, baby," I said softly, "let me take care of you."

I maneuvered us until he was on all fours on the mattress, his perfect ass up and his face buried in the pillows. My cock strained towards him, throbbing with desperation to be inside him, but I wasn't going to fuck him yet.

In a move that was probably more selfish than selfless, I parted his round cheeks and took in the sight of his thoroughly lubricated hole, puckered and dusky pink, shining with the copious amounts of slick his body was producing.

"Fuck, baby," I murmured, watching his hole twitch with anticipation, "look at you. You're dripping for me."

The pillow at his face muffled the long, low moan he responded with.

Unable to resist, I bent my face to his ass and nipped at his left cheek and then his right, grinning against the smooth, plump flesh as he keened out loud. But the sound was nothing in comparison to the cry he tried to strangle when I applied the flat of my tongue to his hole and licked a firm stripe upwards towards his crease.

If tasting his slick from my fingers had been heavenly, the flavor explosion as I sampled it directly from the source was beyond description. My intention had been to pleasure and tease, but I couldn't stop myself from lapping at his hole, searching out more of his honey.

Ollie bucked against my face as I went from sensual licks against his rim to spearing through the ring of muscle with the tip of my tongue. I worked him open as he cried, begged, and moaned, babbling incoherently all the while.

My balls were full and heavy, my cock painfully hard, my knot already threatening to swell, but I could not get enough of Ollie's ass. And the more I fucked him with my tongue, the slicker and looser he got, and the more intoxicating his honey was. It was a vicious (but thoroughly delightful) cycle.

"Alpha please," he sounded wrecked, his voice muffled by the pillow, "please, please fill me…I'm so empty, Alpha. Mate me. Please. *Please*."

My inner wolf preened and urged me to comply. I wanted my mate happy, after all.

With a hint of reluctance, I pulled back, wiping my face on his ass cheek because I just could not resist the contact. "I've got you, baby," I promised before guiding him onto his back. "I want to see your face, Ollie."

Even though knotting him would be easier from behind, I needed to face him first. I needed to watch his eyes flutter shut as I parted his legs and slid inside him with no resistance. I wanted to pepper kisses over his chest, then his neck and cheeks. I wanted to feel his legs wrapped around my waist. I wanted his hands around my neck or clutching at my shoulders and back. I wanted to watch his perfect bow lips part as he panted and babbled.

I got all of that and more.

"You feel unbelievable," I told him, his wet heat unlike anything I'd ever felt before him. Hot, slick, and tight, it felt like his ass was made for my cock. "So perfect for me, Ollie."

We rocked together and he arched up, claiming my lips with his. Our kiss smothered his blissed-out cries, but I was pretty sure Brandi would still be able to hear us. Not that I cared if she did, but I knew Ollie would.

"I'm so close," his declaration was a ragged whisper spoken with his lips still touching mine, "Beck, fuck, I'm going to come."

"Yes, baby. Come for me. I want to watch you. Show me how good you feel."

I reached between us and stroked his cock. Once, twice…his orgasm rocketed through him on the third stroke.

"Oh fuck, oh fuck, oh *fuck*." His final curse was long and drawn out as ropes of his cum landed between us, splashing both our bellies and his chest with the force of his release.

But, more than that, I felt his pleasure inside me as if it was my own, our bond sending the feedback to me much like every other strong emotion he had felt since we first mated. Between the echo of his orgasm inside me and the tightening of his passage around my cock, I couldn't prevent my own release even if I tried.

I came with a roar, barely muffled as I bit down over his mating mark on his neck, electric shocks of pleasure zipping and zapping through my body and through the bond. It was almost overwhelming, and I felt his hole spasm as he came again, probably from feeling the depths of my pleasure coursing through the bond as well.

My knot swelled, locking us together, and his tight heat squeezed it so perfectly. It was almost as though we became locked in a feedback loop of pleasure, with every intense squeeze to my cock releasing a burst of cum inside him.

No longer thrusting against each other, we rocked gently.

The winter chill was completely gone now, the room warm from the fire, and our bodies heated by our physical exertion. The window at the side of the room had fogged over, and the room smelled of fire, sex, and the scent that was uniquely *us*.

"Wow," Ollie breathed against the shell of my ear, his previously scrabbling hands now petting my shoulder blades with soporific satisfaction. "That was —*ungh*— fuck, I love it when you come."

I grinned and licked at the red skin of his neck. I hadn't broken the surface this time, but my teeth had still abused the flesh in my enthusiasm. He moved underneath me and the action pulled another minor orgasm from me. Between us, his cum smeared our bodies. His cock was softening, but it still twitched as I swelled and released inside him for the umpteenth time.

"Come on, baby, let's get you more comfortable," I urged as his eyes turned heavy lidded and droopy.

We gasped and kissed our way through the rolling and shuffling until I was propped up against the headboard with a pile of pillows at my back and Ollie seated on my cock, arms and legs still wrapped around me, clinging like the sexiest of limpets. My knot was still keeping us locked together and, with the amount of cum I had shot into him as we moved into this new position, I marveled that my body had any left to give.

Instinctively, I moved one palm from Ollie's back, placing it between us, over his belly. Was it just me, or was there an ever-so-slight roundness to it that hadn't been there before?

"That's how much cum you've pumped into me," my mate grizzled, but when I looked up he was smiling shyly. "It'll go down when I, uh…" he gestured towards the little en suite bathroom with his head.

"Seriously?" I asked in wonder, smoothing my hand over the tiny distention. "I thought cum inflation was an exaggeration."

Ollie shrugged, the action shifting him enough to send another shock of sensation through my knot. We both moaned quietly and rode it out. "Well, it's not the...the..."

"Pregnancy?" I offered softly, sure to keep my hand right where it was. "Babies?"

His Adam's apple bobbed as he swallowed roughly and avoided my gaze, nodding by way of answer.

Oh no, I wasn't letting that slide.

"Babe," I reached up to cup his cheek, shuddering as our movements stimulated my knot again, "look at me." I didn't like the guilt or shame splashed across his pretty face when he finally met my gaze. "Oliver..."

"You didn't ask for any of this." I would have missed his whispered words if not for my recently enhanced hearing.

"We've been through this, Ollie. You didn't ask for it either. It's not your fault. And you know what?" I waited until I was certain he was actually listening, his green eyes locked on mine. Then I stroked his belly, so faintly distended by my seed, and I imagined what he'd look like in a few months' time. My lips curled upwards into a genuine smile. I probably looked stupidly sappy. "It's not a bad thing. I know I never wanted kids, but...baby, I'm getting excited about it."

I didn't need the bond to tell me how shocked he was by my pronouncement. His eyes went wide with disbelief. "Really?"

I nodded, still smiling like an idiot. "Really."

Almost losing Ollie to his pack had made me realize just how attached I was already. Not just to Ollie, but to the babies inside him. My babies. My family. *My* pack. I was already envisioning a future with them in it, and I was terrified when I thought it was in jeopardy.

"Don't get me wrong," I admitted when Ollie had yet to say anything else, "I'm scared shitless of being a dad. But I'm starting to imagine what life is going to be like. You and me and our two hell-raisers." And they would be. I was sure of it because they had caused so much trouble already. But I loved them for it.

Was it even possible to love people you didn't know yet? Who hadn't even been born? Hell, who hadn't even grown large enough to be felt from the outside of Ollie's womb? It had to be possible because that was how I felt.

Ollie sniffled, but his features lit up with a smile as his hand landed on mine. "I'm getting excited, too."

"C'mere," I wrapped my arms around him and moved him until he was lax against me, his head pillowed on my shoulder. It was worth the tugs against my knot. "Rest up, baby. Growing our tiny shifters has got to be hard work."

He made a sound of agreement. Then, just as I thought he was about to drift off to sleep, he murmured, "Beck?"

I shivered at the feeling of his breath on my skin and reminded my cock that Ollie needed rest, especially after the day we'd had. Plus, as pleasant as it felt having my knot lodged inside his warm channel, I was looking forward to it deflating so we could snuggle more comfortably. "Yeah, babe?"

"I…" He paused. Then, in a soft tone that seemed to say so much more than the actual words, he said, "Thank you for the parade. For…for everything."

Could he feel the rapid beating of my heart? It was thudding hard and fast at the timbre of his words. He mightn't have said what he'd really meant, but I heard the message loud and clear. And I was falling just as hard for him in return.

"No, baby," I eventually replied, my voice cracking, "thank *you*."

Only after I spoke did I realize he was already asleep.

Chapter Seventeen – Oliver

❧

"Good morning," Brandi greeted me with a shit-eating grin when I stumbled into the combined kitchen-lounge area of our cabin on Sunday morning. Her long blonde hair was tousled from her night spent on the couch, but somehow it just made her look sexy rather than bedraggled. She looked like she was prepping for a themed photo shoot rather than rolling out of bed with crease lines on her face (like I had). I hated her a little for that.

I had woken up nauseated and covered in dried, flaking cum, with Beck the octopus wrapped around me in an almost suffocating fashion. It was nice to feel wanted, but not while I was feeling so overwhelmingly gross.

Thankfully, sucking on a sour candy had helped with the nausea before I'd tossed my cookies, and a shower had made me feel less outwardly icky, too. But I was still exhausted and in desperate need of caffeine.

Eric had told me to limit my coffee intake to one cup a day, and I was going to enjoy the ever-living fuck out of my sole cup of caffeinated goodness.

I grunted a greeting to my BFF and went in search of the coffee pot.

Her footsteps padded after me. "Aww, did someone stay up all night?" she teased. "It sounded worth it."

Closing my eyes, I groaned and felt my cheeks heat up. Brandi's hand landed between my shoulder blades, patting consolingly over the soft material of my sweater.

"I'm actually jealous," she said on a sigh. "Beck's hot. And it sounds like he's got the skills to back that up."

I thought back to the things Beck had done to me and couldn't help but sigh. "Yeah," I agreed, knowing that my face was contorting into a goofy, satisfied smile despite my best efforts to keep it contained, "he really does."

There was no point playing coy with Brandi. We'd always shared details of our dating misadventures, so why should this be any different? I was more embarrassed that she had been an audience to the audio performance of the previous night, though. That part was new.

She wrapped her arms around me from behind and rested her chin on my shoulder. "I'm glad you're happy, you know. He's a good guy."

I thought back to the previous night again. To Beck caressing my belly and telling me all the things I desperately needed to hear. I was falling for him hard and fast. With how sweet and considerate he was, I was fairly certain I would have fallen for him without the bond as well.

Clearing my throat of the lump suddenly lodged there, I nodded. "He is."

"Hey," Brandi sounded concerned. "What's wrong?"

I shook my head, certain that if I opened my mouth, I'd

169

cry. The extra hormones were already coursing through my system, making me more emotional than I was used to. Was it supposed to happen so early, or was the fact that I was growing two pups making this all so much more intense?

"Ollie, talk to me," she demanded. "I didn't read this all wrong, did I? He's not…coercing you or anything?"

I shook my head again. "No," I croaked, and a traitorous tear slid down my cheek. "No. I…he's perfect."

He was my alpha. My protector. My mate.

And I was falling head over heels in love with him, despite only dating him for a couple of months. Hell, not even that long. A month and a half, tops.

Brandi shuffled around until she was standing in front of me, her eyes searching my face as she held me at arms' length. "Then what—"

"I'm pregnant," I blurted. In the stunned silence following my impromptu confession, the rest of it started to tumble out. My summary of the past week left me in a rush as the tears came right along with them. "I'm pregnant, and I was freaking out, and he freaked out, and then yesterday happened and it was scary, and he was so perfect and…and…and…"

"Whoa, babe. *Whoa.*" Brandi was hugging me again, rubbing her hands up and down my shaking back as I heaved in gulps of air and tried to feel relief at having told her the final pieces of the story. But I hadn't. Not yet.

"…I think I love him," I finally finished. "And I'm scared because this is all happening so fast, and what if he doesn't feel the same way?"

If my life had been a romance novel or movie, that would have been the moment that Beck would have swept into the room with a firm declaration that he did indeed feel the same way. But my ears could hear the shower still running in our room, so that wasn't going to happen.

Brandi just squeezed me tighter. "Honey, did you not *see* him yesterday? He would have done anything to keep you safe. It might be fast, but I'm pretty sure he's falling just as hard as you are. Which is good because can we cycle back to the whole pregnancy thing?" Her voice went up a few octaves with her question. I could hear her bewilderment and it brought me back down from my anxiety attack.

Finally feeling the relief wash over me, I let out a watery chuckle. "Coffee first."

* * *

Brandi listened attentively as I gave her the abridged version of my story. Alphas plus omegas equals babies etcetera, etcetera. The questions she asked weren't as invasive as I imagined they'd be, and she mostly focused on the logistics of where I would get prenatal care (Eric), how I would give birth (fuck only knew), and whether Beck and I would be moving in together to raise our pups.

"We haven't discussed that yet," Beck said, picking *that* moment to saunter down the short timber clad hallway. He dropped a kiss to the top of my head where I was seated at the quaint little dining table and he headed into the kitchen to pour himself a cup of coffee from the pot.

Brandi and I watched as he added creamer and sugar and then came to sit beside me, slinging his arm around the back of my chair as he sipped at his morning brew. "So, you told her everything, then?" There was no accusation in his tone, just curiosity.

171

I nodded. "I, um, it just…" bringing my hand up to my mouth, I mimed an explosion and made the noise to go along with it.

Beck chuckled. "Yeah, I get it. I want to tell Sandy the next time I see her, too."

Considering he had spent the bulk of the last week practically plastered to my side, it made sense that he hadn't seen his best friend-slash-sister since we had learned about the babies. I leaned my cheek against the hand he had draped over my shoulder. "I'm sorry you haven't had a chance to debrief with her yet. It helps," I smiled at Brandi who was observing us with obvious amusement over the top of her own mug, "trust me."

"She's going to give me so much shit," he groaned, but I could tell he didn't actually mind.

"But then she gets to be Aunt Sandy," I reminded him. "Use that as a bargaining chip."

"Emotional manipulation! A man after my own heart," Beck teased, caressing my cheek with the backs of his knuckles.

"Do I get to be Aunt Brandi?" Brandi demanded from across the table. She set down her mug and folded her arms, blowing a lock of loose hair out of her eyes as she glared at me expectantly. "Or, *oooh*! Godmother?"

I laughed and nodded. "Aunt, yes. Godmother?" I shared a conspiratorial look with Beck. "We'll have to talk about it."

It felt good to be discussing our impending parenthood like this. Without the eggshells we had been walking on. If anything good could have come from almost being kidnapped, this was it.

"But, on the subject of living arrangements," Beck steered the conversation back to where it had been when he joined us, "I think…I think it might be best if you came and stayed at

172

my place for a little while. I'm probably being paranoid, but your pack know where you live and I want you close. I want you safe, baby."

My stomach turned over at the thought of my pack sending goons to my apartment. To rough me up and kidnap me from my safe space. I'd been so caught up in getting away the previous day, and then reconnecting with Beck, that I hadn't considered the long-term issues we might face now that my pack was sending people to grab me off the street. Worse still, they knew Beck was an alpha. He'd told me that he'd revealed it in a bid to distract John and his thugs when Brandi and I had run away from the café.

It wouldn't be long before my pack came at us with reinforcements. Beck had been able to stall them using some sort of alpha compulsion magic before he ran to catch up with us, but that wouldn't work if they came en masse. Hell, it hadn't really worked on the three goons on their own, either.

"I want you safe, too," I told him, hearing the wobble in my own voice. "They know you're an alpha. They'll want to take you out or try and use you as some sort of...of...weapon? Political pawn? Science experiment? Ugh, you know what I'm getting at, right?"

"They're not going to be able to find me in the city," he said firmly. "Not easily, anyway. We'll just have to be careful. But..."

"We're not going to be able to go back and get my stuff from my place." The realization was a rough one. I didn't have many worldly possessions, but I resented having to start over from scratch.

At least I had my laptop with me. My clothes weren't quite as important in the grand scheme of things.

Beck shook his head sadly. "Not at first, no. Maybe we could send Weldman? I get the feeling he could defend himself just fine against a pack of wolf thugs."

I imagined the shock on John's face if Eric shifted in front of him. Not that I had ever seen Eric shift, but he was a dragon. He could eat John for breakfast if he wanted, right?

"Yeah," I nodded, smiling at that thought. "And they know I work with Eric, so even if they followed him back to the clinic, they still wouldn't find your place."

It was still a risk, though. I could be followed from the clinic. Even with the scents of New York City and its thousands of tourists and inhabitants, I could still be tracked. The best I could hope for would be to lose them on the subway or in a cab.

Beck bent his head to mine, nuzzling our faces together. "We'll work it all out, I promise."

I could only hope he was right.

* * *

Sandy was sitting on the couch in Beck's apartment when we walked in hours later. After dropping Brandi off down the street from her place and returning the rental car, then the trip home on the bustling subway, I was exhausted.

"Ollie," Sandy sat upright with surprise as we entered, "Hi! I wasn't expecting to see you."

I immediately felt guilty for invading her space without even asking. "I'm sorry." To my horror, my voice cracked. Between the stress of the weekend finally catching up to me, my hormones, not being able to go back to my own apartment, and my bone-deep exhaustion, I was on the verge of another meltdown.

Oh God, is this how the rest of this pregnancy is going to go? With me crying all the damn time?

It was getting old fast.

Sandy shot up off the couch and pulled me into a hug. Somehow, that made my eyes prickle more. "Hey, no, you're always welcome here, I just woulda' cleaned up the place first."

"There's nothing wrong with your place," I argued, shaking my head.

"Let's agree to disagree, hmm?" Sandy said, then dragged me over to the couch. It was old, the floral material faded and worn thin from years of use, pilling and fraying in spots. But it was soft and the cushions hadn't lost their integrity. I sat down with relief, my entire body sagging once I was no longer on my feet.

"Jesus, Beck, what did you do to him?" Sandy joked.

I was not expecting Beck to respond honestly. "I knocked him up."

Silence fell.

"Say what now?" she asked when neither of us laughed or told her it was a joke.

Beck sighed heavily and sat on the solid timber coffee table in front of me with a dull thud. "He's pregnant, San."

Her head swiveled between us comically. Well, it would have been comical, had the whole situation not been so damn serious. "I'm sorry," she began slowly, pinning her stare back on her foster brother, "what?"

"It turns out when an alpha and omega lust after each other very much…" Beck started, then ducked as a frayed, lumpy cushion went flying his way.

"How are you joking about this right now?" Sandy demanded of him. "This…this is huge. A *baby*, Beckett."

"Two," I lazily held up two fingers for emphasis, my exhaustion now bone deep. My eyes felt heavy, and even though the conversation was important, and I knew that Sandy's support meant everything to Beck, I was struggling to stay awake. "Two babies. Twins."

"Holy fuck," she declared.

"And that's about where we're at," I agreed, then closed my eyes.

Chapter Eighteen — Beckett

Ollie didn't even stir as I hefted him from the couch and carried him bridal style down the short hallway and into my poky little bedroom. I longed to lie down beside him on my bed, but Sandy was expecting me to return to the living area and talk about everything going on.

Micah came out of his room just as I was shutting my door behind me. We both stopped short, scenting the air.

It struck me, as the unfamiliar scent registered, that I hadn't actually seen Micah, or even missed him in close passing, in weeks. Months, even. He kept odd hours and often stayed with friends or family, using our little apartment as a crash pad more than a home.

Now I felt marginally betrayed by Sandy all over again because Micah wasn't human.

"She could have told me you were a shifter, too," I grumbled as that thought filtered through my brain.

Micah just arched an eyebrow. He was tall and lanky, the perfect build for a basketball player, assuming he had the coordination to back it up. (He did not.) His blonde hair was longer than I'd last seen it, with the ends curled upwards, resembling a 1970s glamour model. His dark brown eyes glinted as he said, "Last I saw you, you were human." Tilting his head back, he sniffed delicately at the air with his long, straight nose. "Not beta. Certainly not omega…" I watched as his eyes widened and he whipped his head back into position to stare at me. "*Alpha?*"

Was I going to have to do this with every shifter I met?

Exhaling, I nodded. "Looks like it." I sniffed at him. "Beta?" He bobbed his head.

"Horse?" I questioned, trying to pick the scent.

Micah smiled. "Got it in one, but we don't usually go around asking each other that kind of thing. How did all this—" he motioned over my body with a wave of a hand "—happen?"

"It's a long story," I admitted, starting to walk towards the living area, where I knew Sandy would be getting impatient. "The short version is I met a guy. Ollie. He's an omega. Only, I didn't know about any of this stuff until we hooked up."

I sat on the couch, leaving a space between myself and Sandy, and Micah sat cross-legged on the floor. "And then?" he prompted.

I rubbed the back of my neck. "My, uh, body changed. Um," my cheeks heated, "it locked us together. Then all of a sudden it turns out I'm an alpha, and my foster sister is also a shifter, and apparently so are you, and just as I'm wrapping my head around all of that, I find out that the whole knotting, bonding, mating thing is *actually* a legit biological thing."

"Whoa, whoa, whoa," Micah's eyes were wide again. "*Bonding?*" His gaze flickered to my neck, covered by my turtleneck and scarf. "Like…*bonding* bonding? With the biting and the foreverness?"

"With the biting and the foreverness," I nodded.

"Oh my God, Beck. What's that like?"

I was about to respond when Sandy impatiently demanded, "Can we get back to the whole pregnancy deal?"

"*Pregnancy*?!" The sound of Micah's usually mellow voice flying up at least three octaves would have been hilarious in any other situation. "Holy actual fuck, dude!"

I still chuckled a little, much to Sandy's obvious bewilderment. "How are you so calm about this?" she asked.

I shrugged. "There's no changing it. What's done is done. Plus, I've had some time to get my head around it. And having your knocked-up mate almost kidnapped from right under your nose really makes you reevaluate your priorities, I guess."

Sandy blinked. "What?!"

I looked between my friends and sighed. "Let me start from the beginning…"

To their credit, Micah and Sandy stayed quiet while I explained everything that had happened over the course of the past week. It felt like it had been longer, and it was a shock to my system to realize that it really only had been a handful of days.

As I wound the story down, I felt just as exhausted as Ollie had looked earlier. "So, yeah. That brings us to now. We need a place for Ollie to lie low for a while. I know this place is tiny, but…"

"He's your baby mama. Your bonded mate. Dude, we're not gonna complain that you want to keep him safe from his batshit insane pack." Micah insisted before Sandy could say a thing. "I can go crash at Jesse's place anyway if it gets too crowded. Plus, I'm being sent out to LA for a photo shoot in a couple of weeks." He scratched behind his ear, clarifying, "Just after New Year's."

Micah was a makeup artist who mostly freelanced but had an ongoing relationship with some of the fashion designers based in New York. The blasé way he spoke about the lifestyle he led had once made me kind of jealous. Now, though, I realized it was just another job with long hours and demanding clients, and he didn't get to enjoy the travel nearly as much as I had originally imagined.

I smiled gratefully at him, leaning forward and reaching my closed fist down towards him for him to bump. "Thanks, man. I appreciate that."

"This is only a short-term solution, though," Sandy worried her bottom lip between her teeth. "His pack will eventually find him here."

"I know." I scrubbed my hand over my face. I'd been stressing over our long-term plans even before John and his thugs turned up. "Even without the complication of his pack wanting him back for God only knows what reason, there's no space to raise a kid —let alone *two*— in his tiny apartment, and there's not much more space here, either. We'd probably need to look at getting a place in Jersey or something."

I worried about how I would support a whole family on my own freelance salary. Some months were tight enough as it was, let alone adding in the costs of raising kids or paying rent by myself. I couldn't expect Ollie to work – with the cost of daycare for two kids, I doubted we would break even if he did. Or he could work, and I could pull back my freelancing while I stayed at home with the kids…but I wouldn't ever force him to work if he didn't want to.

I was getting ahead of myself.

We needed to deal with the immediate issue of his pack causing trouble.

"Anyway," I circled back, "his pack know I'm an alpha now. Ollie seems to think they'll want to nab me, too. Well, nab or eliminate."

"Eliminate?" Micah shook his head. "This is *wild*. You were human and now…" He made an exploding gesture with his hand and the sound to accompany it. It reminded me of Ollie doing the same thing only that morning.

"You're telling me," I agreed.

"We'll work it out, Beck," Sandy assured me, reaching over to squeeze my thigh. She looked pale beneath the bright pink pixie cut of her hair. "I'm with you through this. Through all of it. Even if you moved across the world, I'd be right there with you."

A lump of emotion lodged in my throat. It made my voice come out tight and croaky as I held her hand and squeezed it back. "Thanks, San."

* * *

It took all of three days for the pack to close in on Ollie, which was terribly unfair. With less than a week to Christmas, I had hoped that we might be able to enjoy our first Christmas together in peace. But it was not to be. That just made me even more mad for him, knowing how much he loved the holidays.

I felt his trepidation through our connection as I worked on a website design for a new client, and I just knew it was because they had come for him at work. I was glad that we'd been working on controlling the bond. Now, we could turn the emotional connection on and off, save for the really sudden, strong emotions when they hit us. We were working on sending specific feelings to each other, like comfort and reassurance and love. Not that either of us had used that word yet.

Being able to tell when Ollie was upset or needed me helped settle my inner wolf in a way I couldn't quite grasp yet. It wasn't that I liked knowing my mate was upset, but if I was able to help him, I felt useful. Like a good alpha. A good mate.

Sure enough, after his feelings bubbled through the bond, my phone lit up with a text. It read *'Pack's here. They've come in force. I'm locked in Eric's office. I hope he shifts & eats them all.'*

I couldn't help but snort at the last sentence. I could only imagine how the mostly human populace would react to a dragon appearing in the middle of Manhattan. I could also imagine the destruction something like that might cause. I doubted it would be easily fixed or forgotten. Plus, even though humans knew that shifters existed in theory, the majority were unaware just how many were around them. Shifters had hidden their natures for a reason, after all. Humans, when they felt threatened, could wipe out entire species if they so wanted.

Texting him back to tell him that I was on my way, I grabbed my coat and keys and raced out of the apartment. I called Sandy as I ran down the street, hailing a cab. I threw myself into the back seat of the first car to pull up and spat out the address for Weldman's clinic.

When Sandy picked up my call, I breathlessly explained what was happening. We had a vague plan of what we would do when Ollie's pack came for him, and I needed her to grab my laptop from my desk and add it to the 'go bags' Ollie and I had put together.

Basically, we were going to run away for a little while. Sandy would grab our bags and meet us when we knew we were safe. It wasn't ideal, but it was the best we could come up with at short notice. Well, the best chance of keeping Ollie safe, anyway. At least until we could work out something more permanent.

After the cab pulled up outside the brownstone housing Weldman's clinic and lab, I raced up the front stairs, then up the next set leading to the clinic. I could scent the shifters, all wolves, before I burst through into the reception space.

There were at least twenty men in the room, all dressed in black combat gear, large and imposing. They turned as I barged inside, some of them shouting orders to grab me as soon as they scented me.

"Stay back!" I ordered, trying to channel my alpha power. I didn't know if it would work against so many of them, but I had to try. My concern for my mate and my innate dislike of crowds pressing in too close to me fueled my adrenaline, which, in turn, seemed to aid that weird ability to compel them.

"Beckett!" Weldman's voice called out to me from where he was standing in the middle of the cramped hallway on the other side of the crowd of wolf shifters, doing his best to keep them away from his office. He seemed to have partially shifted, his skin now covered in red scales, his previously muscular body seemingly even bigger than I recalled. And he had a tail, shimmering red with gleaming white spikes down its center.

He could do some damage with that, I thought moments before he actually did, whipping the extra appendage at a shifted wolf who was attempting to belly crawl past him. The wolf yelped and whined as the tail lashed at him, its spikes tearing at fur and muscle beneath. A faint spray of red now dotted the previously white hallway wall at Weldman's side.

I ducked and weaved attempts to grab me, issuing demands to let me go when hands managed to grip me or my jacket. I made my way to Weldman's side and he let me pass, whipping his tail at another shifter —this one still in human form— as they attempted to follow me.

"Is there a way out of this place that isn't down the stairs?" I asked, already knowing the answer.

"Not unless you want to jump out of a second story window," he answered, his voice more gravelly than usual. I wasn't prepared to watch him turn back to the encroaching hoard, inhale deeply and then let out a jet of flames.

Ollie's pack ducked for cover, and I gagged at the smell of burning fur and flesh from the guys who had not been quite so lucky to avoid the blast.

"Neat trick," I observed, knowing I should get to my mate, but also unable to move from the spot. One of the fuckers who had evaded the fire pulled out a gun and *that* sent me running. The sounds of bullets flying, lodging into plaster or whizzing past me, was terrifying. I was torn between checking on Weldman and getting to my mate.

"Weldman!" I looked over my shoulder before I turned the corner, "Are you okay?"

"The scales are bulletproof!" he called back. "I'm fine!"

Well, that's convenient.

I kind of wished that I was a dragon. Fire breathing powers and bulletproof skin combined with the ability to partially shift? Sign me up!

I got to Weldman's office and the door flew open before I could even knock.

"I felt you coming," Ollie said, rubbing at his chest. He slammed the door shut behind me and locked it again before turning to throw his arms around me. He was trembling and I wanted nothing more than to fix everything.

I checked him over, needing to make sure he wasn't injured, even though I could tell he was physically fine. Even his panic had receded from the bond once we were together.

"We're gonna get you out of here," I told him, still not quite sure how Weldman and I were going to pull that off.

He pulled out of our hug and eyed the window over Weldman's desk contemplatively.

"No fucking way," I informed him. "You're pregnant, Ollie. I don't think throwing yourself out of a second story window is conducive to maintaining a healthy pregnancy."

"Neither is getting abducted by a cult wolf pack," he sassed back.

I shook my head vehemently. "I would rather let Weldman set every last one of those assholes on fire than risk you or our babies like that."

"That's...actually kind of sweet, in a disturbing way."

"Funnily enough, that's how most of my exes described me, too."

Ollie groaned and smacked at my chest. "Now's not the time for joking about your exes."

Despite his complaining, though, my words had had the desired effect. He was calming down, which made it easier for me to think clearly. I still couldn't come up with a safe mode of escape. We were trapped, relying solely on Weldman to hold the contingent of armed shifters back.

The ridiculous thought I'd had a few days earlier materialized in my head again, only this time it didn't seem quite as ludicrous. Now, with no other viable options forthcoming, it was beginning to seem like the only option available to us.

Because Weldman's office was soundproofed, we couldn't hear the commotion outside. The room was quiet, almost eerily so. Even when I strained my enhanced hearing, I could only hear a murmur from the other side of the door: nothing distinct, nothing to tell me if Weldman was still holding his own.

"Are your colleagues still in the downstairs lab?" I asked my mate, the skeleton of a plan forming in my brain.

He shook his head and held up his phone. "They ran as soon as my pack turned up. I was manning reception, so I didn't even know about it until Eric burst in. I only had a few seconds before the first guys came up behind him."

Cuddling him close again, I reassured him that he was safe. That I would do everything in my power to keep him safe. "I need you to stay here, baby. I'm going back out there—"

"What? No!"

Ignoring his protesting cries, I continued, "I'm going back out there to talk to Weldman. I've got a plan."

He grabbed for my hand, shaking his head. I could feel his panic welling again, just as sure as the tears in his eyes. "Please, Beck. *Alpha*. Don't go. Please."

My heart ached, but I knew that I couldn't give in. If Weldman still had the upper hand, we still had a shot at all three of us getting out of this mess alive.

I cupped his face between my palms and forced him to look into my eyes. "Baby. Trust me. I'll be fine. Stay here."

He sobbed as I opened the door and slipped back out into the hallway. The assault on my senses was immediate. I smelled smoke and burnt fur and flesh, and there was a cacophony of yelling and growling. I inched to the corner and carefully peeked around it, finding that Ollie's boss had ceded ground but was still holding the group back.

"Weldman!" I yelled at him. "You're going to have to shift!"

"If I shift, the building will come down!" he called back, not bothering to turn his head and direct the reply over his shoulder. He knew I'd be able to hear him clearly.

"That's what I'm counting on!" I shot back. "Fall back!"

I watched him hesitate for only a moment before he nodded and literally turned tail, swiping at the nearest shifters with the appendage before he raced down the hall towards me. We ran back to his office and Ollie let us in, slamming the door in our wake. He locked it, and Weldman and I started piling furniture and filing cabinets against the surface as the thumping of bodies against it started up.

"You're going to shift," I told Weldman, "and you're going to carry Ollie out of here. Out the fucking window if you have to."

"What?!" Ollie demanded.

"It's the only way," I told him.

My mate scowled. "What about you?"

"I'll be fine."

"You can't promise that!"

I turned to Weldman. "Do it."

It looked as though he wanted to argue, but at the sound of the door cracking under the most recent body ramming it from the other side, the dragon shifter nodded. He threw his wallet and phone at me, and I deftly caught each item, sliding them into my pockets one after the other. "Tuck yourselves in the corner," he said. "It's your best bet to avoid the tail during my shift."

Ollie and I huddled in the corner of the room, watching with wide eyes as Weldman's body morphed and grew before our eyes. As expected, he was huge. His torso alone took up the bulk of the little consulting room. He did his best to tuck his wings against himself and keep his tail curled under his large, rounded belly, between his crouched legs which looked more like wide tree trunks than legs. Razor sharp claws glinted in the sunlight from the window, poking out from beneath his massive, hunched frame. His scales gleamed ruby red, the spikes along his spine pearlescent white. Glass smashed as he was unable to keep his long neck and giant head contained in the room with his body. The brickwork surrounding the window's frame crumbled down towards the street.

"Holy shit," Ollie breathed.

Holy shit was right.

There would be time to admire the enormous mythical beast later, though. I pushed Ollie forward when I was certain Weldman's shift was complete, and we made our way around to Weldman's front claws. Ollie stroked the shiny scales of Weldman's chest to let him know we were there.

In a blink, the dragon gave a roar, unfurled his wings and pushed up against the ceiling with his back. Around us, the building trembled and groaned. Ollie and I hid beneath Weldman's chest as he sheltered us from the roof which was now coming down around us.

I couldn't see the other shifters, but I could hear their pained screams and I assumed they had been caught by falling debris or by the large, lashing tail.

Then, before I knew it, Ollie and I were being encased by

scales, cradled by a palm in a dark space which was still large enough to hold the two of us comfortably. Then we were moving, and all we could do was cling to each other and hope that the dragon didn't drop us.

Chapter Nineteen – Oliver

ric's scaled palm was warm and dark as he held his clawed hand in a loose fist around us. This was by far the most surreal moment of my entire life, and I was including a lot of recent events in that assessment.

Being knotted. Learning alphas still existed. Finding out I was pregnant. None of that compared to my boss turning into a giant ass dragon and scooping me up into his claws for safety.

Beck and I held each other as we were jostled about in the small space. With Eric's talons closed around us, we had about as much room as we might in the front seats of a very small car or a tiny supply closet. It wasn't comfortable, but it wasn't completely terrible either. I was glad that I couldn't see out to the ground below. Heights weren't really my thing at the best of times, and flying in something other than an airplane was a disturbing concept.

My stomach swooped with the same sort of sensation that I'd only ever felt while riding a roller coaster and it took a moment to understand that Eric had moved his hand in flight. I could hear his large wings beating the air, and I wondered what onlookers were thinking. Shifters weren't exactly a secret, but I didn't think humans would react well to knowing dragons existed among our kind.

"You okay, baby?" Beck asked and I wasn't quite sure how to answer him.

"We can't go back." The realization tumbled out of my mouth and a wave of grief threatened to overwhelm me. The damage to the clinic and lab would be extensive, but that wasn't the only reason we couldn't return. My pack was rabid. They'd stop at nothing to get me and Beck now. Life in New York as I'd come to love it was over.

Even though I was safe from my pack, they'd still managed to take that from me. My job. My friends. My research. All gone.

I stifled a sob and Beck squeezed me tighter against him. "I'm so sorry, Ollie."

That was all it took to break the tight hold I had on my emotions. I cried deep, heaving, ugly sobs as I released the stress of the past couple of months. I mourned for the family I'd never really had, the mother whose love I'd felt as a child but had lost by my teens, the life I'd built for myself and had just seen destroyed in the blink of an eye. I cried for the uncertainty of my future, for the twin babies I carried, for the panic and fear building at the knowledge that we had nowhere to go and no real funds to speak of. I railed against the guilt that this had not only upended my life, but Beck's as well. And Eric's, Sandy's, Colt's and Lacey's, too. Hell, even Brandi's.

Brandi.

Thinking of my best friend only made me cry harder. Would

I even get to see her again?

I don't know how long I wept for, but Beck held me through the whole meltdown. He offered me support and comfort, but he didn't try to calm me before I was ready. He was a good man. A good mate. For all that I felt guilty that his life as he'd known it had fallen apart because of me and my pack, I was glad to have him with me.

Eventually, the tears ebbed away. I was left feeling drained. So drained, in fact, that my eyelids felt heavy, and my body slumped. Beck kissed the top of my head, still holding me close, and the steady *thump thump thump* of his heartbeat guided me into sleep.

* * *

"…any dragon worth his salt has a hoard of some kind. Mine has evolved over time from jewels and gold to stocks and investments," Eric was speaking as I came to.

I felt groggy. My eyes were gritty and my mouth felt as though it had been stuffed with cotton wool. I groaned, and both men turned from their places at a small, café-style dining table to look at me.

"Hey sleepyhead," Beck said softly, pushing back his chair and crossing the room in only a few strides, sitting down on the edge of the mattress I'd woken up on. It was then that I realized I was lying on a faded floral comforter. We were in a motel room, I guessed, judging by the layout of the space.

It was all one big room with two twin beds separated by a dated wicker nightstand. Against the wall directly in front of the beds there was a matching wicker dresser and a TV which looked to be at least twenty years old. The kitchenette was just off to the side of the main door, and I guessed the bathroom was behind the door on the other side of the bed I wasn't lying on. The carpet was old, frayed and graying. There was a sad, stale scent in the air, like mildew or mothballs or some unholy combination of both.

"Hey," I croaked out, still feeling a little like I'd been run over by a Mack truck.

Beck ran his hand through my hair then down my face, cupping my jaw gently in his palm. His thumb rubbed soothingly across my cheekbone. "How are you feeling?"

I thought back to the way I'd broken down and cringed. "I'm fine. I'm sorry. I feel like all I've been doing lately is cry."

"You're pregnant," Eric said from where he was still sitting at the dining table. I glanced over, noting the too-tight white t-shirt he was wearing over a pair of sweatpants that looked more like yoga pants on his big, broad frame. He didn't seem bothered by the ensemble, instead focusing on me. "Not just that," he continued gently, "but you're carrying twins, Ollie. Between the stress you've been under and the influx of hormones, I'd say the crying is completely understandable."

I couldn't be bothered arguing with him, so I just nodded. Desperate to change the subject, I looked around the room again. "Where are we?"

"We're in the only motel in a little no name town maybe fifty miles north east of Sioux City," Eric supplied easily.

"Sioux City?" I repeated in question, frowning before my eyes widened and I sat upright, startled. "Iowa?!"

Eric nodded. "We flew for almost two hours. It'll take them a while to find us all the way out here."

My throat tightened, reminded that I'd left my life behind. "I...I have no money. No clothes. N-no home..."

193

"I was just telling Beck that I've got all that covered." Eric's tone was gentle and reassuring.

I shook my head. "I can't take your money."

"*We* can't take your money," Beck agreed, and I caught him nodding his head out of the corner of my blurred vision.

Eric made a *pffft* sound and waved dismissively. "I've got far more than I'll ever be able to spend. Even in my extended lifetime. And this," he started to smile, "*this* is worth it, Ollie. You're making history. I want to be here for it. I want to be a part of it."

"Eric…"

"Plus," he continued, steamrolling over my attempted protests, "I've got a plan."

That had my attention. "Go on…"

And he did.

Chapter Twenty – Beckett

Weldman's plan was to stay in Bumfuck Nowhere, Iowa. Apparently, the town we'd landed in was once a refuge for outcast shifters, mostly omegas. They'd had alphas once upon a time, according to Weldman. An entire council of alphas, who would happily take in any and all shifters who sought sanctuary within the town's boundaries, offering them freedom and compassion in exchange for whatever services they could offer the pack as a whole.

"It was more like a commune than a pack," the dragon shifter told us excitedly. "And we could rebuild it."

"We?" I asked him incredulously. "Is that the royal 'we', or…?"

"I mean us specifically, Beck."

I blinked at him. "The three of us? Are you completely insane? Does turning into a dragon kill your brain cells?"

"Funny," he rolled his pretty blue eyes. "Beckett, I'm serious. Firstly, running is not the answer. Your mate will slow down as his pregnancy advances, and he will need somewhere to settle down to give birth and-"

"*Lalalalala,*" Ollie covered his ears and sang like a five-year-old, "I can't hear you."

I snorted and pulled him against me for a sideways hug, kissing the top of his head. I knew that he was anxious about his body changing. About what laboring and birthing our kids entailed. Hell, *I* was terrified, and I wasn't the one going through it.

Weldman sighed and shook his head, choosing to ignore Ollie. "All I'm saying," he explained, "is that there'll come a point where you will have to stop running. It makes more sense to do that now. Give ourselves time to brace and prepare for the attack. They won't be expecting that. And next time, they *will* come prepared to take down a dragon."

I let his words roll about in my head. Even though I was the Alpha, Weldman did have a couple of hundred years of life experience and knowledge that I did not. And what he was saying did make sense.

Licking my lips anxiously, I nodded slowly. "Okay," I drew the word out, "but we're going to need reinforcements."

Weldman's lips drew up into a wicked smile. In that moment, I could see the dragon lurking behind his handsome expression. "Oh, I've got that covered."

* * *

"When you said this place used to be a shifter refuge, you didn't say the population was still *all* shifters," I complained uneasily the day after Christmas.

To say that my desire to give Ollie a Christmas to remember

had not gone according to plan would be an understatement. We had spent the day in the little motel room with his boss with no fanfare, gifts, or even decorations. I felt as though I had failed my mate, even though he told me that us being alive and together was the best gift he could have asked for.

I vowed that the next year would be different. It would be the first Christmas we'd spend as a real family, because our pups would be a few months old by that point. So, I was determined to make the right choices to ensure that could happen. I had to focus in order to do that.

It hadn't taken long for Weldman to throw himself into action once we had agreed to stay, getting the two hundred strong township to assemble in the Town Hall – a barn on one of the farms a couple of miles out from the main (pretty much only) street in town. We'd only been there a few days, but that hadn't set Weldman back at all.

"I thought that was implied," Weldman shrugged.

"This has all come together a lot easier than I thought it would," Ollie added from where he sat beside me on a hay bale, sounding mildly skeptical.

We were separate from the townspeople, whose scents mixed in the strangest way. There were shifters of every sort here. Wolves, rabbits, cats, horses…*hedgehog*? I gave my head a little shake. I couldn't pinpoint them all. But it was an eclectic mix and it seemed to back up Weldman's story that the town had formed from outcasts. And, because they were a pack of outcasts, they eyed us warily, murmuring among themselves. That suited me just fine, because I still wasn't completely comfortable with so many people surrounding me at once. Strangely, though, the people interacted with Weldman just fine.

"Okay, so, I might have been planning something like this for a while," Weldman admitted nonchalantly, causing me and Ollie to both whip our heads around to stare at him. He held up his hands placatingly. "Not *this* specifically. I didn't know we'd find an alpha or anything like that. But there has been unrest in the shifter communities for a long time now. Factions rising up, wanting to control all packs and not just their own..." He trailed off. "It always made sense to prepare for the inevitable. Then when I discovered this place it seemed perfect. The people are already a pack, even if they don't really identify as one, and they always offer shelter and sanctuary to shifters in need. I own a lot of property here now, and I've been traveling out here and helping out whenever I can for the past couple of decades."

I'd known that Weldman hadn't just landed us here by chance, but it bothered me that he'd had this plan in place and hadn't bothered to mention it to me or Ollie. It made me distrustful of him, despite the help he had given us. I felt like a pawn, and I wasn't a fan of that feeling.

I barely got a chance to consider Weldman's revelations before he strode with long, purposeful steps towards the front of the barn and cleared his throat. The crowd of townspeople quietened, turning their attention to him en masse.

Weldman thanked everyone for coming and wasted no time introducing me and Ollie. I felt Ollie's shock through our bond as Weldman casually explained our entire situation, including my being an alpha, our completed bond, and our anticipated pups.

I held Ollie closer as heads swiveled back in our direction, the gasps and murmurs starting up again. We were on display, a curiosity more than we were people in need, and I had every intention of strangling Weldman, dragon or no, as soon as he finished talking.

Then Weldman laid out his plans for us to settle among them.

"Word will spread about our alpha, but we can create a safe haven here," he told the town, turning up his natural charismatic charm. It was obvious that these people already loved him, a byproduct of having earned their trust over the past decades. He sounded like a politician, as though this was a practiced speech. Maybe it was. "This is a chance to build a new kind of pack. To redefine shifters. To make history."

"Has your boss always been so radical, or is this new?" I asked Ollie bemusedly.

With wide eyes, my mate shook his head. "I knew he was passionate about the evolution of shifter society, but I wasn't expecting...well, *this*." He gestured towards Weldman. "I'm trying to decide if he's still the safer option to my pack or not."

I could hear the levity in his voice, so I knew he was joking. But I could also feel the truth in his words. We'd been manipulated and were now stuck between a rock and a hard place. I knew better than to put my blind trust into people, and yet I had done just that, and I'd brought my mate and unborn children along for the ride.

"Does this mean you're staying here for good?" one of the older men near the front of the crowd asked, and Weldman nodded without hesitation.

"If you'll have us," he said genially. "I know I own many of the properties here, but it's still your home first and foremost. If you're not comfortable having us settle here knowing that trouble will come looking for us eventually, we understand."

Well, that was something. At least he was giving these people a choice.

When Weldman turned back to us, he smiled sheepishly. "And the same goes for you two. I didn't mean to railroad you into this. I just got excited."

He looked like a puppy who had just eaten his master's favorite shoe. It was hard to continue to distrust him when he seemed so genuine.

Ollie and I shared a look, trading vague feelings along our bond. When it seemed we were in agreement, I looked towards Weldman again, dipping my head in acquiescence. "Let the people take a vote, then."

And that was that.

Chapter Twenty-One — Oliver

We settled into life in the newly dubbed Shifters Sanctuary, Iowa, disturbingly easily. The community welcomed us with open arms, both figuratively and literally, and it didn't take long for me and Beck to find our places in the town.

Eric had taken us to a well-maintained farmstead and declared it our new home, adding the caveat that he would live elsewhere if we weren't comfortable with him living and operating his medical practice from the grounds-keeper's cottage a few hundred feet away from the main house. It felt a bit weird basically living with my former boss, but I wasn't comfortable kicking him out of a place he owned, either.

In the end, Beck and I agreed that we were okay with Eric living in the cottage as long as we could have Sandy come and live with us in the main house, with an open-door policy for Micah and Brandi as well. Considering the size of the place, even with the four of us living there at once, we still had more space than we knew what to do with.

For a town in the middle of nowhere, Beck and I were surprised to find that it had high-speed internet access, a lively night life, and a very well stocked grocery store. It even had a couple of restaurants in the middle of town, and not just a tiny Mom & Pop style diner, though it did have one of those, too. I wasn't entirely sure how these businesses stayed afloat with how small the town was and with it being distanced from any highways or major roads, but Beck seemed to think Eric was behind a lot of that, too. Besides, despite the fact that it was tiny, the town was still bigger than some of the neighboring communities, so it attracted its fair share of local visitors requiring supplies or entertainment.

"Plus," Beck had mused when we'd talked about it during our first days exploring the area, "those restaurants only open a few nights a week each. They're not spending as much on supplies or staff that way."

It made sense to me, I supposed.

When it came to me, personally, I was a bit of a mess. I'd been forced to throw away my phone's SIM and get another one so my mom couldn't get in touch any more, not that that was all that much of a loss, really. But I worried it would only antagonize my pack to come after us more. Then there was my job. I wasn't sure what to do about work or being at all useful. Beck was able to pretty much pick up from where he'd left off once Sandy arrived with his laptop and our meager belongings in tow, but I was stuck.

My job didn't exist anymore. It had stopped existing when my boss turned into a dragon and brought the building down over our heads. When he had given up the life he'd been living in New York to save me, my mate, and our unborn children. I couldn't just ask him to materialize a new job for me after all that, could I? Not when he'd also given us a beautiful home as well, requesting nothing in return, except our commitment to the town, its people, and his research.

But, after a week or so of roaming the farmstead looking for tasks to keep myself occupied, Eric pulled me into his clinic (which was basically the living room and second bedroom of the cottage) and asked me to assist him with his ongoing research into what he was calling 'Locked Alpha Syndrome'. I was in my element, doing deep dives into old scientific journals, but also lurking on the internet, looking for even the slightest hint that more people like Beck existed out there. Eric also reached out to his network of dragon contacts, arguing that keeping Beck a secret wasn't going to work any longer, not with my pack knowing what he was. Anyway, the whole town knew and we hadn't asked anyone to keep it to themselves.

The townspeople helped, too. A lot visited our new home in those first few days, bringing welcome packages and warm smiles. They were fascinated by Beck, reverently calling him Alpha, asking if he would take a leadership role in the community. Prior to our arrival, they had a makeshift council of betas, but no real government to speak of. Beck told them he'd think about it, but that he wasn't here to rock the boat.

As far as I was concerned, the boat had already capsized.

The rest of the community seemed to think along the same lines as me, because they treated Beck as their Alpha regardless of his vague agreement to take up the post. They came to him with concerns and disputes when the Beta Council was at a stalemate, and they didn't leave until he (reluctantly) helped to resolve them. In addition, they helped spread the word of the haven we were planning for other outcast shifters, reaching out to distant families and friends, telling Beck's story, albeit an abridged version.

Weeks passed, then months.

My belly grew.

I was terrified that my changing body would finally scare my mate away, but it seemed to have the opposite effect. Beck couldn't keep his hands off me. He grew more possessive, not to a dickish and jealous degree, but he made it clear to any man who looked at me appraisingly that I was his and his alone. That made me feel insanely sexy, and it made my inner wolf howl with pride.

At roughly eight months into our relationship and my pregnancy, I'd well and truly lost the battle with myself when it came to pretending I wasn't in love with Beck. I was head over heels...not that I could see my feet anymore.

"You need to tell him, babe," Brandi said over the phone after I poured my feelings out to her for the umpteenth time. I missed her terribly but returning to New York was impossible at that point.

Not only was I afraid of my pack still finding us there, but there had been a bit of an uproar following Eric's flight from Manhattan, and an anti-shifter debate was still raging in the city. Showing our faces after they'd been splashed all over the news for months was not a smart idea, especially when I was heavily pregnant.

"I know," I replied, shaking my melancholy musings from my thoughts. "But it hasn't even been a year. It's too soon."

"You're about to have his babies, Ollie," she addressed me like I was a preschooler, slow and deliberate with her words. "You're permanently and magically bonded to him for life. Too soon flew out the window a long time ago, hun."

Tears prickled in my eyes and I couldn't help asking, "But...

what…what if he doesn't love me back?"

"Don't be stupid," my best friend huffed. "That man is crazy about you. I don't even have to see it to know it. Didn't you say he's hyper-focused on making sure you're comfortable and happy all the damn time? And if the sex is still awesome…"

"Brandi…"

She ignored my groaned protest. "If the sex is still awesome, what gives you any reason to think he doesn't feel the same way? I mean, for fuck's sake, you've got that weird shared feelings shit going on. Can't you feel his love? I'm gonna bet he feels yours."

"It doesn't work like that," I sat back on the couch and rubbed my belly where one of our twins was kicking up a storm.

The movement made me smile, recalling Beck's awe the first time he'd been able to feel them from the outside. His dark eyes had welled with tears and he had pressed kisses to the stretching skin of my abdomen, whispering words of affection to the babies inside me. Even now, his excitement to feel them was practically palpable. I didn't need the bond to feel it. I could see it and sense it in him.

"Well, however it works, you've gotta tell him how you feel. There's no use whining at me about it," she added, her tone teasing, "I'm too far away to do a damn thing."

"Don't remind me," I sulked. "When are you going to come visit?"

"After my godchildren are born. I only get a few weeks off a year. I'm gonna make the most of them!"

I laughed and shook my head even though she couldn't see me. Talking to my best friend always calmed me down. "I think you need to look for a job here."

It wasn't the first time I'd made the suggestion and her

exaggerated sigh told me she was sick of hearing it. "Goodbye, Oliver," she said pointedly, then hung up the phone.

I shrugged as I placed mine down on the gray linen couch cushion beside me and rubbed my belly again. "We'll convince your Aunt Brandi one day," I assured my kids.

A giggle came from the doorway and I looked up to find Lena, a rabbit shifter who Beck was paying to cook and occasionally clean for us now that I was really slowing down, leaning against the doorjamb that led to the kitchen. She was short and brunette, with sparkling blue eyes and a cute button nose. I'd thought she was only fifteen or sixteen when Beck introduced us, but she's actually older than me at twenty-four.

"Are you still naggin' that friend of yours?" she asked in mock admonishment as she bustled into the room wearing her usual outfit of figure-hugging jeans and a checkered flannel shirt. She was curvy and confident in her body. I envied her that, because I was anything other than confident in my round belly at that moment. Lena stopped in front of me and offered me her hand. "Come on. It's about time for those little monsters of yours to dance on your bladder."

Lena took her role in making my life easier very seriously. I was beginning to suspect Beck had asked her to keep a close eye on me whenever he and Eric were unable to. It was sweet even though it was grating. I rolled my eyes but accepted the help getting up anyway. I was mildly resentful that I needed it, but I wasn't so stubborn that I would turn it down.

"You're right," I told her, guiding her hand to where the other twin was now kicking, "as always."

"I'm a rabbit," Lena said, as though that explained everything. "Breeding's a big thing for my kind. We have a sixth sense about this stuff."

"About me needing to pee?" I laughed, then scrunched my nose in discomfort when I realized just how badly I did need to go. "It's hardly a sixth sense when it's common knowledge that I need to go all the time these days."

"Are you sayin' I'm not knowledgeable about havin' babies, Oliver Grayson?" Her pink lips curled upwards with a secretive smile. "Think real carefully on your answer. I've just baked those apple cinnamon muffins you like so much."

"You are all-knowing," I told her with a grin of my own. "I won't ever second-guess you, oh great and powerful rabbit lady."

She snickered and shooed me off in the direction of the downstairs powder room. The house was two stories, all timber accents and polished wooden floors. It had white painted timber walls, both inside and out, and a wraparound porch. Downstairs held the large living room, the kitchen and dining room, a powder room, and a guest bedroom where Sandy was currently living. Upstairs had five other bedrooms and two bathrooms, one of which was attached to the master bedroom. Like I said, it was huge, and even with the twins coming, I didn't think Beck and I would fill the place.

"You keep sassing me, wolf boy, and see how far that gets you," she said while my bladder twinged in protest.

"The next time we shift, I'm totally going to eat you," I grumbled, but even I could hear the affection in my voice.

"Uh huh. I might be a chubby bunny, Oliver, but I can still outrun your wolf self."

"Only because my wolf self is somehow even rounder than my human self." I sulked.

The last time I had shifted, I'd felt ungainly and slow, and I'd wondered why that was the case when wolves could carry whole litters and I only had two pups growing inside me. I put it down to shifter biology, but I resented it either way. I'd eventually spent most of my time in wolf form curled up on the porch of our house under a pile of blankets which smelled like my mate while he ran with the people we were coming to consider as our new pack.

I didn't hear Lena's reply to my grumbling because my bladder was protesting with urgency at that point. I hustled into the little bathroom, decorated in blue and white tiles, and sighed with relief, glad to have made it in time. I'd been regaled with pregnancy horror stories from a number of the town's women and didn't relish the idea of reliving any of them myself.

When I returned to the kitchen a few minutes later, Lena handed me a muffin, still warm from the oven, and a glass of cold milk.

"I take it all back," I told her as I stuffed my mouth, moaning at the taste of her delicious baked goods, "you're a saint."

"There was a time you used to make those sounds for me," Beck's voice was low and full of promise as he murmured in my ear, uncaring of our audience. His large arms wrapped around me from behind and his hands came to rest on my belly, rubbing reverently. It was a testament to how distracted by food I had been that I hadn't felt his approach through the bond.

I smiled and turned my face towards his, nuzzling his stubbled jaw. "That's exactly how we got into this mess," I told him.

"And they say rabbits are prolific breeders," Lena snarked, washing dishes in the sink overlooking the crops growing in the fields. "Mark my words: these pups will be the first of many."

Beck's chest rumbled with his laughter, vibrating through my back. "Hi to you, too, Lena. Thank you for keeping my mate fed in my absence."

The longer Beck spent with shifters, the more easily it seemed he fell into using the lingo. He was a natural alpha, so charismatic and born to lead. He wasn't power hungry, but he certainly liked to be in control of most situations. I was so proud him.

The feeling bloomed in my chest and flooded me with warmth. And, courtesy of my hormones and Beck's proximity, the way he tensed briefly before cuddling me even tighter told me that he'd felt it through the bond.

"Well, now that you're here, I'm going to take off," Lena told him as she wiped her hands on a tea-towel, oblivious to the moment we were sharing. "You two enjoy your evening." She smirked. "Make use of what little child-free time you have left."

"Oh, I plan on it," Beck nipped at my mating mark gently, and the feelings suffusing my body turned from PG to X-rated in a blink. I wasn't entirely sure if they were my own, or Beck's, or the mingling of both.

I didn't particularly care.

I felt my slick begin to pool as my cock swelled rapidly to life. I would have been embarrassed by how quickly I became so deeply aroused had it not been for the fact that I could feel Beck's cock turning to steel at my back.

I paid little attention to Lena leaving, too wrapped up in the insatiable need coursing through my veins. My erection was turning painful, trying to escape from the confines of my sweatpants by force alone, and my slick was going to make a mess of my boxer briefs soon.

Inside my belly, the babies did somersaults, clearly picking up on my excitement.

Beck chuckled and turned me around, dropping to his knees in front of me. My cock seemed to strain even harder towards him, but his intention was not to greet it, but the large distension of my abdomen instead.

My mate pushed my shirt up and kissed my stretched skin. "Hey, babies," he greeted, his voice soft and sweet and full of awe. It was the tone he always used when he spoke to them, and damned if I didn't tear up every single time. "Did you miss your daddy? I missed you."

They kicked, little feet and hands pushing outwards towards the sound of his voice, turning the roundness into a weird lumpy surface. The first time they'd done it, I had freaked out and imagined scenes from *Alien*, but now I was used to it.

Beck was, too. His grin widened and he peppered even more kisses to the pushed-out spots where their limbs were pressing hard. "God, I can't wait to meet you both. And you can stop terrorizing your Papa from the inside."

"Instead they'll terrorize us both from the outside," I nodded. "And because I'm suffering through this," I pointed down to my belly, feeling my cock still throbbing but unable to see it beneath the bulge of my abdomen, "you're on night shift for the first month."

It was an idle threat and we both knew it, but Beck nodded his agreement anyway. "Sounds fair." He nuzzled his stubbled cheek against my too-tight skin.

I needed his mouth lower. I whined.

"Aww, feeling neglected, babe?"

Courtesy of my hormones, tears flooded my vision and my

throat tightened. I'd gone from flirty and turned on to so horny that I was going to cry in the blink of an eye. I could only nod.

Beck's expression shifted immediately. His smile dropped and he was full of sympathy within seconds. "Aww, honey," he moved to stand up, clearly wanting to comfort me, but I shook my head.

"Hormones," I promised, my voice coming out strained and wobbly. "I'm just so horny..." My voice cracked and a sob tore from my throat, quickly followed by a bark of nearly hysterical, though watery, laughter. Covering my burning face with my hands, I lamented, "I can't believe I'm crying because I'm horny. *Jesus.*"

I cried over a lot of random things, to be honest.

TV ads. The ducklings down at the pond at the back of our property. Not having enough blue marshmallows in my bowl of Lucky Charms. Stupid shit, really.

"It's okay, Ollie. Let it out. I'll make it better." Beck soothed, running his hands over my thighs. I felt his fingers tugging into the elastic waistband of my pants and I closed my eyes as he eased the clothing down my legs, my underwear following soon after. Eyes still closed, I kicked both items off once I felt my pants around my ankles, then widened my stance to ease some of the discomfort in my lower back.

A full body shudder ran through me when I felt Beck's warm breath on my cock, and I knew I was leaking for him. Slick threatened to drizzle down the inside of my thighs, too. But I didn't care.

I whimpered and thrust forward, seeking relief. I was crazy with need. I felt almost like I had that first night with Beck: desperate and unhinged. But if that had been a mating heat, as Eric and I both speculated, what was this? I was already mated and pregnant.

It felt so intense, surely it couldn't only be pregnancy related, could it? But who could I ask? I didn't exactly relish the idea of talking to the well-meaning, over-sharing women in the town. They were still basically strangers, and I wasn't interested in lending additional material to the gossip about their Alpha and his pregnant omega.

My thoughts snuffed out into nothingness when a haze of pleasure overtook me as my cock was enveloped by warm, wet heat and suction. I cried out at how good it felt, squeezing my already shut eyes even tighter. Spots of color danced behind my eyelids like miniature fireworks.

Beck hummed his approval and the vibrations of it traveled through my rock-hard shaft and down to my balls. My knees wobbled with how close I already was to losing control.

The obscene slurping sounds Beck made tapered away and he pulled off my dick with an audible *pop*.

I whined my complaint, fingers reaching out and threading through Beck's short hair, trying to get purchase, trying to encourage him back down onto my aching cock.

My mate laughed lightly and surged to his feet. His hands came to rest under the curve of my ass and he lifted me from the ground with an ease I couldn't fully comprehend, not with how huge my belly was. He shushed me when I protested.

Alphas.

With my legs wrapped around his hips, Beck walked us across the kitchen and to the sturdy timber dining table. Its surface was smooth but scuffed and worn from years of use. At that moment, though, it was also clear of plates, cutlery, or even the little potted plant Lena kept trying to leave on it for decorative purposes. And that was a good thing because, before I could think, I was being laid out on my back across the cool, golden-hued surface, with my ass only just hanging off the short edge.

"Beck," I admonished half-heartedly, raising up on my elbows to glare at him. "We eat here."

He gave me a roguish grin and a wink, spreading my thighs wider as he stood between them. "I have every intention of eating here, babe."

I groaned, half at his awful joke and half at the idea of having his mouth at my dripping entrance. I knew he loved to rim me, that he went crazy over the taste of my slick, but I was still so desperate to be fucked and filled, I wasn't sure I could handle his mouth on me at that point.

"Later? Please?" I could hear the wobble in my own voice again and cursed it as the hunger in Beck's gaze turned soft once more. Don't get me wrong: I loved the softness, too, but I didn't want him treating me like glass just because my hormones had my emotions going haywire. I canted my hips upwards. "Fuck me. I need it. I need...*Oh!*"

Two thick, practiced fingers slid into me before I could even finish my plea. I couldn't see over the mound of my stomach, but I could see Beck's arm moving as I felt those fingers thrusting in and out of my channel.

He kept his dark eyes on mine as he pleasured me, his other hand moving to wrap around my cock. "That better, baby?"

"*Nnngh.*" It wasn't a coherent answer by any means, but I think it got my feelings across as I writhed on the tabletop.

"I love how wet you get for me, sweetheart. You feel so fucking good around my fingers. I'm almost popping my knot just thinking of sinking my cock into your perfect hole."

Jesus. Fucking. Christ.

I opened my mouth to beg, but he chose that moment to add another finger and I keened with the overwhelming, intense desire to be filled and fucked. Bred. Claimed. Possessed. The stretch of his fingers was exquisite, but it wasn't his knot.

I needed his knot.

Nothing else would feel as good.

A broken sob tore its way out of my throat and I managed to follow it with: *"Please*, Alpha."

Beck sent me waves of reassurance couched in pleasure through the bond as he finally removed his fingers and unzipped his jeans. The metallic sound was loud in the otherwise quiet kitchen, audible over my pants and whimpers. I shivered with anticipation while I waited for the relief I'd been promised.

Thankfully, I didn't have to wait long.

The head of Beck's cock felt scorching as he dragged it through the mess of my slick and teased my hole. I bucked my hips, wordlessly encouraging him to thrust inside me. My chest heaved while I tried to rein in my desperation. Tears slipped down the sides of my face and trickled into my ears as he finally made his way inside me.

"Oh God," I breathed, ecstasy igniting in my veins. I felt whole again. Completed by my mate. "Yes, Beck. Right there. Fuck. More. More, Beck, please." I was babbling, overcome by the relief of getting exactly what my body had been craving.

But now that he was inside me, my mate wasn't rushing me to the finish line. Instead, he moved slowly, dragging his perfect cock back out until the crown was only barely inside me, then easing back in again. Over and over he repeated the languid roll of his body, but it was enough. I didn't need fast and rough. I just needed him.

"You're so beautiful, baby," Beck said when my babbling subsided into happy sighs of bliss. "If you could only see what I see," his hands pushed my shirt up my belly again and then smoothed over the miles of skin he exposed to the warm early-evening air. "Filled with life that we made together. Our babies. Our pups. Your body is gifting me a family, Ollie. You've made that happen."

I'd been enjoying his ministrations with my eyes closed again, but his voice was so strained and emotional that I couldn't help the way they flew open and met his gaze.

Beck's expression matched his voice. His eyes were shining and wet, but his smile was full of affection and something deeper still. He stretched over me, keeping one hand on my stomach as he braced his elbow on the table's surface, bearing most of his weight there. The timber beneath us groaned as he leaned down, still slowly moving his hips, rocking his cock inside me at the gentle pace he'd been maintaining since he first slid in. Bringing his lips to mine, he barely brushed our mouths together.

"I love you, Oliver," he whispered. Even with my enhanced hearing, I almost missed it.

My heart squeezed and a joy I'd never known warmed my insides, making me feel giddy and light. More tears flooded my vision and spilled over my temples. My hands clutched at Beck's shoulder blades and I wasn't about to let him go just to wipe at my eyes.

"I love you too, Beckett," I managed to reply, matching his whisper with my own. It was as though the weight of the words held us back from saying them any louder. Perhaps he was just as scared to be vulnerable as I was. We really were

215

perfectly in sync if that was the case. I swallowed roughly. "I love you so, so much."

I wanted to say more. To tell him that he'd changed my life in the best of ways. That I wouldn't change a thing of what we had been through together, even though those early days had felt crazy. I wanted to tell him that I was the luckiest omega on the planet, that he had my heart and soul and body, and that I would give him anything within my power to give. Confessing my love had taken a weight from my chest that I hadn't even realized was there, but I couldn't make the rest of the words come.

It didn't matter. Beck seemed to understand, if the surge of emotion I felt through the bond was any indication. I melted into the deep, passionate kiss he initiated as the intensity of our feelings washed over and between us. It was harder to control the sharing of our emotions when we were intimately connected, but I didn't want to prevent it anyway. Not in that moment.

Joy, affection, desire, warmth, protectiveness...it all swirled inside me until I was unsure where my feelings ended and his began. Added to that was the feedback loop of our physical pleasure; sparks of bliss that ignited in the pit of my belly and sent shock waves through my extremities. I could feel the same building inside Beck, his orgasm growing right there next to mine, entwining with it, teasing it, taking me to new heights even though we were rocking so slowly together it was almost lazy.

Beck tore away from our kiss, still so careful not to lean his weight on my belly, though his hand rubbed slow circles over the babies rolling about inside me. "I'm gonna come," he warned.

I nodded and moaned, arching my back as best I could, regardless of the unyielding surface beneath me. "Yes! Please, Alpha. Fill me up. I need it."

I couldn't express *why* I needed to be filled to the brim with his cum, only that my instincts demanded it. It wasn't as if he was going to put more pups in me while I was already heavily pregnant. At least, I hoped not.

There was so little concrete information out there about omega pregnancies that Eric and I had been playing it by ear, documenting mine as we went. There was no way to know if I was a textbook case or, if because Beck had only presented as an alpha after we first mated, whether we were paving a whole new path. If this new heat-like impulse meant that I'd be somehow carrying more pups, I'd probably lose my mind.

My gut and all of my years of research told me it wasn't going to be that way, though. Yes, cases of superfetation could potentially spontaneously occur during a pregnancy, but those events were anomalies, not commonplace events. They were rare within humans, so there was no reason to think the likelihood would be different for shifters.

No, my hormones were likely the cause of my current instincts. Hormones and the mystical bond that Beck and I had accidentally formed when we'd bitten each other. If I assumed that my pregnancy was textbook for a bonded omega/alpha pairing, then what I was feeling was probably my body's way of maintaining and strengthening our bond. That was my hypothesis, and I would explore my thoughts later when I wasn't inching ever closer to glorious release.

As it was, all I could think about was getting my strong, sexy mate to knot me and flood my insides with his seed. We kissed just as languidly as we moved, the whole situation far more romantic than I had anticipated when he first laid me out on the table. But it was perfect, even if the surface beneath me was cold and hard, and my eyes continued to leak tears of combined happiness and desperation.

Our breathing was heavy and I could feel myself starting to perspire despite our movements remaining so unhurried. My fingers clung to the material of Beck's shirt at his back as my orgasm neared closer still. I panted into his mouth, gasping as he adjusted his angle and seemed to slide in even deeper.

"Fuck, baby," he exhaled against my lips. "I need you to come. I need you to come on my cock. Untouched. Come for me, Ollie. I'm going to knot you and I need—*fuck*."

His filthy, perfect words had pushed me over the edge and I spasmed around him while ropes of my own cum splashed the underside of my belly and over his abdomen. Cussing and groaning, Beck pushed into me and ground his hips as my orgasm finally drew his out. I relished the additional stretch of his knot inside me, locking us together.

It was a feeling I would never get sick of.

Chapter Twenty-Two – Beckett

I hadn't thought the situation through when I knotted Ollie on the kitchen table. There was no way I was going to be able to hold my position for as long as it took for my knot to deflate. But I hadn't been thinking clearly. From being unable to keep my hands off his body, to his hormone-addled desperation, then finally to our shared declarations of love, logic had not been my friend.

But I'd needed to take him immediately. Even the short walk into the living room would have taken too long for both of us. And the table had been *right there…*

I sighed as I came down from our mutual high and steeled myself for the discomfort of overstimulating my knot. But there was nothing for it: we couldn't stay on the table. I didn't want to risk accidentally hurting Ollie, and I didn't like the idea of lying down on the table together while my knot subsided, either.

"Beck, what—?" Ollie started, then squealed as I took a deep breath and tugged him with me as I tried to shuffle back off the table.

I grunted as my knot caught and my balls tightened and unleashed another load into him, causing my knees to wobble with the pleasure/pain of it all. Gritting my teeth, I guided Ollie's legs around my hips and hefted him from the table, carrying him from the kitchen and back into the living room as quickly as possible. Every step bounced him on my knot, pushing short growls of pleasure from my lips with every motion. I'd wanted to be able to take him to our bedroom, but after taking three steps, I knew there was no way I was going to make it up the stairs.

The couch was our best option. I got us there in record time and sat gingerly, trying not to cry out at the additional stimulation.

"God, that feels incredible through the bond," Ollie told me as another burst of nearly painful bliss shot through me like lightning.

Between us, I felt one of our kids kicking up a storm. It made me smile even while I struggled to catch my breath, the pleasure of coming and coming *and coming* taking its toll on me.

"Mmm, it feels pretty damn incredible in person, too," I said, then took another moment to brace myself before guiding Ollie to lie down on his side, his head tucked beneath my chin and my body curled around him protectively.

I yanked the throw blanket off the back of the couch and draped it over our connected bodies for privacy, just in case Lena returned or Sandy got back from work before we were able to separate. My heart beat almost frantically, but I had never felt so calm and happy.

The past months at the farmstead had been idyllic. I'd had

to admit as much to Eric, even though it had pained me. Hell, just calling the guy by his first name had been struggle enough, but I couldn't deny that he'd gone above and beyond to help us, even if he had his own motivations as well.

Being slowly roped into becoming the town's Alpha was also something I was getting used to. Eric and Sandy both told me I was doing a great job, and I could literally feel Ollie's approval through the bond, but I still wondered if there wasn't someone else better suited to the role. After all, I hadn't even been a shifter for a year. Just because some weird twist of fate or genetics landed me into a designation I couldn't control, it didn't mean I was fit to lead. But even though we were creating a pack unlike any other the world had seen before, the community clung firmly to the notion that my designation gave me additional ranking.

In the end, I just went with it.

Seven months in, I was even kind of liking it. We'd built on the town's council, turning it into as much of a democratic pack hierarchy as we could. I made sure to include omegas as well as betas, making it clear that I saw all designations as equal. I refused to treat omegas the way Ollie's pack and their ilk did.

Because the town was a group of outcasts, they had no qualms with my reasoning. The majority had fled their own packs because either they, or the loved ones they'd brought with them, were mistreated omegas searching for better lives. And then there was Eric, an a-typical omega, who owned half the properties and, combined with his place as the town doctor, held a lot of esteem among the people.

It had made the transition almost too easy.

Obviously, there had been some grumbling from a small

contingent of shifters who didn't like change and weren't happy about the trouble we were inviting to follow us, but even they had quietened down over the past months.

All-in-all, life was good, and I had never felt so happy.

But, as the glow of my multiple orgasms began to fade and Ollie drifted off to sleep in my arms, I couldn't help going back to my thought that things had fallen together too easily.

His pack hadn't yet shown up again, and that was beginning to concern me. I knew that our location was becoming common knowledge, as was Ollie's condition, as people were beginning to seek us out. Firstly, it had started with phone calls and emails from all around the country, asking if the rumors were true and whether we had space for more people in the town. Then they had started showing up.

Most surprising of our newest members of our little society were the three humans who arrived, two with similar backstories to mine who hoped that they might also be alphas behind their human facades, and another who had been born to shifter parents only to present as completely human. Eric had shuffled them off to a house of their own which we were all jokingly dubbing the Frat House, on account of the potential of these men being alphas just like me. They all picked up jobs in the community and allowed Eric to poke and prod them in their free time, which took some of the attention off me and Ollie.

So, with confirmation about our whereabouts spreading, it was only a matter of time before Ollie's pack acted, and I was getting anxious. With every day that passed, the likelihood of Ollie going into labor increased. Eric was estimating that we shifters gestated at a similar length to humans, but with twins in the picture, a premature birth was almost to be expected.

My inner wolf hated the idea of my mate's former pack biding their time until he was at his most vulnerable. I agreed with my wolf. I wanted Ollie's former pack to act now so that the threat could be eliminated before my pups were born.

But it didn't seem like that would happen.

"Ugh, typical." Sandy complained with a mutter as she stepped through the front door, hanging her light jacket on the stand just inside. "This whole place smells like—*oh!*" She blinked as she finally noticed us. I shushed her and fought the urge to growl, holding onto Ollie a little more tightly and shuddering through another small orgasm courtesy of the movement I'd caused.

"Beckett," Sandy dipped her voice into an admonishing whisper, frowning at me as she gently shut the door. "You couldn't have taken this," she waved a hand over us, "upstairs?"

I felt my cheeks burn under the weight of her scrutiny. "Um…no?" I felt like an errant teenager and not the pack Alpha. It was a feeling that only my big sister could induce. I bit my lip and tried to explain. "His hormones…"

Sandy rolled her eyes. "Would have survived the minute it took to get to your room." She huffed and shook her head again. "*Men.*"

"It's a mating thing," I tried to explain again, careful to keep my voice low.

My sister laughed lightly and nodded. "Yeah, I got that."

"No, I mean…ugh, never mind."

I knew she was being deliberately obtuse, but I didn't have the energy to play along. My thoughts returned to the issue of Ollie's pack and the impending birth of our children.

"What's wrong?" Sandy asked, settling in to the plush, floral armchair across from the couch. Her brows, which were dyed lurid green to match the newest color of her hair, furrowed. "Aren't you supposed to be all relaxed and glow-y after sex?"

Checking the bond and Ollie's face to confirm that he was still asleep, I sighed and then quietly unloaded my concerns. If there was anyone in this world who I relied on to help me sort through my thoughts (well, anyone other than my mate), it was Sandy. She listened patiently and, when I was done, smiled softly.

"The whole pack -and that's what we are now, Beck: your pack- has your back. And we have some pretty impressive shifters among us, including Eric. He's taken them down once; he'll do it again."

Despite her reassurance, I felt antsy. "They'll be ready for a dragon this time," I argued.

"Hmm, maybe. But will they be ready for three?"

I startled, wide-eyed, then had to shut them as my sudden jolting had teased my knot again. Letting the sensation pass, I looked back at Sandy. "Three?" I demanded. "Who are the other two? And how come nobody told me that there were new dragons in the pack?" As the Alpha, shouldn't that have been something I deserved to know?

She grinned. "Well, they only just arrived. I was coming to tell you so you could come meet them, but you were otherwise indisposed." Her pointed chin jerked towards Ollie's blanket-covered ass.

A little placated by that, at least, I felt some of the tension in my shoulders drain. "Okay. Well, when my knot subsides—"

"Gross."

"When my knot subsides," I repeated, ignoring her childish gagging sounds, "I'll get dressed and come meet them. I can only assume they're at Eric's?"

My sister pushed to her feet and bobbed her head, brushing her palms down over her jeans. "Yep. I'll head back there and let them know you're on your way."

"Thanks." She left the way she'd come in and I pressed a kiss to the top of Ollie's head, already feeling lighter. Eric had called in reinforcements, and that went a long way towards settling my worries.

* * *

The new dragons were just as physically imposing as Eric. Tall, muscular, and sharp-eyed, the two new omegas greeted me with firm handshakes. They were both men with heart-shaped faces like Eric's, but one had vibrant red hair tied back in a ponytail at the nape of his neck, and the other had dark brown hair cut in a 'more on top' style. In the cozy living room of Eric's cottage, they took up a significant amount of space. Adding in Eric and then myself, the room almost felt suffocating.

"These are my brothers," Eric introduced us properly, smirking at the surprised expression I must have given him. "This," he gestured to the redhead, "is Sage. And this," he waved the same hand at the other man, "is Brandt."

"It's nice to meet you both," I said genuinely. "I didn't know Eric had siblings."

"Eric always has liked to be the center of attention," Sage shot Eric a smirk. His voice was softer than I'd anticipated. More effeminate. Sassy. "Typical of the youngest, really."

Eric rolled his eyes. "It never came up in conversation."

"Uh huh." Brandt scoffed, but his blue eyes were lit with the same sense of humor. His voice was deep and rumbling; a stark contrast to his red-headed brother's. He appeared older than the other two men, with fine lines around his mouth and the creases of his eyes. Laughter lines. When he spoke, I got the hint of an accent…something European, maybe? I never had been good with picking accents. "You just wanted to keep your discoveries to yourself, little brother. I know you too well."

"I sent word," Eric was as close to pouting and petulant as I'd ever seen him. Watching his interactions with his brothers was fascinating. "Eventually."

Brandt snorted and reached over to ruffle the mop of golden curls on top of Eric's head. He was batted away by the younger man who scowled at him.

"Anyway," Eric sniffed and tried to smooth out his hair, "you're here now." He turned to me and explained, "Brandt's a doctor as well, which will help with our increasing numbers and with my research. Sage is a jack of all trades—"

"But master of none," Brandt chuckled and ducked the fist Sage half-heartedly slugged at his shoulder.

"—And he'll help out wherever we need him to." Eric finished, ignoring his siblings. Then he sighed. "But, more importantly, they've agreed to help keep Ollie and the babies safe. With all the attention we've been getting recently…"

"It's not just Ollie's old pack we need to worry about." I finished, feeling horrified.

I hadn't stopped to consider that our existence might encourage other old-school packs to challenge us, but I should have. We were offering their castaways and mistreated shifters a safe haven and an escape from their control. We were a threat.

Eric nodded. "Exactly."

Whatever relief I'd felt about having the additional fire-power (pun totally intended) in my pack was dampened by the fear that we had more than just one potential attack to fend off. Plus there was the ongoing debate within human society which we had inadvertently rekindled with our flight from New York. With humans just as afraid of shifters forming packs and defenses, it was possible they'd come for us as well. After all, history had shown that they'd done it before.

"It'll be okay," Eric assured me, and I tried to feel bolstered by his confidence. He grinned sharply. "Three dragons, especially in the prime of our lives and at our size, aren't easy to take down."

"And I reached out to Dexter," Sage told his brother. "He's living it up in Australia, of all places, but he said he'll see how many of the old crowd might be interested in coming to stay for a while. Just until things stabilize."

"I wasn't aware you were still on speaking terms with Dex," Eric responded with an arched eyebrow.

Sage's shoulders lifted and dropped with nonchalance and he sat himself down on Eric's two-seater couch, propping one booted foot on the coffee table and then the other over the top of that, crossing his legs at the ankle. "We were kids. A couple of hundred years apart was all we needed to get over it."

"Sorry," I interrupted, "who's Dexter?"

"A dragon we grew up with," Brandt supplied when neither of his brothers answered.

"I thought you were solitary creatures? Ollie said you don't do packs." I cocked my head to the side, genuinely curious.

Brandt sat down carefully on the armchair which was positioned kitty-corner to the couch. It was almost comical to see him treat the beige furniture so gingerly, like he thought his bulk might break it. "Once upon a time we tended to keep to smaller groups, but as the alphas started dying out and our numbers dwindled, we became a little more insular. Well, until Dad disappeared and then…" His face fell as he trailed off. "We scattered. It's easier to face the end of your species if you're not watching everyone die off one by one."

"Well, thanks for bringing the mood down, Bee," Sage snarked. He turned a bright smile on me. "So, kids, huh?"

Understanding that it would be best to follow the change of topic, I smiled genuinely and bobbed my head. "Yeah. Two. Now that I've wrapped my head around the concept, I'm excited."

"I'll bet." There was something melancholy in Sage's green eyes and the set of his shoulders, and it took me a moment too long to understand that he was an omega and his brother had just reminded him that, without alphas, their species was dying off.

Awkward silence descended.

Damn it.

I cleared my throat. "Anyway, you're a jack of all trades, right? Any chance you're good at building stuff? Like…cribs?"

Sage brightened again and the tension from our conversation finally dispersed. As I admitted that I couldn't follow instructions or build furniture to save my life and he teased me, I got the feeling he and Ollie were going to get along like a house on fire. That would be especially good for Ollie, who I was beginning to suspect was going a bit stir crazy being housebound with only Lena for regular company.

"Anyway, I'd better get back to Ollie," I drew back from the conversation as it began to dwindle down. "Come up to the house tomorrow morning so I can introduce you."

The guys agreed and I left the cottage feeling a little more confident that we'd be able to protect our strange, fledgling pack from most threats.

That proved to be my biggest mistake.

The walk between the cottage and main farmhouse was about half a mile, separated by a copse of apple trees which provided additional privacy to both homes. In the darkness, it also provided additional cover from the moon's light and, with my guard down and mind distracted, I realized too late that I was walking into an ambush.

The strange shifters surged at me from their hiding places behind trees, their scents muted by the synthetic scent blockers Eric had told me existed for times of shifter warfare. Dressed as they had been when they came for Ollie, in dark fatigues and balaclavas, they blended with the shadows. Even with my alpha strength and the strange commanding voice I could wield, I was outnumbered.

Blind panic seized me as I thought about Ollie in the house unprotected and alone save for Sandy. The tether of the bond we shared told me he was still there, but his emotions were dim. He was asleep. Well, he had been until my terror woke him.

Through the bond, I tried desperately to urge him to run. To flee. To hide. I yowled and tried to shift, knowing I had a better chance in my wolf form than I did in my human one. But the men converged on me, distracting my thoughts and movements enough that I couldn't do it.

Through the bond, I felt Ollie's answering panic. He knew something was wrong. I couldn't even send reassurance because it would be a lie.

Run, I thought with urgency, hoping the command would translate into feeling. *Hide. I love you. I need you to be safe*.

He wouldn't hear the words, but if he could only grasp the emotion...

The butt of a shotgun caught the side of my head, pain blooming where it struck. The blow made my head snap back and sent me to my knees. Ollie's fear spiked.

Just as we could feel each other's extreme pleasure, it seemed we could share high-intensity pain, too.

Run, baby, I thought at him again.

He sent a wave of determination through the bond, even while his own anxiety twisted and churned inside me. I could tell the difference from my own, the feelings from the bond carrying a sense of otherness with them.

"Stay down!" a gruff voice demanded of me when I tried to push to my feet.

Even though I wanted to leap up and fight, I obeyed. If all I could do was stall them from going after Ollie, after my mate and unborn children, then that's what I was going to do.

"Fuck you," I spat, craning my head and wincing against the sharp pain building behind my temples. I squinted up into glowering dark eyes, the man's face otherwise hidden behind his woven mask. "You make me sick."

"Shut the fuck up and stay down," he snapped, aiming the barrel of his gun at my head.

I wisely opted to obey. I wouldn't be any use to Ollie if I was dead.

Inside me, Ollie's fear calmed slightly, and the sensation of him settling was coupled with a deafening roar from the direction of Eric's cottage. Two more followed directly on top of each other.

The dragons were on their way.

"Well," I smirked up at the guy holding the gun, "you've really done it now."

The men surrounding me burst into a flurry of activity. It sounded like they'd been expecting one dragon, but not multiple, just as we had suspected.

"Cuff him," the guy with the gun to my head barked at another bulky man nearby. "Get him to the van. Boss wants him alive."

That meant the chances of him shooting me in the head had just dropped substantially. If shit went completely pear-shaped, they might kill me out of necessity or spite, but for the time being I would live long enough to stall them some more.

Gravel bit into my chest and cheek as I was shoved down hard onto the ground, the second guy's knee digging into my spine as he wrestled my arms behind my back. The cold metal of the cuffs closed around my wrists and I tried not to panic. The dragons were coming. They would guard Ollie. It didn't matter what happened to me as long as my mate and pups were safe.

Finally restrained, the two men yanked me to my feet and shoved me off the path and into the copse of trees. They shoved me forward, marching me in the direction of the little dirt road that ran behind the farmstead. The sound of gunfire erupted behind me, followed by another roar.

My captors cried out and dove to the ground as the sky lit up in red and orange, and I felt the heat from the epic burst of flame behind us, even if I hadn't seen it.

Gun Guy rolled onto his back on the uneven ground just a touch ahead of me. I watched as his eyes widened in abject horror as he stared over my shoulder. "Mother fucker, that's bigger than the one in New York," he growled, then turned to his buddy. "We need to get the fuck out of here now."

"But the others…" the guy who had cuffed me protested.

"Are not our problem. Getting the alpha back to the boss is the priority."

I considered shifting, but with my arms behind my back, I could sense that would end badly for my wolf form. With my captors on the ground I could run, but they could shift and outrun me easily. Instead, all I could do was concentrate on the bond that tied me to my mate. To his emotions and to his physical location. As long as Ollie was safe, nothing else mattered.

Gun Guy and Handcuffs Guy scrambled to their feet as the dragon swept overhead, turning in a wide arc in the sky, his dark scales glinting under the light of the moon. He aimed for the trees again, bellowing out another roar that shook the ground and vibrated through my entire body.

"Grab him and get going now!" Gun Guy yelled. Handcuffs gripped the front of my shirt and yanked me roughly to follow.

We raced further from the farmhouse and the sounds of battle, and I felt the rubber band inside me tighten the farther I got from Ollie, and I felt his accompanying burst of panic. I tried to send reassurance but, as I was shoved into the back of a black panel van, intense pain that was not my own rippled through the bond, forcing me to double over.

"Ollie!" I cried out, terrified.

But of course there was no answer.

Then the sliding panel door was slammed shut, and I was plunged into darkness, our bond now a feedback loop of panic and terror unlike anything I'd experienced before.

Chapter Twenty-Three — Oliver

Eric was quick to act after I called him. He assured me that he and his brothers would take care of whatever had gone wrong with Beck, and then the distant sound of a dragon's roar rent the air. Strange how something so scary could be so comforting.

I tried to calm myself, for Beck's sake and for the babies. I wasn't about to do anything dumb like go running into the fray at over eight months pregnant, but I was worried and restless. And I needed to pee.

Even though I'd promised Eric that I would stay put, my bladder waited for no man. Hoisting myself from bed, I waddled into the bathroom, ignoring my body's twinges and complaints. The kids were oddly still despite my panic, and I wondered if they were sleeping.

It figured that the one night they finally synced their sleep schedules with mine would be the one when shit went down. My luck was awesome that way.

Having made it to the bathroom, I sat down to pee, my

back aching far too much for me to bother standing anymore. Gravity, and the kids' current position low down in my belly, forced nature to call in other ways, too, which I was grateful for. If my pack did manage to break into the house, at least I wouldn't soil myself in fear.

But reaching under myself to wipe once I was done led me to a new, wholly horrifying discovery. There was something different about the stretch of skin between my balls and my ass. It felt wrong. It felt like the skin was thinner and more sensitive to touch when I accidentally brushed it with my wrist, and it damn well hurt when I prodded at it with the tips of my fingers.

This was definitely the kind of thing I needed to talk to Eric about, but he was indisposed at that moment.

I trembled in fear and tried to focus on Beck through the bond. He was anxious but doing his best to send determination and reassurance my way. I needed to stay calm for him, I reminded myself. If I distracted him at the wrong moment, I would never forgive myself.

Swallowing back bile, I ran through the motions of tugging my pajama pants back up and washing my hands. Then I waddled from the bedroom and strained my hearing, listening to the house for any signs of infiltration. The house was silent, except for its usual creaks and groans.

Padding down the stairs, I gripped the timber balustrade and took each step one at a time. With my center of balance off, I had to be careful. At the bottom, I made my way to the little hallway which led to the powder room and the guest room. I tapped at the door of the latter lightly.

"Sandy?" I asked meekly and pushed the door open, tears welling in my eyes as another wave of fear and panic threatened to overwhelm me.

Sheets rustled and I flinched and squinted as the bedside lamp flickered to life with a click. "What's wrong?" With her neon pixie cut, Beck's older sister didn't look half as formidable as she sounded. "Ollie?"

"I...Beck..." I swallowed roughly and tried again. "I think my pack came. He's out there," I waved vaguely in the direction the bond was tugging me towards, "somewhere. He...he felt so panicked and I..."

I would not break down. I would not break down. I would not—I gasped as an intense cramp-like pain stole across my belly. It was unlike anything I'd felt before. I didn't want to think about what it meant.

"Ollie?" Sandy sat up straighter, throwing back her thin blankets and revealing the light pajama pants she wore beneath the covers. They were pink and covered in kittens. She ignored my babbling about my pack and Beck, her focus on my belly. "Is it—"

"No," I shook my head vehemently, clutching at the expanse of firm, distended skin. "Nope. It's too early."

"And it's twins," she offered gently, as though I'd forgotten. "Eric did say—"

"I know what he said!" Another cramp built slowly and traveled through my abdomen with increasing intensity, causing the muscle beneath my hand to tense up.

To be honest, we had all anticipated that I would go into labor before I even made it to eight months. Or maybe Eric was right about our shifter sides being built for carrying multiples. Either way, the intense cramping could only be one thing, not that I wanted to admit it.

I hissed through my teeth, "Fuck. Fuck fuck fuckity fuck."

"Come lie down," Sandy urged me, patting the space beside her. "Stressing yourself isn't going to help right now."

I wanted to roll my eyes and say something sarcastic like 'Gee, why didn't I think of calming down?' but I bit my tongue and ambled into the room, rubbing soothing circles over my belly as I went. It wasn't until I was reclined against a mountain of pillows that I realized I hadn't been paying attention to the bond or to Beck's proximity through it.

My heart leapt into my throat when I realized he was further away than I had expected and pulling even further still. Pressing my fingers into my breastbone, I gasped.

"What?" Sandy demanded. "Is it the babies?"

I shook my head, terror icing up my insides. "Beck…" It was hard not to break down, but if he'd been taken, I couldn't let my emotions get the better of me. Swallowing roughly, I looked back up at Sandy and met her gaze head on. "I think…I think they've taken him."

I gritted my teeth against another contraction as she got up and paced the room. There was no fucking way I was going to give birth without my mate at my side. No way. I refused.

But there would only be one surefire way to track him down and rescue him quickly, too.

Sandy was thinking out loud, explaining what she thought the best course of action should be, but I already knew what I needed to do.

I pulled my phone from my pocket and dialed Eric, praying that he would pick up. With all the dragon roaring I could still hear, I wasn't sure he'd be in human form. But, as the town's only doctor, I assumed he would try to be on call for anyone caught up in the attack.

He sounded tense when he answered. "Ollie?"

"They've taken Beck," I tried not to cry. "I can feel it through the bond."

Over the line, he sighed and waited a beat before admitting, "I know." He hesitated again then added, "Brandt's gone after the van. He'll get him back, Ollie, I promise."

With the distance between us increasing quickly, I could feel Beck's absence like a physical ache. "I need him back now, Eric." Rubbing my belly through the onset of another contraction, I extrapolated, "I think I'm in labor."

There was a sharp inhale and then clatter on the other end of the line. "I'll be there in five minutes."

I don't want you, I wanted to scream, *I want my alpha.*

But the line went dead before I could protest.

* * *

"Get on the bed," Eric folded his arms across his broad chest and raised his eyebrow at me. "Now, Ollie."

Sandy had let him inside the house only a few minutes earlier and the pair of them had ushered me back into her downstairs bedroom, away from the front door through which I'd wanted to leave to chase after my mate.

"The contractions aren't even regular yet," I argued, rolling my shoulders back as I raised my chin defiantly. I probably would have appeared far more intimidating if I wasn't wearing my soft cotton pajama pants emblazoned with rainbows and a loose graphic t-shirt which read 'Jingle My Bells'. Beck had bought the shirt as a gag gift and, even though it wasn't even close to Christmas yet, I wore it every single night (when it wasn't being washed). Then, to top all of that off, a searing pain between my legs had me crying out, my knees buckling from the unexpected agony.

Eric caught me before I hit the ground. "Contraction?" he asked.

"N-no," I groaned, unable to fully describe the sensation which I was still feeling. "It…it feels like…like I'm shifting? You know how, like, our bodies rearrange our organs and stuff when we shift and it kind of hurts? But not completely like that, either. It's like…like I'm being stretched and torn apart. It *aches* and *stabs* and…ugh. It's, um, near my ass."

"On the bed," he repeated his earlier command as he gingerly pulled me back to my feet, trying to be gentle while I continued to whimper as the movements amplified the pain. "Now."

This time, I complied.

Eric helped me out of my pajama pants and directed me to spread my legs once I was on my back. I was in too much pain to be concerned about modesty. Besides, he'd been monitoring my pregnancy from the beginning: there wasn't much of me he hadn't already seen.

I closed my eyes and focused on my breathing, yelping when one of his gloved fingers ran over my taint. As I had discovered earlier, it was sensitive to touch and not in a pleasant way.

"Fascinating," he muttered.

"What's fascinating?" I asked, not entirely sure I wanted to hear the answer.

I did not.

"If I'm not mistaken, and my most recent research leads me to believe that I'm not, your body is preparing for delivery by developing —or, rather, opening— your birth canal."

"My *what?!*" I pushed myself up on my elbows to glower at him over the quivering mass that was my belly. "Did you just say *birth canal*?"

He nodded, unfazed by my incredulous tone. "As you know, most records of omega labors have been lost to time, so the information I've found has mostly been anecdotal and vague at best, but stories I have come across all alluded to the body 'creating the passage' for the birth when the time comes. I wish I had my ultrasound equipment. I'd love to document this properly."

"Of course you do," I grizzled. "Please tell me this...*passage*... goes away again after the birth."

He shrugged. "I think so? Like I said, the information is vague at best. Your guess is as good as mine as to what will happen afterwards. But if the birth canal only appears when you're close to birthing, then I think it's safe to assume that your body will conceal it again when all is said and done." He cocked his head. "It's interesting that you likened the pain to shifting. Perhaps as an omega, part of the process is to shift into a different creature..." Looking back at me, Eric smirked. "You have to admit, it sounds better than the alternative."

"True..."

To be honest, I had spent a lot of time doing research of my own. Working out the science behind my ability to conceive was actually extremely interesting. Using Eric's aforementioned ultrasound equipment, we had been able to study and document the connections that allowed for sperm to travel to my womb, even though trans-anal ultrasounds are not the most pleasant thing I have ever experienced in the name of science. But it made sense that being able to shift my physical form would allow for an easier birth than, say, trying to get the kids out through the same path that put them inside me in the first place.

"So," I eventually asked, resigned to the changes my body

was going through, "does it look...okay?"

Eric snorted. "With noting to compare it to, sure."

"That does *not* help me."

"I mean, the skin is super thin," he ignored my renewed yelping as he ran his finger over the tender spot again, "and kind of translucent? It's absolutely fascinating, Ollie. I wish you could see this. Oh!" He stood and held out his palm. "Pass me your phone."

"You are *not* taking photos of any of this," I insisted, cuddling my phone to my chest. "Gross."

"It's for science," he insisted. "Nobody will know that it's your—"

"Oh, sure, because there are how many other pregnant omegas running around out—*owwww!*" Another contraction stole my breath and had me lurching forward, curling over my belly. "Mother fucker, that *hurt*."

Eric scrunched his nose. "I don't envy you." He held his hand out again. "Now. Phone, please? I'd rather take the photos on yours than on mine so you can see them and decide which ones to send to me."

Perhaps it was the conditioning of the time spent as his employee, or perhaps he had appealed to my scientist brain, because I handed the device over to him. Within moments, he opened the camera app with a swipe of his thumb and bent between my spread thighs again. I closed my eyes and prayed for the humiliation to end.

Meanwhile, I'd been doing my best to keep tabs on Beck through the bond, even while I freaked out about going into labor too early for my liking. The tether inside me felt stretched so thin, I was worried it might snap or blink out of existence, but he was still out there. Still alive. Still mine.

He was too far away to feel his emotions, though. Or perhaps he was doing his best to keep calm, not wanting to distress me any more than I already was. I was almost certain that he'd felt the pain of my contractions when they had started, and I hoped he wasn't driving himself crazy with worry for me, either.

The fact that he was still alive gave me hope. If my old pack had wanted to kill him, they wouldn't have taken him away to do it. They wanted him alive for whatever their plans were.

I'd wanted to be the one leading the charge to rescue him. I'd wanted to guide Eric and his brothers to the assholes who had taken him from me and let them rain down a world of fire and pain. I'd wanted to be the hero, to prove that omegas could be brave and strong and useful. It sucked that I couldn't do any of those things.

But it wasn't my fault and I knew it. Just because I wasn't going to be flying in with a dragon army to save the day didn't mean that I wasn't brave or strong. Hell, I was about to give birth without my mate by my side: *that* took bravery and strength, I was certain of it. Additionally, I would keep our babies safe until my alpha was returned to me. That meant something, too.

My thoughts were interrupted by Eric asking, "Do you think you're up to walking around for a little while? It might help speed this up. Gravity and all that."

I didn't want to speed the process up. In fact, if I could have crossed my legs and held my children inside me for as long as it took for Eric's siblings to bring Beck back to me, I would have. However, the biologist inside me knew better than to say such a thing out loud.

I sighed and nodded. "Sure. Help me up."

* * *

The pain of having one's body literally tear itself a new orifice was not something I wanted to repeat ever again. I was glad that Eric was with me, because the blood and the wholly bizarre feeling of suddenly being aware of an entirely new body part almost sent me into a panic attack, despite having been forewarned.

"It's time now, right?" I panted and basically begged from my reclaimed spot on the bed. "Please tell me this will be over fast."

It had been hours since Eric had come over. Hours since Beck had been abducted. Hours since the contractions had started. Hours since life as I'd come to enjoy it had all gone to shit.

Beck was still too far away to feel his emotions, but I took solace in the fact that he probably couldn't feel mine, either. Just knowing he was alive helped keep my head in the game, though I did consciously check the bond every few minutes, hoping that he would start moving in my direction again. If I could only feel him getting closer to home, I would be happy.

Well, as happy as I could be with the onset of active labor.

"You know as well as I do that labor can take hours and hours, Ollie." Eric still sounded chipper and patient, even though he had been listening to me whine, cry, and complain for hours on end. "And you don't seem anywhere near dilated enough yet."

I flopped back onto the pillows with a huff and grit my teeth against another contraction.

If Eric's brothers did manage to save my alpha? He was never *ever* sticking his dick inside me again.

I liked that thought so much I said it out loud. Eric chuckled. I wasn't aiming to amuse him. I growled.

"And this is why I have no intention of finding an alpha of my own," my not at all helpful doctor friend responded with a blasé shrug. His blonde hair was tied back from his face, but I noticed that it was beginning to look a little frazzled. Wisps of it escaped and flew about his head in a 'crazed genius' sort of way. "I firmly believe more exist and that there's a fated or, at least, compatible mates component to the awakening of their alpha designations…but I would rather stay on this side of the research." He grimaced. "Sorry."

"Well it wasn't like I —*Jesus Christ!*— planned this." I curled forward over my tightened belly as another contraction built and seized me. I tried to modulate my breathing as I rode it out, but the pain was starting to get to me. Tears slid down my cheeks and I brushed at them angrily as the tension subsided. "Fucking fuck."

"You're doing well, Ollie. You can do this."

"Oh, shut the fuck up."

There had been a time when I wouldn't have imagined it possible that I could be so disrespectful to the man who was my boss…but that was before he became my delivery nurse or OBGYN or whatever term he wanted to use.

He chuckled again and suggested, "How about taking another walk around the room?"

Groaning, I nodded. It was better than languishing in bed, I supposed.

* * *

"Eric?"

"Hmm?"

More hours had passed and Eric had decided that we should both try and rest. I'd agreed, if only because I needed the only medical professional available to me to have enough energy to deliver my babies safely.

"I…" I grunted and panted through another contraction. They were coming harder and faster than before, and I was almost delirious with pain. "I need to push."

My waters had broken earlier, but even then Eric had said I wasn't dilated enough. Now, my body was demanding that I was ready, fuck whatever Eric said.

My boss-turned-friend sat up quickly from the armchair he'd been lazing in and hurried over to the bed. I whined and cried out as he checked me out, the intrusion on my new (hopefully temporary) body part painful beyond words.

"Yeah," he breathed, sounding awed, "you're good to go, Ollie. On your next contraction, I want you to bear down." He glanced back up at me over the swell of my belly. "Are you sure you don't want Sandy in here?"

I shook my head and tried not to cry. The only other person I would tolerate sharing this moment with was still missing. Checking the bond again, I cried out in earnest, realizing that the connection had dimmed out entirely.

"What's wrong?" Eric asked me urgently. "Was that a contraction? It didn't look like one."

Shaking my head, I allowed the tears to stream down my cheeks. "No," I sobbed. "No. I checked the bond. Beck's gone."

I could feel the mounting wave of pain and tension as another contraction built and instead of fighting the pain, I fed off it. I lurched forward and pushed, screaming as I did. But I wasn't screaming because of the pain. I was screaming out my fear and panic, and the deep sense of loss and anger in my chest.

Beck was gone and there wasn't a God damned thing I could do about it.

Chapter Twenty-Four — Beckett

I bounced around in the back of the van for countless hours. Shrouded in darkness, I couldn't tell you which direction we traveled, nor for how long. It seemed to me that the van was taking backroads and country trails with how turbulent the drive felt. The metal floor beneath me felt gritty and smelled of rust and dirt, with the lingering, unpleasant scent of manure.

There weren't any windows, nor was there a screen or slide away partition between the rear of the van and the front cabin. It was dark and claustrophobic and I considered trying to throw myself against the side panel to dislodge the door, but with the bumps and twists and turns in the road, I didn't think I'd get enough force behind my run up.

I stayed as calm as I could, trying to focus on Ollie and whatever the fuck was happening back at the farmhouse, but the further we drove, the harder it was to feel him. I could sense the rough direction of his location, but everything else was impossible.

Every so often, a roar would sound overhead, and I wondered if Eric or one of his brothers was tracking the van, trying to scare the driver into stopping. I knew they wouldn't spray it with fire, not with me in the back, and they probably didn't want to risk rolling it for the same reason.

I strained my hearing, hoping to catch any piece of information I could from the guys in the front of the van, but there was nothing to be heard.

Debating whether I should try to sleep to conserve my strength, or stay awake in case we stopped suddenly and there was a chance I could get the drop on my captors, I sighed. There were pros and cons to both options, but with my adrenaline finally flagging, I decided rest would be the better choice. I had to trust that the dragon following us would have my back if we did stop suddenly.

I managed to sleep, however fitfully. I don't know how long I was out for, but I woke to the van coming to a stop. Climbing to my feet, I eyed the side panel door and readied myself to rush whoever opened it.

But the door stayed shut.

Dimly, I could hear sounds that gave clues to where we were. The sound of something on the side of the van being unscrewed? Metal clanking? A rushing liquid sound?

Then it hit me: they were refueling the van. I wondered where my dragon tracker was, assuming there had ever been one to start with. Had he tired out? Lost sight of the van? Was he perched somewhere just waiting to make his move? I hadn't felt quite so powerless and desperate for answers since I was a kid stuck in the foster system.

There was some more murmured talking and then the sound of both of the front doors opening and shutting. The engine rumbled back to life and then we were moving again.

Whatever hope I'd carried inside me began to wither and fade, but I refused to give in to the negative thoughts that encroached on my brain.

I could feel that Ollie was still out there somewhere. As long as he was alive and well, I would do everything in my power to get back to him.

So, despite it going against every fiber in my being, I settled back down on the floor of the van and willed myself to rest some more.

* * *

The next time we stopped, the door to the van slid open and I was immediately blinded by one hundred thousand lumens. The sunlight was ridiculously bright after being confined to a dark space for so long that I hissed and squinted, unable to make out a thing.

My captors had obviously been banking on this because they grabbed me and yanked me from the van before my eyes could adjust to the searing sunlight. The sun felt scorching on my skin and I wondered where we were.

I was jostled forwards, stumbling over my own feet and craggy ground, trying to use the rest of my senses while my vision sorted itself out. We walked for five, maybe ten minutes before we came to what I could only describe as a mansion. The place was huge and looming, blocking out the sun from where we stood in front of it. Three visible levels, too many windows to count at first glance, and a giant garage to the side.

It looked like some sort of oversized Tuscan villa, all

terracotta shades and stucco siding. The sort of place Hollywood producers present as home compounds for drug lord characters. Up close, I could understand why. It was massive, pristine, and intimidating as fuck.

Then the front door swung open and an older beta stepped out onto the front porch, flanked by two buff dudes in suits carrying assault rifles.

Yeah, Hollywood drug lord was pretty much exactly where my brain went.

The beta between the armed goons was of average height. He was lean, with a long face that seemed to have a permanently pinched expression. He had short, tightly curled, ashy-brown hair with flecks of gray that caught the sunlight, and dark eyes that sat just a tiny bit too close together on his face. Unlike his goons, he was dressed down in a pair of navy business pants, a white business shirt and an ugly as sin argyle sweater.

The weather was too fucking hot to justify that sweater.

If his whole demeanor didn't scream 'I'm the villain, hear me whine', the off-seasonal attempt to appear unassuming and harmless did it.

"Mr. Morstein, sir," Shotgun said, shoving me closer towards the house, "we got the alpha."

"And the dragon?" Morstein asked, tilting his chin so he could look down his large nose at my captors. I couldn't scent his species from where I stood, but I was willing to bet the guy was a weasel or a snake. My hackles rose at just the sound of his smarmy voice.

"Lost it somewhere in Ohio," Handcuffs shrugged at my other side, trying to play off how proud of himself he was for doing so.

My spirits fell as the likelihood of being rescued slipped away. Also, "Ohio?" I asked before I could stop myself. My voice came out gravelly. My mouth and throat were dry from spending hours without water and without fresh air, and the heat of the sun blazing over us wasn't helping. We were further away from home than I'd thought we would be.

Shotgun raised his weapon and clocked me in the back of the head with its butt. "Nobody gave you permission to speak."

"Hey now," Morstein interrupted, *tsk*ing at Shotgun. "The alpha is our guest, Ramsay. Is that any way to treat a guest?" He turned his beady, slimy gaze on me. "I'm terribly sorry for that, Mr. Smith. Ramsay gets a little trigger happy sometimes." His words oozed falsities just like any other stereotypical villain's might. I was going to have to rethink just how ridiculous Hollywood made bad guys seem.

"How's about you uncuff me if I'm such a valued guest," I suggested, only for Morstein to laugh and shake his head.

"I might not want to see you harmed right now, Mr. Smith, but I'm not an idiot."

"You kidnapped a bonded alpha from his pack and mate," I argued with him, my tone going dark with the promise of retribution. "I'd say you are much dumber than you look."

"Such a pity," Morstein sneered and straightened his spine. "Oliver's pack was looking forward to meeting you, but I can't in good conscience let someone with manners as poor as yours meet anyone right now." He looked to his goons. "Get him out of here. The cellar has been prepared for his arrival."

With the confirmation that Ollie's pack were involved, I couldn't prevent myself from mouthing off. "Aww, you didn't have to move all your overpriced alcohol for little old me."

He ignored my admittedly lame jibe and waved for Shotgun

and Handcuffs to take me away. "Maybe some time down there will make you rethink your options, Mr. Smith. I'd like for us to come to an arrangement. We could be great together. Think of the power we could wield."

Is this guy getting all his lines from Hollywood? It's like Villainy 101 up in here.

I scoffed, barely refraining from telling him to find some original material, and turned to Shotgun. "Just take me to my cell."

The goons took me around the rear of the house and opened a timber door set into the ground which led to a darkened space filled with sharply descending stairs. Handcuffs stepped in first and led the way, while Shotgun stayed true to his name and held the barrel of his weapon to my back as I followed Handcuffs down. This was clearly not their first rodeo.

The cellar, it turned out, was not actually a wine cellar. I'm sure the house probably had a real cellar somewhere else beneath its sprawling floor plan, but this space was dank, dark, and contained cells befitting a third world prison. I was shoved roughly into one, landing onto the dirt floor with a thud, and locked inside. The clanging of the metal bars echoed in my ears, but Shotgun took obvious pleasure in snapping the padlock shut.

"How do you expect me to go to the bathroom?" I demanded, climbing back to my feet so I could turn my back on them and wiggle my still-cuffed hands.

"There's a bucket, your highness," Shotgun sneered.

"I can't take my pants off if I'm cuffed," I reminded him in the same annoying tone.

For a moment, I thought they were going to laugh and tell me to just shit in my pants, but Handcuffs sighed. "If we don't uncuff him, we'll be the ones havin' to clean him up, and I ain't doin' that."

"And if he shifts?"

"He's a wolf, ain't he? He's not gettin' through the bars, and he can't dig his way out."

I glanced over my shoulder to watch Shotgun consider the logic behind Handcuffs's assessment. Eventually, he rolled his eyes and exhaled with irritation. "Fine. Whatever. But if uncuffing him leads to his escape, I'm makin' sure the boss knows you're responsible."

"He ain't gettin' out," Handcuffs reiterated, speaking to Shotgun as though the other man was worrying over nothing. Then he barked, "Get your ass over here if you wanna be uncuffed."

I backed up to the bars and felt Handcuffs grasp the metal around my wrist and then fiddle with the lock. It gave way with a tiny *click* and he pulled the loosened cuffs away. My wrists were chafed and my shoulders protested as I brought my arms back to their natural position at my sides.

"You try any funny business at all, and I'm puttin' a bullet in you," Shotgun warned as they backed away from my cell.

"And here I was going to try my latest stand-up act out on you," I sassed back.

Handcuffs snorted, then smoothed out his expression when Shotgun growled at him.

"You guard him," Shotgun demanded. "I've got other shit to take care of."

"I'll sit on top of the door," Handcuffs responded, following his partner back in the direction we'd come from. Their voices faded as they started up the stairs. "This place gives me the creeps."

I didn't hear Shotgun's reply because the door at the top of the stairs slammed and I was once again plunged into darkness.

At least I was able to use my bucket in peace.

* * *

After a while spent pacing back and forth, I opted to shift into my wolf form, reasoning that I had a better chance of making a break for it as a wolf than I did as a man. I plotted and schemed, considering what limited assets I had at my disposal.

By the time they came for me again, I would have a rudimentary plan in place. It wasn't likely to succeed, but I wasn't going to go down without a fight.

I whined as I considered my mate and the surge of pain and terror I'd felt all those hours earlier. Even though we couldn't communicate telepathically or at all through the bond any more, my gut told me that I needed to get back to him. Whatever had happened, he needed me.

I would try every trick up my sleeves to get back to him.

More time passed. I had no way of knowing how long, but Morstein eventually arrived, flanked by his two goons. Sunlight spilled down the previously darkened staircase, providing enough light for me to take his appearance in properly. With a hint of amusement, I noticed that he'd shed the sweater. I also noted that his goons still carried their assault rifles. The risk I was about to take was a big one, but I had no alternative.

"Shift back," my captor instructed lazily. "Don't think for a second I'll be opening this gate until you're cuffed again."

Having been banking on such a demand, I huffed as dramatically as my wolf form would allow and turned away, my body morphing back into my human form. I reached for my clothes and tugged them back on slowly.

Behind me, I heard the metallic sounds of the padlock unclicking and sliding out from the latch of the gate. In no rush to face them, I continued to re-dress myself.

Morstein's impatience won out. He made a sound of frustration and I heard the cell's gate swing open as footsteps moved my way.

Bingo.

Everything happened in rapid succession from there. I grabbed my toilet bucket and spun around, flinging the contents over Morstein who shrieked and shielded his face, diving aside and clearing a path to the gate. His goons also flinched and I threw the bucket at one while I lunged for the open gate, shifting back into wolf form and tearing my clothes as I went.

The sound of gunfire erupted behind me, but I didn't turn back or allow it to distract me. Adrenaline coursed through my veins and I freed myself from the remnants of my shirt, bolting for the stairs. Morstein was yelling but the sound of bullets bursting out from those rifles echoed around the cement walls, drowning him out.

I could feel the deadly projectiles whizzing past me, pinging off metal, breaking unseen objects, ricocheting off walls. Pumping my legs harder, I bowed my head and ran as fast as I could through the space, yelping as searing pain tore through my rear flank. I'd been hit, but the adrenaline kept me going.

I raced up the stairs and burst through the thankfully open door at the top, not stopping to look at my surroundings. In the distance, I could see a tree line. I knew my pursuers could also shift, and that they could track me through scent, but I didn't care. I had high hopes that I could find a stream or a river: a body of water to dive into and end the scent trail.

I raced in a zig-zag pattern, my muscles burning, my rear left leg twanging with pain. My heart thudded within my furry chest, and it was only the thought of making it back to my mate that forced me to keep up the pace.

The trees inched closer too slowly for my liking.

As an alpha, I had the gift of enhanced speed on my side, but with how dehydrated I was, and my injury, it wouldn't be long before I slowed down.

Overhead, there was a *whoosh* of giant wings and an unmistakable roar.

Dragon, my brain supplied, relief making my legs wobble. *Ally*.

Still I ran.

I ran, regardless of the flush of heat that scorched the earth behind me. I ran, despite the yelps and renewed gunfire. I ran, ignoring the revving of engines and human voices yelling indistinguishable words in rage.

I ran and I ran and I ran.

The trees called to me, their height growing with every step forward I took. I panted and forged on against the pain and encroaching dizziness in my head until the line of forestry towered above me like an oasis in a desert. I wanted to howl my victory.

The sound of an engine, rumbling and aggressive, seemed to come out of nowhere.

Despite my focus, I turned my head slightly and caught the movement of a large, black truck barreling in from my left side. It was close. Too close. The trees were only a couple of hundred yards away, but I started to doubt that I would make it.

I bowed my head again and raced forward, new determination flooding me.

The trees got closer still, their shade cooling my overheated fur.

I was going to make it! I was going to—

Yelping, I rolled as the vehicle clipped my injured flank, sending me rolling across grass and gravel. My head spun and I knew before I stopped moving that my leg was broken.

This time, I did howl. It was a mournful sound, bursting forth from my chest and up out of my throat. It rattled my own teeth and I flattened my ears atop my head.

I'd been so close.

I'd failed.

I'd failed my mate.

All that was left of my adrenaline at that point was tremors. My vision darkened from the pain in my leg. Defeat set in.

The vehicle stopped and booted feet raced towards me.

I let them come, not even bothering to growl.

I'd failed my mate.

This time when darkness came for me, I let it, barely registering the beating of large wings or the roar of a dragon drawing near.

* * *

I found myself enclosed in darkness again the next time I woke up, but it was familiar in a way that I was not expecting. The walls and floor of my space were warm, smooth, and curved enough that I was cradled along the whole length of my body. Slivers of light came in through gaps in the ceiling of this space and I shifted back into human form with a cry of pain.

That's right, I thought too late, *broken leg.*

It was a broken leg which had also been shot, but who was counting?

At least I knew I was safe. There was no way to mistake the feeling of being carried by a dragon, and I could only assume that the dragon in question was Eric or one of his brothers and not a rogue dragon working with Ollie's pack.

My stomach swooped as we descended and, minutes later, the large claws cupping me like I'd once carried mice to release them into the crappy half-dead garden beds outside my foster home parted and I was set carefully on the ground.

The dragon, who was bigger and darker than I recalled Eric being, waited patiently until I was as balanced as I could be on my uninjured leg before he shifted back into his own form. Brandt. Relief swept over me all over again and I lunged, hugging the man who had been a stranger when I'd met him hours (or was that days?) earlier. It didn't matter that we were both naked, or that I was filthy and stank from my ordeal.

"Thank you," I said, my voice reedy and weak. "You saved me. I don't know how and honestly? I don't even care. You saved me. I owe you. Whatever you need, whenever you need it, I've got your back."

Brandt chuckled and he patted my back. "Eric would have my hide if I allowed anything to happen to you. Aside from your value as the only known alpha, you're *his* Alpha. You mean a great deal to him."

"Oh," I pulled away, scrunching my nose, "No. No, we're not like that."

Brandt's chuckle became a deep laugh. "I meant his pack Alpha, you twit. I'm well aware that you're bonded to a different omega." His expression shuttered. "Speaking of, we need to get your injuries mended and then get back in the sky."

My elation and relief at being rescued faded. Guilt immediately seized me. *Ollie.* I hadn't asked about him. I hadn't stopped to think if he was okay.

"He's fine," Brandt assured me, wrapping his arm around my waist and assisting me down the empty street. We'd landed in the parking lot of what once must have been a box store of some kind, but was now abandoned and empty, its windows and doors boarded over, its walls graffitied. The street it sat on was just as eerily quiet. "I made a stop an hour ago to call Eric, but you were still out cold."

"Where are we?"

"Not far from home," he assured me. "You need a hospital. It's only a ten minute flight back from here." After leading me to a nearby bench, Brandt cocked his head and listened intently to something, then instructed, "Wait here. I'm getting us some clothes."

Covering my junk and hoping no-one else would stumble across me, I did as told. Brandt returned ten minutes later, wearing sweatpants that were too small for him and a tight black t-shirt, carrying a bundle of fabric.

"God bless the inventor of clotheslines," he declared, handing me a huge pair of jeans and a flannel shirt which had seen better days. I put them on without a fuss.

"The hospital is a few streets away," he told me as he helped me back onto my feet. "It'll be easier if I carry you."

Exhausted to my marrow, I agreed. We probably looked

ridiculous to the few cars that passed us on our trek, but I didn't care. I wouldn't have been able to walk the distance, and the buildings in the middle of the town were too clustered together for Brandt to shift and fly me to the hospital.

The hospital itself was only small. I'd been anticipating a giant, modern building with many windows and floors, but it was only three stories high, constructed from red brick, with a peeling sign declaring its purpose over the double doors at the front of its façade.

Brandt carried me inside and over to the triage desk, where a wide-eyed nurse popped a bright pink bubble of gum and then gaped up at us. I could only imagine how we looked.

"My friend was shot in the leg and then hit by a car," Brandt said, his accent smooth and his tone so charming, I almost did a double take of my own. "Can you help him? Also, can you do it fast? His, uh, partner is currently in labor."

I'd been smiling at the nurse sadly, trying to appear as pitiful as possible while I nodded along with Brandt's explanation. It took a few moments longer than it should have for my drained brain to catch up with what he'd said. But when it registered, I jolted in his hold and stared at his strong jaw in shock while my heart beat frantically.

"Ollie's *what?!*"

Chapter Twenty-Five – Oliver

I sobbed and begged and cried my way through the first hour or so of active labor. It was all a blur of pain on pain with extra pain…and without any baby to show for it. I had two of the little fuckers inside me, but neither one had made an appearance.

When Eric's phone rang, he looked up at me from between my legs and said, "That's probably Brandt."

"Answer it!" I screamed at him, desperate for any news about my mate. Neither of my kids seemed interested in making their appearance yet anyway, as though they were hanging in there for their father to return first. That was as good a theory as any to my pain addled brain.

Ditching his nitrile gloves, Eric stood up with a grimace and rubbed his back with one hand, pulling his phone from his pocket with the other. "Hello?" I watched as he seemed to slump with relief as he listened to whoever was on the other end. "Oh, thank God. Where are you now?" His blonde brows pinched and he glanced at his watch. "So…what? An hour away?" He paused for more talking and I watched his expression carefully, but he kept it blank...until he cast a quick, concerned glance at me. "Oliver's in active labor, Bran. Try to hurry."

Eric ended the call there, then his face broke into a small, but genuine smile. "Beck's alive," he said and I immediately reached for the bond, still finding it blank. My panic must have shown on my face because Eric rushed to explain, "but he's unconscious. They're about halfway here. Brandt stopped to find a payphone once he'd put some distance between him and Beck's abductors." Pulling on a new set of gloves, he continued, "It sounds like Beck's been through a lot tonight. Brandt's taking him for medical treatment before he brings him here. It's completely necessary, but thankfully his injuries don't sound life threatening. You heard me say they need to get here as fast as possible."

Tears slid down my cheeks and I nodded, sobbing my way through another contraction and half-heartedly pushing when my body demanded it. "He's coming home," I cried, relief washing over me like a tidal wave. "He's coming home."

Eric nodded. "He is, and he's going to be okay. Brandt's a doctor, and I trust his judgment. So," he settled back in between my spread legs, "let's make sure he comes home to safely delivered babies, huh?"

I groaned but nodded again, my determination renewed.

My mate was coming home.

* * *

"That's it," Eric urged excitedly what felt like a lifetime later, "the first one's crowning. I can see hair."

"It *burns*," I cried, once again bent forward over my distended, seizing belly. "Oh my God, it burns! I'm being torn in two!"

Is it always like this? I wondered. *Or is it only because I'm an omega? How do women do this over and over again? How did my ancestors?*

"You're doing so well," Eric assured me. "Bear down as hard as you can on the next contraction, okay?"

What the hell did he think I'd been doing?

"I'm fucking *trying to*," I hissed back.

"I know."

"Don't patronize me….*aaargh*!"

"Keep pushing, keep pushing, keep pushing!"

I wanted to tell him that him chanting it on repeat wasn't going to help me push any harder, but the door burst open just as the contraction waned and the pressure in my new (hopefully temporary) orifice gave way a fraction.

"Holy shit," Beck's voice was filled with equal parts horror and awe. "Is that—"

"Head's out," Eric declared triumphantly. I attempted to lean forward to catch a glance and immediately regretted all my life choices.

Then it hit me that I had heard Beck's voice and, having been so distracted by the pain of giving birth, hadn't noticed him through the bond. My eyes shifted from the vernix covered scrunched up alien face emerging from between my legs and up to my lover's.

I burst into tears and made grabby hands towards him, unable to speak.

Beck looked like shit and I gasped as he hobbled towards me on crutches, his left leg encased in a plaster cast. My pack had done that to him. Guilt ate at me and I cried harder, only for him to flop down on the mattress on my left, landing on his seemingly uninjured right hip. He gathered me into his strong arms, holding my head to his broad chest, and he kissed the top of my head with reverence.

"Ollie…" his voice cracked. "Ollie…we're having a baby."

"Babies," Eric corrected him.

"Babies," he acknowledged, sounding overwhelmed but happier than a man who looked as beaten and exhausted as him had any right to sound. "What you're going through…I can't imagine. But I'm here. I'm here, and I'm not going anywhere. Wild shifters *literally* couldn't keep me away."

"Too soon," I hissed. "At least…*argh*…give it twenty-four hours before you start joking about being abducted."

Another contraction built and crested and I pushed, not even bothering to snap at Eric when he told me to 'push softly' because the shoulders were the widest part and the likeliest to cause tearing.

How the fuck was I supposed to push *softly*?

Nevertheless, with Beck's arm around my shoulders and his warmth lending me strength, I tried.

I closed my eyes and screamed as the burning agony returned. Bearing down with as much restraint as I could muster, I followed Eric's guidance. Finally, I released a guttural sound from the back of my throat which wasn't human as, with a great *whoosh*, the pressure between my legs suddenly vanished.

"Oh my God," Beck's voice wobbled moments before the warbling cry of a newborn rent the air.

Exhausted and plastered with sweat, I peered over my stomach to watch as Eric adjusted his hold on a bloodied, vernix covered baby.

"Congratulations," he smiled up at me and Beck, "meet your firstborn daughter."

My heart somehow hammered and seized all at once. "Daughter…" I echoed in awe.

"Uh huh. Daughter," he repeated, looking her over. "We'll measure and weigh her after baby two joins us. Beck," he said pointedly, "will you hold her? Or can I call Sandy in here?"

"I've got her," Beck's voice was thick with emotion and the overwhelming feelings flowing through the bond were hard to distinguish from my own. Joy, terror, excitement, love…we were mirrors of each other.

Eric gestured at Beck. "Take off your shirt. Skin-to-skin bonding is incredibly important right now."

Beck hurried to comply and then sat back against the headboard of the bed, gingerly accepting the tiny, crying bundle of flailing limbs. He held her close to his chest, his large arm warming the side of her body not pressed against his body, and he murmured a soft greeting. "Hey, sweetheart. I've been waiting for you."

Tears streamed down my face unchecked. I leaned over to meet our baby girl, but another contraction built and I groaned, startling Eric back into action.

"Okay," he repositioned himself, "bring on round two."

"That's easy for you to say," I grumbled, but seeing the result of my efforts cradled so lovingly in her father's arms gave me the boost of energy I needed in order to deliver her twin.

The second round of pushing was much faster than the first. Within ten minutes, baby number two was squalling right next to his sister. I barely noticed as Eric guided me through delivering the afterbirth, too focused on my children.

A daughter and a son.

Beck held them both carefully on his furry chest, large palms shielding their seemingly too-small backs from any potential breeze. He growled low in his throat when Eric explained that he had to cut the cords and clean our children up a bit, and a surge of love hit me so hard that I was glad I was already lying down.

My mate. My pups. My pack.

Mine. Mine. Mine.

"She looks like you," I told Beck softly, feeling my eyes droop despite how badly I wanted to stay awake and spend time with my babies.

"Mmm," he agreed, "but he looks like you." He jerked his chin towards the baby in Eric's arms.

I yawned. "They need names."

"That can wait," Beck assured me. "You need sleep."

He wasn't wrong. I'd been laboring for so long that I'd lost track of what day it was.

"I need to feed them." I looked down at my swollen pecs, glad that biology had provided a way to nourish the children I'd birthed. We'd switch them to formula within a few months, but my inner wolf begged to be able to feed and bond with my babies in a primal way.

For the first time in my entire life, I was proud of my secondary gender. Not that I bought into any of that misogynistic crap about people who were able to breastfeed vs people who couldn't, mind you. But I felt good about who I was. There was no shame in that, either.

Beck passed me our daughter and, after some readjustments and some trial and error, she latched on to my nipple and drank with greedy, snuffling sounds. My heart overflowed all over again.

"Uh, gentlemen?" Eric said cautiously, which made both my and Beck's heads snap to attention. The doctor was looking intently at our son's right thigh. The baby had been carefully wiped clean of a lot of the mess from birth, but still looked to me as though a bath would do him good. "His birthmark…"

"Omega, beta…we don't care as long as he's healthy," Beck told him.

"Well, good. Because he's an alpha." Eric sounded mystified. "The first marked alpha born in hundreds of years." He finally looked up and at the baby on my chest.

She'd fallen asleep while nursing. We traded babies and I watched as he put her to his shoulder and burped her in sleep before setting her on the mattress to cut her cord and wipe her down as he had her brother.

Bringing the tiny boy to my other aching pec, I ran my index finger over the misshapen moon-mark on his thigh. It matched the mark on Beck's ass perfectly. Next to a crescent like my own, the pair made a perfect circle or, as we saw it, a full moon.

"Wow," I breathed, trying not to let the anxiety of what it might mean for the news of his existence to reach other shifter communities.

"Um…guys?" Eric squeaked. It was so uncharacteristic that I snorted before I looked up at him. He was looking down at our daughter's left arm with wide eyes, his shock almost palpable.

"What?" Beck demanded, already shuffling forward across the mattress, heedless of his bum leg.

Eric stalled him, holding out his palm. He swallowed and gestured down at the sleeping baby. "She's got the same mark."

He looked back at us. "She's an alpha. A female alpha."

I closed my eyes and tried to stay calm.

Somehow, I knew that our lives were only going to get crazier. But it was okay because Beck and I had each other. We had our unconventional pack in the form of the close-knit community of the town as a whole. And we had Eric, who looked like he was itching to return to his research at once.

"Well," I eventually said, yawning widely. "All the more reason to make sure we give her a kick-ass name."

And that was that.

Epilogue – Beckett

In the weeks following the twins' birth, our house felt like a revolving door had been installed for the townspeople. They came in small groups, everyone wanting to meet the new additions (whose designations as alphas we were keeping to ourselves for the time being, grateful that their scents wouldn't develop until puberty) and wish us well. The upside to the constant parade of people was the food they brought. Our freezer was stocked with enough meals to last us six months at least, and neither Ollie nor I were going to complain about that.

Rory and Duke, whose names I'd thought were a little on the nose but on which Ollie's heart had been set (and seeing as he birthed them, I wasn't going to take his joy), were showered with gifts and promises of endless hours of babysitting. We accepted the former and politely declined the latter from most of our eclectic pack, trusting only a few select people with our kids' safety.

Being a dad was every bit as exhausting and terrifying as

I'd imagined it would be. Our babies were adorable, but they were hard work. You wouldn't think that two tiny humans would be that disruptive, but they refused to sleep on the same schedule and they took turns crying, eating, and pooping. It felt like Ollie and I were constantly with one or the other.

But they were so worth it. Their cute, squeaking sounds when they stretched, their wide blue eyes as they took in the world with bobbling head movements, their surprisingly tight grips when they wrapped their impossibly small hands around our fingers...I was besotted. Exhausted, but besotted.

By the time Brandi finally came to visit a month following their birth, I felt that we had settled into a routine. Life was good. And, when I managed to convince her to stay for Ollie's sake, it got even better. Of course, I wasn't sure whether she chose to stay because I had used the cuteness of our children to manipulate her, or because she'd become tongue-tied and unexpectedly flustered in a 'I wanna bone that person' kind of way from the moment she'd met Lena. Either way, it worked in our favor and Ollie was over the moon with happiness about it.

I would do anything to ensure he was always happy.

* * *

Ollie's mouth on my dick was *everything*.

I moaned and wound my fingers into his soft hair as he worked his tongue over my shaft before suckling at the head, flicking the tip of his tongue in my slit the way he knew I liked it. At six weeks post giving birth, Eric had given Ollie the all clear to have sex again and Brandi had immediately offered to babysit for us.

I was going to shower that woman with gifts the next time I saw her.

"Fuck yes, baby," I did my best to resist rocking my hips into the perfection that was his mouth. Hot, wet suction had my eyes rolling back in my head. Unfettered pleasure rolled through the bond we shared, not all of it my own. "Suck it. Suck my cock. So good for me."

Having watched him suffer through labor, there had been absolutely no way I was going to pressure him for sex until he was ready. But as soon as he'd handed Rory over to Brandi while Lena had taken Duke, Ollie had grabbed me by the front of the shirt, dragged me upstairs and slammed me against the closed door the second we were inside our room.

I was not complaining.

The vibration of his own moan traveled through my cock and into my balls, sparking entirely new tingles of pleasure.

"I'm going to come," I told him on a gravelly rasp, squeezing my eyes shut in a futile attempt to keep my release at bay.

Ollie took me to the base of his throat and *swallowed*.

I was done for.

With a muffled cry, my cock pulsed and I came hard, feeling his mouth and throat convulse around me as he tried to contain every drop of my orgasm.

"Jesus," I muttered, slumping against the painted timber at my back as Ollie finally pulled off me, licking his lips and looking smug and disheveled. His light brown hair flew in all directions, his lips were swollen, and his cheeks were flushed with exertion. If I hadn't just come harder than I had in weeks, the sight of him alone would have tipped me over the edge again. "Thank you, baby."

"You've been so patient," he said softly, allowing me to help him to his feet. "Waiting on me hand and foot, getting up for the babies…I wanted to do something just for you, y'know?"

Shaking my head, I pulled him in for a tender kiss, enjoying the taste of myself on his lips and tongue. "I'm not doing anything special by looking after my mate and kids. What kind of monster would make you do all the work when those babies are mine, too?"

How could I make him see that I wasn't acting from a sense of obligation, but from how happy he made me? From how in love I was with him and our little family? I didn't think I could. Not in that moment. All I could do was continue to try and show him and to tell him how much he and our babies meant to me every single day.

Honestly, I had no idea how Ollie's pack, but especially his parents, could have treated him so terribly. As a new parent myself, I only wanted to shower my kids with love. Hadn't they ever felt that for Ollie? Assuming they had, what had changed so terribly that they had come after him and then abducted and threatened the man he loved?

On that note, I didn't think we had heard the last of Ollie's pack or any other potential threats to our history-making existence, but with three dragons and a growing pack of multi-talented shifters at our beck and call (no pun intended), we would be ready to face them again when the time came. In the meantime, focusing on our family and our continued happiness was my highest priority. Especially when Ollie was making his need and desire so obvious. Any outside concerns could wait.

Grinning, I swept my mate off his feet bridal style. I laughed as he squealed and I carried him to the bed, depositing him down softly and then covering his body with mine. He squirmed and turned pink.

"I know it's all healed up down there, but..." he trailed off and sighed. "I don't feel the same as I used to. My stomach's still all pooched, and I have stretch marks, and—"

"And you're gorgeous, Ollie." My tone was affectionate but firm. I made sure to look him in the eye, to push my feelings through the bond so he could feel how genuine my words were. "Your tummy and your stretchmarks?" I lifted his shirt and peppered light kisses over the shiny striations. "These are proof that you brought our kids into the world. Every time I look at you, all I want to do is carry you up here and practice knocking you up all over again."

He gasped and looked horrified, even as he laughed and hit at my shoulders. "Don't you dare. You're not putting any more babies in me until these ones are old enough to fend for themselves."

"Yes, sir," I agreed happily. Then my expression softened again and I crawled back over his body, nuzzling his nose with my own as I gently rocked my rapidly re-hardening cock against his still clothed one. I'd stepped out of my pants on my way to the bed, and now I wanted us both naked. "But, baby, you are even more attractive to me now than you were when we met. Your strength, your resilience, your personality... getting to know you properly has made you even hotter than the flirty twink whose dancing almost made me come in my pants. I need you to understand that."

Biting his lip, Ollie looked up at me from beneath his thick lashes. "I get it," he eventually told me, then trailed his hands beneath my shirt. "I get it, because I feel the same way about you." A lone tear rolled down the side of his face, but I could only feel joy through our bond. "I love you. So, so much."

"And I love you. More than I thought I'd ever love anyone."

With no more words necessary, I set about showing him the best way I knew how.

Almost a year earlier, I'd thought I was human. I'd had great friends and had been starting to think about dating seriously, but I never would have imagined the path my life would take after one chance meeting.

Having my inner alpha unlocked and discovering I was so much more than the no hope foster kid I'd been had given my life purpose in ways I was still learning to embrace.

I had a family. Pups. A pack.

I didn't know what else life would bring, be it more drama from Ollie's pack or more supernatural surprises, but in that moment I was happier than I thought I had any right to be.

Bonus Epilogue – Oliver

◈

"I can't believe you did this," Brandi's eyes were wide as she surveyed the main street of our little town. She turned to her girlfriend, Lena, and gestured wildly. "He's nuts. Tell him he's nuts."

It had been the biggest surprise of all to watch my previously man-crazy best friend fall over her feet when she'd met the short, curvaceous rabbit shifter. The two of them had been drawn to each other in a way that reminded me of the night I met Beck, unable to keep their eyes off each other. It had taken a couple of months before they'd acted on it, though, and then worlds had once again been upended.

The subsequent discovery that female omegas existed had been a big surprise to all of us. Eric and I had theorized it, of course, what with Rory's alpha birthmark suggesting that secondary designations had once been universal across all gender combinations, but learning that your human BFF had presented as an alpha shifter after she finally gave in to her urges and took her girl crush to bed was something else.

Eric was naturally thrilled to have new test subjects to validate his theories on shifter evolution, while Brandi and Lena were still trying to work out what it meant for them. Brandi was spending a lot more time with Beck, Sandy and Eric, learning to embrace the changes to her physiology, and I was spending a lot more time with Lena, sharing our stories of mating with an alpha, though she and Brandi had not accidentally bonded. Yet.

I gave it a few more weeks. I had money on Lena popping out cute little rabbit babies within nine months, but both women had been curiously tight-lipped about how the whole knotting and breeding thing worked without a penis involved. Eric and I were still trying to coax it out of them for research purposes.

For the time being, Beck had distracted me by allowing me free reign over the town's holiday decorating. With Rory and Duke strapped to me in a twin carrier, I'd thrown myself into the task with more enthusiasm than anyone had bargained on.

Really, Beck should have known better. He'd seen my poky apartment in New York the year before. He couldn't have thought that my addiction to all things Christmas was going to wane just because I had endless space to fill.

With access to Eric's unlimited credit card, his brother Sage's ability to build things, and Prime Delivery at my disposal, I had outdone even my wildest dreams.

"It looks like Santa's Workshop threw up over Main Street," Brandi continued to decry when her girlfriend refused to back her up.

"I know," I grinned and bounced on my heels, careful not to disturb the sleeping infants strapped to my chest. "Isn't it awesome?"

"It's *something*," she replied, uncertainly.

I clapped my hands together. "Wait until you see what I have planned for the parade!"

With the twins only a couple of months old, it was too early to try and live out the fantasy life I'd imagined when Beck had taken me to see the parade in Rhinebeck. However, I could create real memories and start my kids' Christmas addiction early, and that was what I planned to do.

Brandi groaned dramatically. "Don't you remember what happened the last time we went to a Christmas parade?"

"All the more reason to make our own," I insisted. "We can't live in fear forever. I want these guys," I brushed my hands through the downy soft hair on my babies' heads in illustration, "to grow up as normally as possible. I'm not building walls around our house and never leaving. I want them to make friends and feel safe in the town. I want—"

"Okay, okay," my best friend held her hands up in surrender, once again directing her gaze down the street lined with an abundance of tinsel, fairy lights and fake snow. She glanced up and noticed the oversized fake bells strung from the power lines, the green tinsel-covered wire stretched in a zig-zag pattern across the street and sighed. "I get it. And I'll concede; it is pretty."

I smiled, closing my eyes to envision my plan coming to life. The town's tiny school had roped the families and few teachers in on parading with the children, dressed in homemade costumes of their own choice. A few of the local businesses were also on board, and the music teacher had even promised to try and get a small marching band organized.

It wouldn't be anywhere near as fancy as the parade in

Rhinebeck, and certainly not as large or long, but it would be the first time our entire extended pack of outcast shifters celebrated as a united front. We'd even complete the event with our own little tree lighting ceremony.

I was so excited, I could burst!

* * *

It turned out that the reality of my plans culminating was even better than I'd imagined. In early December, the whole town came together for the biggest festive street party they had ever seen. It was cold, but we all bundled up in thick coats and puffy jackets, and the stalls selling hot cocoa and eggnog made a mint. But, as predicted, it was the parade that stole the show.

Beck and I stood at the closed-off end of the street, near the large tree Eric had paid for and Sage had decorated under my guidance. He wrapped his arms around me from behind, our babies cooing and making adorable sounds from their aunts' arms at our sides. Resting his chin on my shoulder, I could feel pride and adoration swelling through the bond, as well as a touch of amusement when I bounced up and down on my heels, craning forward to try and see the procession before they reached us.

"This is magical, Ollie," he murmured into my ear, squeezing me for emphasis. "I can't believe you arranged it all."

To be honest, it hadn't been difficult. As omega to the pack's Alpha, most of our townspeople had been more than willing to volunteer time or services to my cause. Besides, almost everyone loved a party.

News of the parade had even spread to nearby towns. While that worried Beck a little in terms of security, it was good to see a small influx of visitors to our otherwise sleepy town. They spent money in our stores and made connections with our locals which I could only think would benefit our pack in the long run.

Besides, we had three dragons. I figured that was what was keeping any attacks at bay. I wasn't certain it would keep us safe forever when even humans could amass weapons to hold the dragons at bay, but we were just going to have to continue on living and stay vigilant. There was no sense getting bound up in the fear of attack, and I refused to do so at Christmas.

"What can I say?" I shrugged. "I love Christmas."

"And I love you," he nipped at my scarf-covered neck, over the mating mark. I shivered with pleasure.

We watched as the parade came down the street, and I cheered and clapped along with everyone else as candy was tossed out into the crowd. Joy lit everyone's faces and I couldn't help but feel like this was what my pack growing up should have felt like. At least Duke and Rory would grow up in a supportive environment where everyone was treated as though they were valuable, regardless of their secondary designations.

When the troop of schoolchildren and their guardians came to a stop in front of the large tree, I nudged Beck to stand on the makeshift stage which Sage and a couple of the local farmers had built for the event. He was the pack Alpha after all. He needed to make a speech.

"Welcome to the first annual Shifters Sanctuary Holiday Festival," my mate spoke into the microphone we'd set up, pausing as the assembled audience —including the crowds who had been lining the main street—pressed in closer to cheer and applaud.

He looked so handsome and confident as he spoke to the crowd, as though he had been practicing the art of public speaking his whole life. Considering how reserved and closed off he'd been the night we met, it was as though unlocking his inner alpha and his shifter side had set his inhibitions free.

He could very well have run away after we'd mated. I knew he'd been understandably freaked out, and I imagined that the urge to escape the world of crazy he had stepped into would have been a strong one. But he'd stuck it out. Even after we discovered I was pregnant, he'd still stayed. It was a testament to his own resilience, no matter how often he talked about mine.

My mate was everything I had ever wanted in a boyfriend and then some. He'd come along right when I had needed him to and had been a rock to cling to amidst the turbulence of my life. In the span of a year, he had changed, but so had I, and we were both so much stronger and happier for it.

"...and, obviously, none of this would be happening without Ollie," he was saying as I tuned back in, and I blinked in surprise at the sound of my name. "Come here, baby," he said, holding out his hand. In front of our pack and a few outsiders, I stepped up to his side. He grinned at me for a long moment before he slowly dropped to one knee in front of me, to a chorus of gasps and quiet squeals.

My brain went blank. "Beck. What...?"

"Just over a year ago," he said, still speaking into the microphone but directing his dark, soulful gaze directly up at me, "I saw you across a crowded dance floor and I was enraptured. Through you, I've learned a lot about who I am and what I am capable of. We've been through a lot of crazy sh...er...stuff," he chuckled and so did the crowd, but I only had eyes for him, "since then, and I'm betting we'll go through some more in the coming months and years, but I'm asking if you'll do me the honor of formalizing the bond we already share. Will you marry me, Oliver Grayson?"

My throat was tight. Tears clung to my eyelashes. My sinuses prickled.

All I could do was nod and croak out my emphatic, "Yes."

Confetti canons exploded as the whole town roared with delight. But I was oblivious to all of it, too busy tugging Beck back up to his feet and slamming our lips together.

"I hope you know," I whispered against his lips when we parted for breath, "that this has only made me love Christmas even more."

His laughter was like music to my ears.

"What can I say?" he responded happily. "I've been converted."

"Really? You love Christmas now?"

Pulling back further to look me in the eye, Beck cupped my cheek with his gloved hand. "It makes you happy, and that's all I ever want to do for the rest of our lives."

THE END

Thank you so much for reading *His Alpha Unlocked*. This was my first foray into writing an original Omegaverse story and I am so excited to keep the Shifters Sanctuary series going from here.

I'd love it if you could leave a review on your retailer of purchase or on Goodreads.

Reviews not only tell the algorithms that our books deserve attention, but honest feedback also encourages and inspires me to keep writing. Even a star rating helps, and I greatly appreciate you making time to do so.

Speaking of my writing, if you want a glimpse into Book Two of the Shifters Sanctuary world, titled *His Prodigal Alpha*, keep turning the pages because Chapter One is waiting for you.

And if you'd like to follow Ollie and Beck into a 3,700 word extra epilogue/additional steamy scene, you can find that by signing up for my newsletter at:

https://annasparrows.com/newsletter-subscription/

If you're already signed up and still want a copy, email me at:

annasparrows.author@gmail.com

I'd love to hear from you!

Love,

Anna

Sneak Peek: His Prodigal Alpha

Prologue – Damon

The Christmas festival was in full swing when I parked off the main drag of the infamous little town. Shifters Sanctuary had become notorious in shifter circles since the news of an alpha had begun circulating. According to rumor, he was the only one of his kind, but I knew that to be untrue.

How did I know he wasn't the only alpha in the world?

Well, the obvious swell of my belly wasn't from indulging in too much pie.

There was another alpha out there somewhere, but fuck if I knew where he had run off to. He hadn't taken his body changing mid-orgasm very well and, the second his knot had deflated, the fucker had run out of the bathroom stall in which we'd had our anonymous tryst without so much as a backwards glance.

Apparently my being a shifter hadn't bothered him, but the idea that he wasn't human had been too much to handle. I supposed I couldn't blame him for that.

I'd been too mystified by the entire encounter to consider the fact that I, an omega, had been knotted during unprotected sex until the vomiting had started six weeks following the experience. Then I had been in denial for a while after that. It wasn't until my stomach started to curve outwards in a very telling way that I accepted what had happened.

I'd unknowingly found an alpha in a random bar. We had been *incredibly* interested in each other. I would even go as far as to say that we were inexplicably drawn to each other. I had begged him to fuck me hard right then and there, desperate for him to fill me and claim me.

And the asshole had knocked me up and vanished.

Okay, okay; he obviously hadn't realized he was an alpha any more than I hadn't realized that he wasn't human, but I still felt as though I had the right to resent him a teeny, tiny bit. After all, I was the one left holding the baby: figuratively and literally.

Unable to hide my condition from my not exactly pro omega rights pack, I'd gotten together as many of my belongings as possible and had made a run for it. As far as I'd known, I was the only pregnant omega in a long ass time, and I had no idea how I was going to make it through the following months, let alone the birth.

And then, while I'd been staying in a small shifter town in Nebraska, I'd heard the whispers.

There was an alpha with a pregnant mate. They'd started to build a pack in Bumfuck Nowhere, Iowa. Word was, they believed there were others out there like them. Like the alpha.

Men with dubious backstories who didn't know their family histories, or those who came from shifter lines but presented human, who needed to find a compatible omega to unlock their inner alphas.

Was that what had happened to me? It sure as fuck sounded like it.

I'd sidled into the conversation as nonchalantly as I could, needing more details. Namely how the fuck could I find the town and were they looking for twenty-five-year-old college dropouts who were happy to earn minimum wage in exchange for any kind of job at all?

A couple of months and a fuckton of effort later, and there I was: Shifters Sanctuary.

I didn't know why I had thought that early December in Iowa wouldn't be cold, but I wasn't prepared for the blast of chilly air that hit me as I climbed out of my beater of a car. It had been all I could afford to buy with the meager savings I'd stashed away over my teens, and I'd only been able to convince my parents to allow me to buy it because I'd been going to college and needed it for the commute. I was glad that I'd bought it in my own name, because nobody could accuse me of stealing it when I ran away from the pack with what few possessions I owned tossed haphazardly into the trunk.

It had once been white, but was rather a mottled mass of scrapes and rust marks and had been since I'd bought it. But I had taught myself a thing or two about mechanics, so the engine ran well, and the heater worked just fine. It was better than having no car, and Ol' Betsy and I had been through a lot together since I was eighteen.

Wrapping my too-thin coat tighter around myself, I made my way towards the central source of the festivities. The street was lit up with fairy-lights and multi-colored Christmas lights both. The ten or so storefronts on either side of the main street also had their windows illuminated and decorated in Christmas cheer. Loudspeakers played Christmas Carols and there were stalls set up selling anything from cookies and hot cocoa to knitted beanies and dolls.

My throat tightened involuntarily as I brushed my index finger over one of the crocheted toys. It was only a few dollars, but I couldn't even afford that for my unborn child. Not while I was homeless and jobless.

"Can I getcha anything, honey?" the lady manning the stall asked. A delicate sniff revealed her to be a hedgehog shifter. The cat living inside my soul relaxed at that.

Well, I called it a cat. I was actually a puma shifter, but I mostly felt like an oversized house cat.

Shaking my head, I decided that if I had any chance of staying in the town as part of their pack, I might as well start trying to make nice with the locals. "No. I...I'm actually looking for the Alpha. Is, um, is he around here somewhere?"

Her nose, red from the cold, twitched. Her eyes narrowed and she looked me up and down. With my coat closed, she couldn't see my bump. I preferred it that way. "Why are you asking?" she sounded less friendly at that point and more defensive, as if a diminutive omega like me could really be a threat.

I wondered if that meant the Alpha was a good man so his pack cared about his well being and wanted to protect him from potential threats, or if it meant that he was a bad man who ruled them all with an iron fist.

"I, um, I kind of...I..." A lump lodged in my throat and I cursed my hormones for making me cry at the drop of a hat.

But it had the benefit of giving away just how pitiful I was, because Hedgehog Lady's demeanor slipped right back to empathetic and maternal.

"Oh, sweetie, I'm sorry. We're just real protective of our fledgling pack is all. Here, come sit," she ushered me to walk behind her table of knitted goods and sat me down on the plastic chair she'd had sitting in the corner of her stall. "I'm gonna get you a cup of cocoa, and I'll get the Alpha. Stay right here, okay?"

At the point of sniffling and fighting my stupid hormonal response, I could only nod.

She returned a few minutes later with the promised cup of hot cocoa and a tall, broad chested man with dark hair and deep brown eyes. At his side was another man, shorter and slender, with flopsy light brown hair and green eyes.

The taller man called for my attention without even having to speak. I could scent the difference in him on the air. It buzzed and tickled my nose.

Alpha.

My lower lip quivered and I ducked my head.

Having guessed that the man standing next to the Alpha was his mate, I was overwhelmed with a moment of irrational jealousy. How come that guy had been enough for the man who had mated him, but I wasn't enough for the guy who mated me?

The Alpha cleared his throat and I forced myself to look up at him with watering eyes. Both men scented like wolves, but strangely, my inner cat had no complaints about that. Perhaps it realized they weren't a threat to me.

The Alpha smiled back at me softly. "Hi," he greeted me casually. "I'm Beck. Jazz said you were asking for me?"

My eyes darted between him, his mate, and the hedgehog lady. *Jazz.*

Weird name, but okay.

I nodded and tried to swallow around the lump of emotion in my throat. "Yeah," I croaked out. "I, uh, I heard about this town. This pack. And I, um, I was wondering if I could join it. The pack, I mean. I...I ran away from my pack. I couldn't stay. If they found out..."

"Whoa," Beck held up his hands to stall my babbling. "Let's start with your name first, huh? And maybe we'll head inside somewhere and get out of the cold. You're shivering."

I hadn't even noticed. I nodded again, dumbly. Then, after a beat of silence, I realized they were still waiting on my name. Stupid baby brain. "Damon," I finally blurted, then blushed. "My name is Damon. Damon Richards. I'm sorry. It's...it's been a really long trip to get here and I'm...I mean, I know I shouldn't just expect that you'll let me join the pack, but I have nowhere else to go and—"

"It's okay," this time it was Beck's mate who spoke. He also smiled kindly at me. "Shifters Sanctuary is supposed to be just that: a haven for outcast shifters and people who don't have a pack or family." He extended his hand. I took it. "I'm Ollie," he said, shaking my hand and then gently tugging me upwards. Standing next to him, I realized he wasn't as short as he looked. In fact, he was at least two inches taller than me. "Come on, let's head inside. Have you eaten? The diner here makes the best burgers."

"You'd think you would be sick of them by now," Beck teased his mate as Ollie guided me back out of the stall and towards the town's diner. "Considering how many you ate when you were pregnant."

The child in my belly rolled over, as if summoned into action by that word. It was a word I hadn't spoken out loud to anyone yet, but Beck and Ollie used it as though omega pregnancies were totally normal.

Having lived through one, I supposed for them they had become as much.

I let their banter wash over me until we were inside the warm building. It was a long, narrow space, with one wall lined with back-to-back dining booths, and the other with a kitchen and counter. Three stools lined the counter space next to the cash register. It looked as though it had been decorated in the 80s to resemble the 50s. The Formica counter tops were chipped and worn, and the bright red vinyl seats of the stools and booths had also seen better days. But it smelled so good. My stomach rumbled audibly and the baby inside me kicked up a storm.

"Come on, let me take your coat and you can take a seat. It's sweltering in here." Ollie was bright and cheerful and he had no idea what kind of anxiety he'd just set off with his request.

I swallowed and turned to face him and Beck, reminding myself that they had been through what I was going through. If I was going to be safe anywhere, it would be with them. They would understand. I needed them to understand. If they didn't, I really was out of options.

"Before I do, there's something else. The reason I ran from my pack. I…um…I…" God, why was it so hard to say aloud. With a growl of frustration at myself, I said. "How about I just show you?"

Giving them no time to respond, I removed my coat.

The threadbare sweater I wore beneath it was stretched tight over my unmistakable baby bump, and the jeans I was wearing were baggy around my legs but growing ever more snug around my waist. I'd found them in a Goodwill during my travels, and the sales lady had looked at me strangely for buying a pair so much larger than I had visibly needed at the time. Standing in that diner, I thought they wouldn't be big enough for much longer.

"Holy shit," Beck breathed, before turning to Ollie with startled eyes. "I swear, I didn't do it."

Ollie just rolled his eyes at his mate. "I know that, dumbass," he sassed, but the affection in his words was more than obvious. "But you know what this means."

Beck nodded, his expression becoming serious. "He's definitely joining the pack."

"Well, duh," Ollie sighed. "But that's not what I meant." He turned back to me, his eyes roving over my swollen, gravid form. "We were right: there's at least one other alpha out there somewhere."

About the Author

I've been writing for as long as I can remember. I started with silly short stories as a kid, moved on to fanfiction in my teens (and still write it now), and am a previously published romance author (under a different pen name).

I've read MM romances of all sub-genres for decades, but when I discovered Age Play romances -by complete accident- I was enthralled. I fell in love with these stories of cute, sweet Littles and their hot AF Daddies. It wasn't long before I decided that I needed to start writing my own. And, when I got serious about it, I really wanted to create a pen name that was specific to this niche genre* to give it the focus it deserved.

And thus, Anna Sparrows was born.

*Though I have since branched out into Contemporary MM romances, and Omegaverse/Mpreg now, too.

You can connect with me on:

◯ https://annasparrows.com

🄵 https://www.facebook.com/AnnaSparrowsAuthor

𝒫 https://www.instagram.com/annasparrows

Subscribe to my newsletter:

✉ https://annasparrows.com/newsletter-subscription

Also by Anna Sparrows

I write ridiculously sweet & steamy MM romance with guaranteed HEAs…and sometimes with a side of kink.

The Littles & Lace Series
The Littles & Lace series is an MM Age Play series, following a group of like minded friends in the BDSM community. You'll find ABDL, light Pet Play, Femme Play and more here.

Book 1: Asher's Answer

Book 2: Matteo's Mettle

Book 3: Ted's Temerity

Book 4: Spencer's Satisfaction

Book 5: Chance's Choice

Book 6: Josh's Jackpot (MMM)

The Dads & Adages Series
Venture to Australia's stunning Gold Coast, where a group of single dads are going to learn a few life lessons on their way to their HEAs.

Book 1: Where There's A Will

When Connor Stark's life is turned upside down overnight, firefighter (and silver fox) Will Bradford finds himself helping his young neighbour navigate his new reality. Will has no intention of falling butt over tea-kettle for Connor or Connor's kid, but life has other plans...